The Truth

By Astrid Cook

Special thanks: Lynn, Liz, Faye, Leah, Andrew, Becca, and, always, N&Y.

Printed and bound by Creative Space.
Cover art by Diane Velletri (ddnystudio.com)

ISBN-13: 978-1480225879 / ISBN-10: 1480225878

For Frank*

I

What do you want?

**A nice new spatula... An inexpensive pair of waterproof, fur-lined boots
that keep out the slush but don't make my feet sweat... An umbrella that
doesn't blow backward in the Hudson River wind gusts...**

Such a funny question: What do you want? If you ask most people, they
will claim to want things that are generally fantastical. *A million dollars. World
peace. A long life of perfect happiness.*

I have whittled my current wants to the most fundamental and potentially
attainable: I own a plastic spatula that my mother gifted to me five years ago.
I live in New York City, thus making the challenge of finding boots that are
practical—let alone warm and dry—a quest of Quixotic proportions. And I left
my nice umbrella... somewhere. On a subway? At the bank? Who knows? It's
gone and there's nothing to do but replace it. Yet shoddy umbrellas are in
abundance and windproof umbrellas in short supply.

My current wants are two-thirds weather related, which reveals something
of the day outside: It is snowing on New Year's Eve 2010. Although the decade
technically doesn't end for another year (technicality schmechnicality), the
change from the aughts to the teens is welcomed by me and probably every
other person breathing in this country. Good riddance to turn of the century
rubbish.

I belong to the resolutionist movement. This hardly makes me unique. The
gyms will be full of fools tomorrow, working off 364 days of over-indulgence
from last year when they hit the treadmill on January two and hit the donut
stand—not to mention pasta bar (or just bar bar)—from January three through

1

the wee hours of this coming morning.

Disparagement aside, however, I applaud my fellow resolutionaries, who truly believe they will change this year. They *will* lose weight, *will* quit drinking/smoking/purging/toking, *will* find new love, *will* spend more time with their kids, *will* pay more attention to their bored spouse, *will* show *will.* High marks for self-discipline. Unfortunately, those who truly possess it are so sanctimonious about how it's just a matter of self-control, anyone can do it, only the weak perish.

Elise and I discuss our resolutions: hers are broad, general, all-encompassing, qualitative. For example, to show more patience. Mine are concrete, quantifiable, specific. For example, drop 20 pounds. Finish just *one* of the many novels I have begun. Have sex at least twice in the coming 12 months.

I am pretty sure that Elise will be among a handful of resolutionaries that will succeed in 2010, not because she is in the "I'm self-disciplined and you should be, too," camp, but because qualitative resolutions are amorphous by nature. You cannot fail at them, because you are bound by self-preservation. Hence, by year's end, Elise will not remember the times she lost her patience; rather she will remember those key moments when she endured. She will—in a year's time—move on to another global improvement and feel better for her real or imagined spiritual growth.

I, on the other hand—despite my journal enumerating ten resolutions—am destined to fall short yet again. I have kept my "10 Resolutions" (a nice round number) journal since the early 80s, when the quest to be perfect became my religion of choice. Each year I consult my journal quarterly, to measure my "success." I consider myself superior to those resolutionaries who are less methodical and have abandoned their mission after a few days, weeks, possibly a couple months. At least I keep going throughout the year. I strictly monitor my shortcomings and tally up annually which goals were tackled—with varying degrees of success—and which had to be moved to a never-satisfied credit sheet of consummate and enduring failure.

It is not that I set unrealistic goals. I do not want to be a millionaire or a movie star. Last year, I wanted to lose 40 pounds. By June, I had lost 35. Then I became distracted. Between Thanksgiving and Christmas, whatever self-discipline I thought I had eroded between the deep-fried turkey and free-flowing red wine; as of this morning, I am 15 pounds heavier than I was last summer. Of course, I could note that last year I wanted to lose 40 and this year I want to lose 20 (yes, weight-loss—the most banal of the resolutionist movement—is yet again on my list for 2010). Thus, I've made progress. But the goal is never attained. Even on a good day I see where I have failed.

When I look down my list and see the magnitude of it all, I feel uninspired. My half-life weight-loss lifestyle will net me 10 pounds, if I'm lucky ("lose 40 pounds" was on my list for five years before I lost the 20). I will not complete my novel this year (or even a tall tale). And I will never *ever* get laid again in my entire life.

Φ

The worst part about the last time you have sex is that you don't know it's the last time. If you knew, perhaps you'd make much ado over it. Throw a Pussy Pity Party. A rather sad but festive moment: a vaginal wake. If you are Irish, you could first felate a bottle of Jameson and then fuck it; should you choose to commemorate the event, a nice wax candle may be fitted in the neck of the bottle towards which you showed such lust. You can then burn it on the anniversary of your final fuck.

For the Asian funeral, you could have a Chinese Cunt Celebration, which admittedly is not as alliterative as it could be. A Cantonese Cunt Cotillion, perhaps? For the Jewish woman, there could be the Missing Muff Mitzvah. The Buddhist could bid bon voyage to her Bored Beaver.

Alliteration is a passion of mine, in case you'd yet to notice. A sort of verbal masturbation, which—considering my otherwise celibate state—is all the poor entertainment I've been left.

You see, I really should not be in the "I don't remember my last fuck" category. I knew my marriage had failed. It was only a matter of months, then weeks, then days before we went our separate ways. I should have been keeping track of the rare liaison. I hadn't initiated sex during that final year we were together, and despite never refusing my husband sex for the first 19 years of our union, I had regularly rebuffed him those final months, weeks, days. Yet sometimes I would acquiesce, if for no other reason than to make our small apartment (not small by New York standards, but small by suburban human standards) less acrimonious. If I bent over every third or fourth request, the vitriol was less vicious (my husband, Ryan-Claude, was quite a virtuoso of venomous vicious vitriol... ahh, that alliteration almost made me come... but I digress). So, yes, I did succumb or surrender or suffer through a sex session or six those terminal months together.

I can narrow the window of the final fuck, but I cannot pinpoint a day or even a time. It could have been dawn or dusk or possibly even mid-day, he having slept off a drunk and awoken with an erection not worthy of self-abuse. It was late July? Early August? And that's all I remember about an activity that once was something I craved and now live without entirely.

Why a Pussy Pity Party and not—say—a Phallic Final Farewell? Simple. Because for men, sex is sex. Porn was invented so men could have sex with themselves. Even a "sexually satisfied" man jerks off. Regularly. It's almost mechanical and subconscious. Men believe that women are frigid or only using sex to trap a man. I don't believe either to be true. In fact, the main difference between men and women is that men have good sex and occasionally great sex. There's no such thing as bad sex for a man (if there were, the porn industry would never have succeeded). For a woman, however, she would rather have great sex or no sex at all. It's almost like a switch that can be turned on or off. Many, many women suffer the pain of never having great sex. They endure the necessity of conjugal coitus and call it "meaningful" sex. However, given the choice of bad (or even average) sex and no sex, women will almost invariably opt for the latter.

Even masturbation becomes redundant: I masturbate because I am alone; I am alone so I masturbate. Eventually, a good book and a cat become a more-than-adequate substitute for the lout who used to take up two-thirds of the bed. The vibrator in the bedside table gets lost in the ennui, its batteries oozing until the damn thing is rusted shut and will never elicit another pleasant moan of longing lustful loneliness.

Richie is an observer of a certain class of this particular female of the species. We met on Craigslist when I was searching for a drinking buddy, and although he doesn't drink, I found him so delightfully diverting that I've kept him around. Richie has observed that there is an entire subculture of women who have abandoned all hope of ever having sex. They tend to have amazingly full social calendars, having banded together into the Coven of Closed Cunts, whose sexuality is so insulated that it no longer even registers as a basic biological need. Richie has encountered many of these women in his newly found promiscuity. He tells me they are all enormously fat, hang out in bars together, never do anything independent of a group consultation, and book cruise vacations *en masse* (about which he genuinely fears for their safety: Their combined heft could tip an aircraft carrier).

Richie is lovely, actually, totally sweet and misguided. He thinks he can will me into loving him, but what I cannot bring myself to tell him is that he's bald and fat and suffers from poor dental hygiene. He claims never to have met a woman like me, and he's smitten. Unlike me, Richie is not prone to prejudice: He will fuck anyone. He'll even fuck a man, so long as the guy doesn't kiss him on the mouth. Richie isn't gay; he just doesn't discriminate, and I mean that in the best way.

Thus it was that Richie found himself dating Kate, a recent convert to the aforementioned Coven of Closed Cunts. One day, six-pack of Pepsi and a super-size bag of Doritos in hand, he made a joke at the checkout counter at Gristedes. Kate was behind him in line, toting a plastic shopping basket containing cooked ham, uncooked rotelle pasta, and a jar of Ragu Alfredo sauce. He liked her eyes, so he struck up a conversation. Of course, Richie could strike up a conversation with a cabbage. His eloquence works wonders on everything save me.

But I digress...

Richie and Kate spent that afternoon together in Battery Park, her ham added to his Doritos and Pepsi for a make-shift picnic. He didn't find her particularly attractive, but she had a marvelous laugh and shining blue eyes.

At dusk, his lips barely met hers in farewell, and he asked to see her again. There were a total of four subsequent dates. On the first of these, she regaled him with stories about "her girls," a group of women as amorphous in body as she, many of whom would accompany her to Karaoke in Tribeca on Friday nights. On their second date, she admitted she hadn't had sex in almost three years; that had been 50 pounds ago. On their third date, he made sweet love to her in her Laura Ashley-adorned queen bed. She told him that he touched her better than she touched herself, and this made him swell with pride, in more ways than one... lather rinse repeat.

On their fourth date, Kate said that her Coven comrade Helen would be really happy for her that she was seeing Richie, but that Jane would be jealous and probably hate her when she found out. Kate was truly scared of Jane, who—in Richie's imagination—was Commandant Crone of the CCC.

Richie said to Kate, "Don't worry about Jane or anyone else."

"Oh, you don't understand at all," Kate protested. "My girls are my *family*. I don't want to disappoint them. Jane is very protective and doesn't want any of us to be hurt."

Richie, dear sweet Richie who never lies to anyone but himself, blurted out without thinking, "Maybe Jane is a miserable old hag who doesn't want any of you to be happy!"

That was the end of his dalliance with Kate, for which Richie wasn't the least bit sorry. On the scale of attractiveness, she was to him what he is to me, but he doesn't discriminate. And I mean that in the best way.

Thus ends the story of how Kate almost left the Coven of Closed Cunts. Almost, but not quite.

I do not want to join the Coven. I do not want to join the Coven. Whatever it takes, I do not want to join the Coven. This is my mantra of late.

So what happens if—please excuse the obvious Lady Godiva metaphor— you forsake what's easy and decide to get back up on the horse that threw you? Suddenly your 20th Century dating experience proves itself to be woefully inept. The world changed, and no longer are you equipped with the Darwinist survival genes requisite for finding a suitable partner or even a quick lay.

THE TRUTH

Suddenly you are a child again, learning how to crawl while everyone around you is uploading at 10,000 kilobytes per second. No matter what you think you know about technology (hey, I'm hip, I'm on Facebook, I'm Linked In, I can Tweet!), you not only do not possess the skills for 21st Century dating but there is no school that will train you in this pair-bonding paradigm.

And the smarter you are, the more complicated, the more dynamic, the more three-dimensional, the less likely you are ever to fuck again.

Unless you can bring yourself to settle for a Richie.

The Architect

It was a masturbatory office.

As she entered the foyer through 20-foot-high, reinforced plate-glass doors, the first thing she noticed was the assembly of rough sketches and finished drawings excreted onto every wall within view. She suspected they were there to illustrate the architect's "great works." Some had won awards, the museum-like notification affixed to each piece declared. To the trained eye—and Hallee fully admitted she had none—these "pieces of art" may have inspired insipid sycophantic awe; to her unindoctrinated self, they left nothing more than a feeling of the ironic. Two thoughts crossed her mind: The architect was compensating for something; alternatively, hither went a man so self-absorbed that justifiable pride had been trampled by pomposity.

Yet Hallee needed the job. And she knew full-well that pomposity was often rewarded. How often had she attended a film that was praised as great art merely to feel that she had wasted a perfectly good ten dollars (not to mention the three hours of her life that she would never regain)? She would walk away questioning her own intelligence. She felt the same way when trying to wade through *Ulysses*. Was this great art or some practical joke? In the case of Joyce, she was pretty sure it was all about drunken rambling.

In what felt like another life, Hallee had obsessed over the ennui of popular culture, even on an historical level. She had noted to musically-inclined acquaintances that Mozart held no authority over anyone during his lifetime and had died only to be buried in an unmarked grave. He was a genius, and 300 years have validated the claim. On the other hand, Andy Warhol pissed on a canvas and painted soup cans, was both lauded and shot at while on earth. Ephemeral fame versus immortality. Where did the axes intersect?

None of this really held any sway on Hallee at this particular juncture. She had traveled 3,000 miles (okay, 2,914, to be precise)—from San Francisco to New York City—with three kids in tow, in an effort to start anew. When her college roommate had thrown her a lifeline, Hallee had grasped at it and this time—contrary to her usual efforts—she was able to catch the rope that would pull her from one end of the country to the other.

The long-distance job interview had been perfunctory. Lauren had told her that the job was hers to have, that the office desperately needed back up, that two young administrators had been let go and quit respectively in the past three months, that the job required a mature and dedicated worker. Having recently turned 40, Hallee tried not to dwell on the possible euphemistic use of "mature." She also accepted the downgrade in status (she had been a project manager before the twins were born), because she was desperate. After relinquishing the career track for role of "wife and mother," she understood that her expectations were nil. She simply had chosen a new life for herself and her kids, and the job was requisite for keeping on this obscure path.

Hallee immediately recognized her old friend as she entered through the second double glass door. Lauren jumped up from behind the two-person desk that encompassed the reception area in a sweeping parabola. The white sheen of the front desk mirrored white tiled floors and blended into the white background. The vestibule was spotless, and Hallee barely had a moment to consider how difficult it must be to keep a busy Manhattan office this clean in appearance before Lauren was taking her coat and offering her a warm hug. Hallee held on longer than necessary, and Lauren pulled away awkwardly and with embarrassment.

They couldn't look more different: Lauren tall and wan, almost sickly in appearance; she had lost a ton of weight since their college days at Oberlin. Hallee on the other hand, several inches shorter and several stone fatter than her roommate undoubtedly remembered her to be. Yet there was a flush and healthy glow to Hallee that showed despite the sadness in her eyes. She knew it was good genes that gave her a youthful appearance, but the pain of the last few years had somewhat negated the effect.

"You look great," Lauren commented, not without irony.

What Hallee wanted to say: "You look tired and ill and two-thirds the woman you were when we graduated; you look, well, old. I know what has happened to me, do you know what has happened to you?"

What she said: "I look fat," which was true. For the past few weeks as she transitioned to this new life, she had consciously decided to address whatever elephant occupied the middle of the room she was entering. It disarmed any malevolent force and quelled those who would feel pity for her. She couldn't mount a reasonable defense in the case of the former and didn't need anyone's condescension in the case of the latter. It also seemed to take New Yorkers off guard, this blatant honesty. Apparently the natives were unaccustomed to the truth.

Hallee sensed that Lauren felt sorry for her, yet the offer of help that had allowed Hallee to start over was sincere, and she was capable of separating Lauren's assessment from her generosity. She quickly forgave her friend the immediate impression; after all, Hallee was also judging Lauren's physical appearance based on too little information.

"Let me show you around the office," Lauren said, hanging Hallee's coat up in the closet (clear plastic hangers) and leading the way. As they turned from the vestibule, past a (white, naturally) couch that probably cost more than Hallee would make in a month, she took in the breadth of David Ormston-Meighton Architects Company, Incorporated. The office was, indeed, impressive. Panoramic views from every window revealed various aspects of the New York City skyline. Large drawing sheets were scattered on desks, which ran down the center of a warehouse-like room. The architects were—to a man (and they were nearly all male)—young. Hallee walked, barely listening to Lauren as she told her the story of the firm's founding and its success in New York City and across the globe.

Hallee knew the name of the company, of course, but to hear the phones ringing and various voices answering, "Thank you for calling David Ormston-Meighton Architects Company, Incorporated. How may I direct your call?" gave her an inkling that David Ormston-Meighton was quite serious about

THE TRUTH

David Ormston-Meighton Architects Company, Incorporated. Couldn't they have come up with some kind of simpler name? Maybe an acronym? Was this company merely a shell around the live creature? Or perhaps an albumen to the yolk that was the eponymous founder?

Had Hallee spoken her thoughts aloud? Because Lauren was saying, "And why shouldn't he be? This company *is* David. He built it from nothing." Lauren was turning a corner, the only walls were those around the elevator shaft. Any other dividers were floor-to-ceiling glass panes. Hallee briefly wondered if anyone ever inadvertently ran into these plate glass walls, à la a flying bird. The forcefield-like enclosures included David's office: a room with a view of the fiefdom.

A view that he presently was not enjoying. As Lauren led her past the glassy vault that contained the Lord of the Manor and towards the kitchen, Hallee saw only the back of her new boss's head. A tousle of strawberry blonde straw pivoted away from her, his Herman Miller armchair supporting the back of his head. He was behind a colossal cherry desk, wedged between it and a large drafting table, which held very little other than his leather-slippered feet. He was on the phone, and despite the glass office door being shut (a single loop of burnished silver served as a door knob), Hallee heard his chortle as he spoke to someone somewhere.

"You know," Lauren continued, with a hushed tone that could elicit either confidence or conspiracy, "I was here at the beginning, when David was first starting out. Only ten architects then. Now we have eighty-two." She placed emphasis on the "two," as though it were particularly significant.

What Hallee wanted to say: "My last job? We had 55,000 in 900 offices worldwide."

What she said: "Wow! An 800 percent increase," which was true. Hallee's newly acquired desire to be truthful was not self-sabotaging. She had learned long ago that stating the blatantly obvious with strong emphasis generally worked in any situation where the listener longed for positive reinforcement or a compliment. The recipient of the message would interpret it exactly as she wanted to hear it, allowing Hallee to be honest without necessarily being forthcoming. Hallee had learned this trick from her sons' pediatrician, who once confided that whenever a parent asked him, *Don't you think my baby is beautiful?*, he would say with great enthusiasm, *That's a baby!* No parent was ever disappointed by this response. Hallee had racked her brain to remember if the doctor had ever said such a thing about the twins, but she could not remember that he had. Although Hallee probably had never asked the doctor to weigh in on more than the babies' general health. Of course, this confidence with the physician pleased Hallee, which was probably what the doctor had hoped for in relaying the anecdote. Keep the parent happy without sacrificing a compliment, whether directly or indirectly.

As she ventured around the office, Hallee was preoccupied by the journey that had brought her here. Jeremy had always been a cruel husband; to admit this meant that Hallee had to admit to being an abused woman. Whenever she had thought about abusive families, she envisioned "cheap white trash" and drunken brawls. It was a prejudice formed more out of self-regard than stereotypes. To admit that she—an intelligent and educated woman from a "good" family—had been abused, had allowed herself to be denigrated, was to admit that she had failed in the worst way; self-preservation should come more naturally. She could have left at any point over the 16 years they had been together, but she hadn't. She had clung to Jeremy with a love too blind, too fantastical. How many years had she cast away on the vain hope of "next year will be better"? Her entire adult life, in fact.

The tipping point had been almost a month earlier. Hallee had long suspected her husband was unfaithful, but she had no proof: only late night returns that at least once had led to a slap across her face when she had confronted him. Then, one night Jeremy suggested the kids stay over at his mother's so that the two of them would have the house to themselves. Hallee objected, since this usually involved multiple dildos he had purchased at a sex shop along with a porn tape acting out the gang-rape of a borderline-legal-aged actress. Yet not giving in to her husband's demands from time to time generally caused even worse treatment in the long run. Thus, she foolishly dropped the children with Grandma and returned home to be the victim once again.

What she walked in on made her trepidations look childish. Jeremy was fully *in flagrante delicto* with a woman 20 years her junior. Her name was Tatiana, and she was a Russian student who had babysat the kids a few times. Jeremy had taught her at the university, and he had introduced her as "a nice young woman" who could help out with the twins from time to time. Hallee had foolishly taken the arrangement at face value, even tipping the girl at Christmas.

When Hallee gasped at the sight, Jeremy had sneered. He commanded that she sit and watch. Unable to run away, terrified to turn her head, she watched while he fucked his lover in every way imaginable, while Tatiana glared maliciously at the wife, knowing full well that her young, supple body was the only weapon she had needed to wield in this battle. In truth, Tatiana seemed to despise being watched almost as much as Hallee despised watching. A new kind of porn to witness. Hallee cried during the entire "show," but Jeremy mercifully did nothing worse than spit at her. He dragged his concubine by her hair, forcing her to dress, still dripping with his scum, and announced they wouldn't be back that evening.

Hallee had sat in shock for a full hour before calling her college roommate, who knew of some of Jeremy's callous treatment, but not the truth, the whole truth, and nothing but the truth. Lauren had always been an early riser, so Hallee wasn't surprised but had been deeply relieved when she answered the phone at what would have been 6 a.m. on the east coast. Hallee had nothing left to closet; she relayed the horrors of the night to the only person she thought might care. It was then that Lauren told Hallee about the job opening in New York City. No longer seeing merely a window of opportunity, Hallee sensed her entire life had been ripped wide; not to step through the craggy aperture would have been to relegate herself to a life of slavery and humiliation. If she hadn't had children, she would have—at that moment—leapt from the Golden Gate. Instead, she said a weak prayer that Jeremy would indeed stay out all night.

As a point of fact, Hallee truly believed in God. She really couldn't help it, having been raised Catholic. Although she no longer attended Church (Jeremy had not been Catholic, so they were married in a civil ceremony; Hallee sometimes wondered if a Church wedding might have been their salvation), she prayed every day and tried to get the boys to pray at bedtime.

She packed the car with only the most important possessions. She thought of it as, "If the house were being destroyed by the 'big one,' what would I grab?" Other than a few pieces of jewelry, she found herself gathering mostly the boys' possessions (in addition to five-year-old twins, she had an eight-year-old son): clothes, a few toys, their aquatic turtles.

In the morning, she picked the boys up from Jeremy's mother. She looked hard into her mother-in-law's eyes. For the first time, she recognized the same tiredness in the older Mrs. Thompson that she had in her own. Jeremy's demented apple had not fallen far from his paternal tree. Perhaps her mother-in-law had seen the overflowing contents of the car; perhaps she saw a younger version of herself that had never had the courage to escape. Regardless, after loading the boys into the back seat, Hallee turned to find her mother-in-law holding out a tattered shoebox, thick, burnt-orange-colored rubber bands holding it closed. She handed it to Hallee without a word and returned to her apartment.

Hallee was five miles out of town, with the rubber-banded shoebox on the passenger seat, before she had the courage to open it. Inside was almost $3,000. One dollar for each mile she would travel into the future to get away from her present. Her mother-in-law was in effect saying, "Run away. Run away while you still can."

At first, Hallee had feared that Jeremy would chase after her. Then, ashamedly, she hoped he *would* chase after her. A week after she found a so-called "flex 2BR" apartment (only in New York City can a one-bedroom with a proper kitchen and a decent-sized living room be called a "2BR"), she received an envelope, forwarded from her old address (she had hesitated before putting in a change of address but she reasoned that she wasn't in witness protection). In it was a check for $1,500. The note attached was perfunctory:

> *You'll never have to sue for child support. I'll send a check each month (set up a PO Box, if you think I'll actually come after you). Goodbye, smelly old cunt.*

Hallee had held such a conflict of emotions upon receipt of her husband's missive. Was he making some kind of tacit threat that he would come after her? Should she be afraid to send him her address? Did the note mean he would file for divorce? Should she? Ultimately, none of these thoughts took hold. The simple truth was that he had moved on, and she had, as well. She cashed the check.

During this reverie, Lauren also had moved on, to David's office. She rapped lightly on the glass door. An effeminate wave ushered them in. David wore round, John-Lennon-style reading glasses barely perched on a wiry nose. His slightly ruddy face he came by naturally: freckled from sunshine as opposed to hung over. His green eyes were clear and sparkled with intense intelligence. He dressed à la Johnny Cash: The Man in Black. The relief of his body against the white and glass surroundings was almost supernatural. His mouth formed a slit that was neither sneer nor grimace. Perhaps this was his version of a smile? Hallee couldn't help wondering if David had any teeth.

She held out her hand in introduction, but David didn't so much as flinch. He held her gaze with his reptilian-like eyes, as Lauren gently lay her hand on Hallee's forearm, pushing her friend's hand back to her side.

Hallee looked to Lauren for a cue: Was Lauren blushing? She stammered slightly, then quickly recovered.

"David, this is my fr... former college roommate, Hallee Thompson. She's starting today."

"Yes," David hissed, a slight southern drawl belying any malice the drawn-out, serpent-like "s" might have evoked. "Lauren tellss uss" (again, the sibilant "s"; David Ormston-Meighton had a lisp) "great thingss about you. Welcome."

Hallee had to admit he had a somewhat disarming charm. He was quirky, odd, and—despite the lisp and flamboyant manners—completely asexual. Lauren had mentioned there was a wife. Hallee tried to detect if he was simply in the closet, but her gut instinct told her he wasn't gay. Perhaps the wall excretions were evidence of a sexuality channeled in a way Hallee had never considered, despite all those years in San Francisco being exposed to pretty much every kind of sexuality creation could produce.

The introduction apparently was over because Lauren was escorting Hallee out of David's office. Feeling she should fill the awkward silence, Hallee said, "He's, uh, a little different."

Again Lauren blushed. Hallee couldn't recall that Lauren ever had turned red from embarrassment in college, despite having been in several awkward encounters. Hallee felt a nearly suffocating sadness wash over her: They both had changed, not turning into the women they had been so certain they were destined to become. She quickly turned her head away in an effort to regain her composure and not burst into tears.

As they rounded the corner from David's office, Hallee noticed an extremely tidy and unoccupied desk. A thought went through Hallee's mind that this was the only desk David would be able to see when his back was turned, as it had been during Lauren's tour of the place. It was also the only desk facing away from what Hallee was coming to think of as the "hall of architects," meaning anyone could look over the shoulder of whoever normally sat there.

"Whose desk is that?" Hallee pointed as she asked.

"Oh," Lauren said in a hushed tone, "that's where Alison sits. She's David's EA Out today. She's been sick."

"So, who is his executive assistant when she's out?" Hallee asked. As if to say, *Why do you think you were hired?*, Lauren rolled her eyes and walked around to her desk. Hallee smiled, since this was the first gesture to remind her of the "old" Lauren, the one who had been (still was?) her best friend.

As if suddenly remembering something of critical importance, Lauren confided, "I'm really sorry about the handshake." Hallee had already dismissed David's refusal to shake hands, but Lauren seemed compelled to revisit the encounter. She adjusted her chair beside the front office work station and motioned for Hallee to sit down beside her. "David works such long hours, you see. Traveling so much, coming in contact with so many people..." Lauren's voice trailed off.

"It's okay," Hallee offered, not knowing what else to say.

"He just can't risk getting sick," Lauren said. "He avoids physically coming into contact with staff. It's for our benefit, honestly. Without David..."

"I know," Hallee interrupted. "The company *is* David." Hallee suddenly noted the hand sanitizer next to Lauren's phone. There was a second bottle next to Hallee's computer. From her subconscious, Hallee retrieved the image of personal-sized bottles on every desk she had seen. The entire office was awash in hand wash.

Hallee could appreciate some of this prophylactic approach to New York City. She herself had never been a germaphobe, but since moving here she had been washing her hands after every jaunt outdoors and making sure the boys had done the same. She had encouraged them to eschew hand rails and banisters; just the thought of millions of hands—those belonging to the homeless, sick and otherwise—was enough to make one aware of contagion. However, the plethora of Purell struck her as overkill.

What Hallee wanted to say: "How the hell will you ever build up any immunity to the germs if you're always bathing in antibiotic cleanser?"

What she said: "I guess you can never be too careful about these things. It is flu season, after all."

Lauren turned to the work at hand, showing Hallee how to log on to the computer and the company's database system. "Now, one of your main jobs will be to answer the phones," Lauren said. As if programmed to prove the need, the phone rang. "Pay attention. This is how we answer the phones."

Before Lauren could continue, however, Hallee reached for her phone's receiver. "Thank you for calling David Ormston-Meighton Architects Company, Incorporated," Hallee said in her naturally sultry voice. "How may I direct your call?"

Lauren exhaled with a smile of relief. Hallee pressed the "hold" button.

"Great job," Lauren said.

What Hallee wanted to say: "Come on. A monkey could do this job!"

What she said: "It's Paul Schneider of City Planning for Jeffrey Charles. Should I put him through?"

"Yes," Lauren answered. "Let me show you the extension list."

Ten minutes and 15 phone calls later, Hallee had graduated from phones to filing. Faxing and FedExing came next.

Thus her day was spent. While not mentally taxing, Hallee had to admit a brisk, intense pace she had never experienced in any of her previous jobs. New York City moved at a speed that few could maintain (cue Frank Sinatra). By 6:30 p.m., she was relieved to turn on the night phone (there was a service that Hallee would have to contact first thing in the morning to retrieve overnight messages) and to turn off her computer. The job was, in fact, physically exhausting. Hallee briefly fantasized about becoming as thin as Lauren in a year's time.

Hallee exited the midtown office to a cold, damp evening. Despite being late February, the week had been rainy and gross. A gray haze shrouded skyscrapers as rain trickled down their façades pooling to a foul swirl of sludge and swill in the street gutter as blackend chunks of snow coagulated in the runoff. At the crosswalk on the corner, a puddle formed from the over-flowing sewer. Grown women paraded through in little-girl-style rubber boots. Hallee attempted to negotiate her wind-blown umbrella while understanding this particular fashion statement. Certainly the boots were practical, but didn't they come in brown or black? She stood amidst a red pair decorated with white cats, and a green pair decorated with purple-outlined frogs that preceded a comparatively unimaginative pair of canary yellow.

A cab clipped the curb, honking at pedestrians who had the right of way. A cascade of opaque filth splashed the women to mid-calf. Hallee's shoes were soaked in only God knew what. Two blocks later, she purchased a pair of rubber boots decorated in faux Burberry plaid. She chucked her $25 pumps in the nearest trash receptacle, overflowing with sodden paper cups, wadded napkins, plastic food containers and some illegally dumped household trash.

Hallee descended the steps to the R train, coveting a taxi cab ride home. Not that she would have been able to catch a cab in the rain even if she could have afforded the fare (she couldn't). Instead, she swiped $2.25 from her Metrocard and headed home. The subway was crowded. Fortunately, the trip to Greenwood wasn't heinous. From work to the Brooklyn neighborhood she now called home took only 40 minutes. Nevertheless, she couldn't bare the idea of having to cook tonight. Fortunately, the corner store—which everyone called a bodega—sold cheap take-out. She got some chicken cutlets, potato salad and a pint of ice cream for the boys to split.

Her three sons were attending a subsidized afterschool program that—despite financial aid—would be costing their mother one-fourth her take-home pay and dismissed almost two hours before she came home from work. Fortunately, another mom of multiples (also twin boys, a year older than Drake and Josh—it had seemed like a good idea at the time—but younger than Gavin) offered to trade babysitting weeknights for weekends. Mary lived in Hallee's building and picked up all five boys from school at 5:30 and fed them dinner. In exchange for the 90-plus minutes each day afforded her sons, Hallee would take Mary's twins every Saturday at 5 p.m. for a sleepover so that Mary and her husband could partake of a date night (followed by—what Hallee imagined to be—wild, noisy sex). This meant Hallee never had a moment to herself, but the trade-off was necessary; she simply could not afford the extra day care for the boys, and she was already uncertain how she would deal with them during the summer. Hopefully things would get easier at some point. For now, Hallee's New York state of mind was basic survival.

In this new life, Hallee had instituted the routine of "family dinner," which basically was 30 minutes at the table with no electronic devices allowed. The boys each took turns relating an anecdote that summarized or encapsulated some part of the day. Hallee frequently felt a pang of regret when she heard these stories second-hand. The only kindness Jeremy had extended her was the ability to raise their—her—children. Now, even that was stripped from her. Instead of caring for her boys, she would be caring for David Ormston-Meighton Architects Company, Incorporated.

"How may I direct your call?"

The boys stared at her, slack jawed. Then they all burst out laughing.

"What?" Hallee looked at the boys incredulously.

Gavin, always the jokester, said, "Mom, I think you're losing it."

"Huh?" Hallee was puzzled. She wasn't aware she had spoken aloud. The boys rolled their eyes, giggled and seemed to speak in a code only they three understood.

Had the wine gone to her head? After the bodega, Hallee had popped into the liquor store where she bought a bottle of cheap chardonnay. Cheap not because she suffered from a lack of oenological appreciation, but because it was all she could afford (and she liked cheap wine better than cheap beer). She was on her second glass and probably well on her way to finishing the bottle. Sleeping alone was not conducive to sobriety. However, the alcohol had loosened her tongue and addled her brain. She really hadn't even heard the boys' stories. In fact, she had barely touched the dinner she was rushing them to eat in an effort to get them all fed, bathed and put to bed by nine (8:30, in the case of the twins).

The boys tucked in in the bedroom, she polished off the rest of the chardonnay in a shallow but blissfully over-heated bathtub. After bathing, she fell onto the futon that doubled as the living room couch by day. As she turned her already spinning head towards her pillow, she smothered her face and sobbed herself to sleep.

II

What do you want?

A *Soda Stream*... A cheap vacuum cleaner that sucks dirt from cheap carpets... A refrigerator with shelves that make sense...

I am cleaning the kitchen. Hardly a Sisyphean task in New York City; in fact, I have to remind myself that this "not quite a walk-in closet" is more culinary paradise than many in this city afford. I could be stuck with no more than a hot plate and microwave, but keeping a small kitchen clean has its own penalties. For one, I can never find what I'm looking for and there's almost nowhere to store food (assuming I want dishes on which to serve that food). So I am cleaning out the refrigerator. Starting from scratch.

In going forward, sometimes it's best to look back. When you are young, you are mostly ignorant about your own beauty. It's only when you see photos of your former self that you begin to grasp the notion that once you were beautiful for no other reason than the fact that you possessed youth. *Youth is wasted on the young*, somebody somewhere once said. I don't believe youth is wasted; it is squandered. We are young for such a brief time. If you do not count the pre-mnemonic years (roughly until five), you have a baker's dozen of childhood with a handful of youthful years beyond. Yet kids are always trying to force adulthood upon themselves. They fail to realize that being an adult is the worst part of the Sisyphean effort that is life. They've forgotten their quest to remain in Neverland.

Some parents think they are protecting their kids by delaying the truth. I think that truth is exactly what today's youth need to hear. They need to know that if they experiment with drugs and sex in their teen years, well,

21

40-something becomes interminably tedious. Pot is for the post-mortem of youth.

If I have one quality of which I am most proud (and, trust me, the list of my qualities of which I am proud is succinct), it is my ability to learn from my mistakes. My timing on this issue is often retarded, meaning that the epiphany follows many months or years after the error. However, to note that I've made a mistake and to appreciate that I should not repeat it (even if the intel into comprehending how not to repeat it is delayed) is probably key to my survival. Many mistakes are not unearthed until the lessons that could be derived from them come far too late. I suppose I learned to blame myself for my own problems (whether fairly or unfairly) a long time ago and, thus, am constantly vigilant in deciphering the moral of my missteps.

Right about now, you may be tempted to whip out that violin that fits well between thumb and forefinger. Poor little rich girl, and that. Boo hoo for you. First off, I admit that I do tend to suffer from "first world problems." If anything, awareness of my privilege has led to self-inflicted guilt that will plague me until the day I die. I know there are places in the world where children are conscripted into working in diamond mines and fighting civil wars. I know there are parents whose DNA alone contributed to birthing a sociopathic child. These sad stories are multitudinous and, to paraphrase Tolstoy, unique in their own way.

Which leads me to a heretofore unknown philosophy established in 1987 by my best friend and roommate from college, Marilynn: *The Brooke Shields' Knee-Sock Theory.* Allow me to take you back to a simpler time. Our enemy was clearly defined: The Soviet Union. We typed on typewriters. There were four main broadcast stations, and one of them was underwritten by the government and no one minded (hint: it was PBS). Gas was relatively cheap. Food still had some food in it. Brooke Shields was the "it" girl of the day.

In fact, Brooke was at school with us, in the class one year ahead of me and Marilynn. Brooke seemed like everyone else in the crowd, but we all knew that she was above us even if she didn't act as though she were. One day I mentioned to Marilynn that I felt guilty for being depressed about my life because I was privileged and going to this amazing college and how dare I not appreciate all I have? Thus it was that Marilynn established the *Theory*. She noted...

> What if one day, Brooke Shields awoke from bed, her perfectly coiffed hair perfectly coiffed, and went to dress herself only to find she had no matching knee socks? She searches high and low, she checks the laundry room, she asks her dormmates, all to no avail. Her world crumbles before her, knowing that she has no matching knee socks to wear. She writes a quick epistle, noting her despair, and hangs herself right then and there. The world will see her as ridiculous; the media will scorn her for killing herself over footwear! We will mock her endlessly. However, what no one will appreciate is that having mismatched knee socks is the worst thing ever to happen to Brooke Shields! She didn't kill herself over her wardrobe; she killed herself over the worst thing ever to happen to her. Who are we to judge anyone's "worst thing ever"?

Of course, as time has shown, Brooke did have far worse issues than a wardrobe malfunction with which to contend. And suicide by hanging seems a cruel thing to mention, given the resulting years and the tragedies she's faced. Nonetheless, this theory has made me a more empathetic person towards the seemingly lucky, even towards myself. As I said, I learn from my mistakes.

Which isn't to say I don't make new ones to take the place of the old.

I was fairly young when I married. A French boy, a few years older than I, wanted to live in America. We were in the Peace Corps together and he was stunningly beautiful. He was not among the young who didn't appreciate his own beauty. But because I was, I thought that marrying him would be as good as it gets. And when his insane (and unfounded) jealousy led him to hurt me, well, I thought that was love. Certainly it was the only love I had ever known.

Affection always was paired with cruelty in my life. From the earliest age I can recall (which admittedly is not particularly early; I've blocked out a lot), there was a constant channel of choler leading to violent outbursts. I was raised on deflection techniques. My technique of choice: be perfect. Strive to please my abuser. Please him (and, indeed, the majority have been "hims") and know that you've served your master to the extremes of your ability. When I met men who could not or would not be pleased, my life would shatter to varying degrees. I had a few of those types of relationships prior to getting married, as well. But I digress...

Quick: What came first, the chicken or the egg? The answer is quite simple: It doesn't matter. Both exist and they cannot be separated from their nature.

Does abuse create victims or do victims gravitate toward abuse? This notion is controversial, but appears more worthy of metaphysical discussion than the aforementioned *ortus pullus*. I do not mean to imply that victims crave abuse, but rather that once you are a victim, to a very great extent, that is precisely *who* you are. You may identify as victim or not, denial often being a last-ditch claim to sanity. I truly do not think that victims seek out or stay in abusive relationships because they want to remain victims. However, comfort in victimhood is the reality that many face. Is it endogenous? Imprinted shortly after birth? Can any victim transcend her (and, indeed, many have been "hers") fate?

At the risk of you, my dear reader, chucking this book into the fireplace, I will suggest that at some point abuse becomes a comfortable existence for the victim. This is not because she wants to be abused, but because it is her *reality*. It's like those prisoners who are released and reoffend not because they weren't rehabilitated, but because life outside of prison comes with no map as to show them how to navigate a world they've never before seen.

I didn't choose to be abused. I am certain of this despite the fuzzy childhood. Whatever happened to set me down this path, after a good long time I became conscious of the fact that I was choosing to be a victim. It was (and is) my reality. I can escape it no more than the Type-I diabetic can escape daily insulin injections. I am a victim. I have exited the closet and I say it with trepidation: *I am a victim.* I am neither proud nor ashamed. I will no longer affect that I am other than I am.

I think about this often: escape. I am aware that this is a treacherous slope, so I skirt the rim of the realm of "disappearing" that can often seem too enticing to deny. For example, I am walking home with a canvas bag full of farmers market veggies: collards, turnips, broccoli. As I am about to turn the corner towards my apartment, I come upon a Harley Hog, one of the guys is on a cell phone. His T-shirt reads: *If you can read this, the bitch fell off.* I turn to him, smiling, and say, "Do you need a new bitch?" He laughs the kind of laugh that comes from truth, goodness, the soul. He tells the guy on the phone to hold on. "Are you volunteering?" I answer, "Absolutely." He laughs some more.

Upon reflection, I have determined that I should have chucked the greens and straddled the bike. What am I waiting for? I've never sought adventure because work, husband, kid, responsibility, society's expectations keep me on the straight and narrow. And what have I to show for it? Would my child's life be worse off had I gotten on that bike and rode away? Would escaping this reality be such a bad thing?

After I was a half-block away, I considered going back to give the biker my card. Seriously. I thought that if he had my *business card* he might get back to me. Ask me to be his bitch. Because, you know, having a card with your contact info at the ready is the surest way to bacchanalia. Sarcasm aside, this is my reality: I pass out business cards to acquaintances on a search for something... different. Anywhere but here, right? I'm still playing the victim. Perhaps I should employ this title on a lightly-embossed, 100# weight card in raised letters:

Victim at the Ready, *call 1-800-ABUSEME.*

I am progressing, however. Now that I have embraced the harsh light that shines on my nasty little truth, I have to step out into this light and determine how to keep myself safe from future abuse. From where do I summon the strength to fight my abusers: the ones I attract, the ones I haphazardly stumble upon, the ones who ingratiate themselves with manipulative trickery until they are past my defenses and I am at their mercy?

I need a creative solution to this conundrum.

Φ

Ironically enough, it was Ryan-Claude who first challenged my assumptions of victimhood. In our early days of courtship, he had doted on me. In retrospect, he was probably more in love with the notion of America than he was in the notion of a life spent with me. However, at the time, his gestures of tenderness seemed sincere. It was only after we had been married a few months that the trickle of disapprobation fomented into a sea of disgust. When I decided to go back to get my Master's degree, he turned unusually cruel. At the time, I believe he worried that I would gain enough leverage to leave him (I am the worst kind of victim: a hopeless romantic; I had worked three jobs while pregnant with our daughter to put him through medical school, my own career path suspended indefinitely), but I also knew he was lashing out at me because I had made a number of friends from grad school. He had forbade me making new friends since our marriage and did his best to strain the few friendships I had from before we met. Keeping a victim isolated is the abuser's first line of attack.

During my studies, he felt abandoned, which was a weird reality to me. He reverted to bachelor slobbism: Mold literally began to grow on the walls of our apartment. He also decided that porn fell into the parameters of marital fidelity, and as the Internet grew in size so did his appetite for free downloads.

A word about fidelity...

Richie asks me about what I hope to find in a relationship. Specifically, he asks if I'm looking for fidelity. I respond, "Fidelity, or monogamy? Because these are two very different things." He nods, but I doubt that he wouldn't cheat on his wife if he were married and thought he could get away with it. That doesn't mean he isn't absolutely *faithful*. On the other hand, I've known men who were addicted to porn and never cheated technically, but their fidelity was undermined by a forfeiture of ever pleasing their partners based on the corruption to which they had been over-exposed. Richie rolls his eyes; it's not the first tirade he's heard from me against pornography. "Look! Men who troll for porn have essentially discovered that one hand and an Internet connection are far easier an erotic undertaking than having to please a flesh-and-blood-and-excrement partner. Monogamy and fidelity are not necessarily mutually exclusive, but they are by no means inclusive." Another revelation delivered to me long after mistakes were made.

THE TRUTH

I suppose I must explain my negative bias towards porn—a bias not on principle but rather owing to the fact that men tend to be unimaginative and lazy lovers as it is, and porn elicits a knee-jerk (okay, cock-jerk) antipathy for all women that further disenfranchises their partners when it comes time to copulate. I have no scruples when it comes to photographing and profiting from the filming of grownups having sexual relations. The problem is that there isn't a porn production available that is more creative than the average woman's subconscious. However, by turning to porn instead of a real woman, the average man simply widens the abyss between himself and a great fuck truly earned. The rise (pun intended) of the Internet has birthed a chasm that may never be crossed: Men are from this tectonic plate, women are from that.

Thus it was that I discovered my husband's secret cache. It turned into a sick game, where he barely hid the evidence of his wide-ranged searches (not to mention peep-show-shop purchases) as if he wanted me to know where he'd been and what he'd seen. Some of his clicks truly sickened me (let's just say he took the dog and pony show a little too literally), but over certain other photos I would linger. I was particularly intrigued by women bound in all manner of restraints. I went from wanting to confront him to feeling aroused, an irony lost on Ryan-Claude who hadn't directly contributed to my female excretions in years. The greatest shock to me wasn't that I could "feel" again, but that it was such an abrupt switch. My dwindling interest in sex had—if you'll excuse the pun this time around—petered out over the run of several years. I had assumed it was a natural result of aging or post-pregnancy physiognomy. I had assumed my state was simply a given, not to be undone. I had assumed ever feeling sexual again would be a gradual thawing, like spring after the ice age.

How wrong I was. I went from disgusted to hypersexual in an instant. So much for my loathing of porn on principle (in case any doubts were lingering in your mind). And since he was my husband and the only man I knew at the time, I pounced. It was a resurrection of our lust, but whatever love had been between us remained unearthed, silent in its grave. Needless to say, my lust for Ryan-Claude was short-lived; he didn't become less cruel. In fact, he accused me of cheating because nothing else would have explained this sudden interest in sex again. Not even his uncleared cache of bondage photos.

The cart of mistakes was set way in front of the steed that years later would bring me clarity and carry me away from my horrid circumstances. Instead of moving on back then, I struggled to find some form of connection, to please him in a way that seemed just. Thus, came our substitute bond: Booze.

There are people who drink tea.

They make it an art (Japan). Or a pastime (England). A ritual (China). An indulgence (Australia).

I have often wondered about protagonists in novels who drink tea. They are so sensible, practical, dependable. Tea time is one of contemplation and reverie. Offer such folk a dose of Sake and their next day is a wasteland of regret and recrimination.

If such people exist, well, I haven't met them. For the post-Prohibition majority of us, there is alcohol. It is the panacea that underlies all peace. Seriously. One may say that drunkenness leads to debauchery. Nay, say I. The drunken man passes out. So does the drunken woman, which may very well lead to debauchery, but not on her part.

I have often wondered if I'm an alcoholic. The reasons for this are two-fold: genetics and practice. As for the former, there is a rather broad range of stereotypical drunks among my extended family (I fall in the happy, loud variety myself). As for the latter, it would be easy to blame Ryan-Claude but not in my nature to do so. Once I took up drinking with him, I never quite mustered the prowess to beat him at his daily imbibes, but certainly I tried my best. Misery and company and so forth. But it was an empty camaraderie and at long last (20 years qualifies as long last, trust me), I threw in the towel and left.

While my marriage went comatose, being fed intravenously, respiration forced into it with great intention, I began to question what is "normal" in any relationship, particularly with regards to sex. While we copulated approximately 3,000 times over one score years of marriage, I could probably count on one hand how many of those fucks were meaningful (especially if you excuse me the first six months of fucking when it still was fresh and miraculous). As I waited out leaving Ryan-Claude, this musing about sexuality was more a philosophical inquiry than any kind of exploratory pursuit. However, I began to wonder who gets to decide the mores: what part of sex is debauched or immoral? The months that have ensued in celibacy have given me plenty of time to think about sex with little opportunity to have any. I'm still waiting for my epiphany.

Indeed, this question is more relevant for me post-marriage than it was when I had a man in my bed with whom there at least was potential for experimentation. I'm not sure I would have been able to discuss any particular longings with my husband, who both was indifferent toward and highly suspicious of my sexual leanings. I don't entirely blame either of us for our befuddlement. Most of us with "first world problems" are driven by mixed messages in the mores of society. Questions of polygamy are over-dramatized on television. Bachelor/ettes frolic with multiple partners for the voyeurs of the world to view (no credit card proving age required to watch). Political and sporting heroes get stung in prostitution rings or barroom toilets. Gay is the new black. Even Iowa is allowing same-sex marriage.

There's a new buzz word: heteronormativity. Although coined as a phrase to describe society in opposition to gays and lesbians, the definition falls short of modern reality. For that matter, it really doesn't describe humanity from the get go (just ask those naked Greeks at the first Olympics!). When did we decide that a man should be one thing, a woman the other and only when a prescribed male meets a proscribed female can bedroom bliss blossom?

A light was shone on the fallacy of heteronormativity more than two score years before the word found its way into the vernacular in 1991. The Kinseys were revolutionary in their approach to sex analysis and widely criticized as a result. The brilliance of the Kinsey reports is not in their accuracy but in their non-judgmental data retrieval. Long before *Deep Throat* hit a seedy Times Square theater and alt.com joined a plethora of Internet "dating" sites for kinky folk, Kinsey and his staff gathered details of sexual "perversion" and recorded it for posterity. Even in post-war America, there was evidence that heteronormativity existed in theory only, a wedge issue if ever one was required to divide people and keep each of us afraid of ourselves. Not to mention unhappy in the bedroom. Add in a bit of Catholic (or Jewish) guilt, and the cycle of circumcision is complete.

On a personal level, I am still wrestling with notions of what is acceptable behavior, beyond the whole "sluts have more fun but aren't worthy of love" trope. As standards of public decency fall like leaves from a dead tree, never to be regrown, we see more and more evidence of what normal isn't. It isn't fidelity. It isn't "till death do us part." It isn't the Missionary position. It isn't a one-man-one-woman union. I wonder where the axes of love and sex meet; I do not believe these to be parallel needs. However, there are times that I sense a complex calculus quandary (forgive the phonetic alliteration: English suffers having no komplex kalculus kwandary); it's like those "approaches zero" problems I never mastered in first-year college math. You get closer and closer to a connection, but you never actually connect at all. Mathematics may build on irrelevancies, but relationships don't function as functions.

I remain certain that intimate relations are merely the symptom of intimacy, that no matter how much "free love" or NSA sex is out there, intimacy can only be sublime or transcend the biological into the artistic if the intimate partners combine the emotional (what most of us would call "love") with the physical (what we refer to as "sex"). To be more blunt: Casual sex is boring. At this point, probably you are telling me I am just too damn picky if I expect my orgasm to border on the rhapsodic. However, I don't think I am picky. I'm just honest. But honesty is not rewarded. The less guarded you are with your sexuality, the more likely you are to be hurt. Just as the more open you are about your deepest hopes and dreams, the more likely you are to see them dashed. How did Bruce Springsteen put it? A secret garden? If you keep it secret, you keep it safe. In effect, that secret can stay locked away and eventually go untended, even forgotten. Then there is no way to explain why you chose to grow lilies instead of roses or how it was that your grapevines were overtaken by poison ivy.

If only we were taught from an early age that there are no bad plots, only pernicious weeds. That even the dandelion serves its purpose. Purslane may overtake the flowerbeds but can be harvested and provide sustenance. There's no such thing as a "bad" garden unless it is neglected or its plants made to feel unworthy. Worse, someone may come along with a scythe to cut down the misunderstood growth, leaving you with a sense that nothing wild should be allowed to grow; you should be satisfied with a nice, safe lawn. A lawn that looks like the neighbor's lawn. Which looks like their neighbor's lawn.

Elise's favorite flower is the tulip, which is a flower that never dies but blooms beautifully for a very limited number of days each year, hibernating for months before finding its way through the last spring snow. So long as the squirrels don't dig up the bulb, the tulip will burst forth every spring without fail. How it occupies itself the other 11/12 of the year remains a mystery.

I prefer hydrangeas. I like the fact that they change color based on the chemistry of the soil in which they are planted. Hydrangeas are totally affected by their surroundings, yet they make the most of those surroundings by being unpredictable. You cannot even be sure year to year what color the hydrangeas will be; blooms on a single plant can vary in appearance. And once the season ends, the blossoms hang on to the stem, frequently becoming dried and tissue-like. They do not blow quietly into the night. Hydrangeas bloom and age. They do not simply drop their petals, bearing no resemblance to their younger selves.

I envy anything that can be beautiful and take advantage of its environment; to remain fresh, always adding something remarkable to its small corner of the world. I like the predictable unpredictability of the hydrangea: It will always make an appearance, but you cannot be sure how it will look when it does. And even as their beauty fades and color turns from blue or pink or white or purple to decaying brown, the flower holds its form until the season comes to an end and intervention will pluck the dried form from its shaft.

I would like to believe that the proper gardener could make the most of my hydrangeas, appreciating a bloom with so much potential at adaptation and differentiation. One season, the blossom would be pink. Another, it would be blue (a color that appears nowhere else in nature). Occasionally, it could go stark white. And in my garden, the altered blooms would be exciting, not a disappointment. I've always been made to feel that I present myself inappropriately, and, as a result, I've kept my garden under lock and key for far too long. Now I'm afraid to open the door and see what nature has wrought.

The Job

Day two at David Ormston-Meighton Architects Company, Incorporated, was pretty much like day one. Day three was identical to day two. Day four, however, brought with it some variety. Variety that made Hallee disconcerted.

"David Ormston-Meighton Architects Company, Incorporated," Hallee answered the phone, managing some inflection in her voice despite the rote reception. "How may I direct your call?"

There was silence on the other end of the line. At first, Hallee assumed the call had been dropped. Then there was the familiar sibilant diction. "Yesss, Hallee. It'sss David."

"Yes, sir," Hallee responded, not sure what else to say. She felt "at the ready," to put it in Army parlance.

"The way you sssay my name," David instructed. "It's OrmsTONE-MeeTONE. You're sssaying it cut short: ORMstin-MEEtin. I need you to practiss thisss."

Another dead silence. Hallee never heard herself mispronouncing her employer's name, but now he was waiting to hear her repeat it back. Carefully, she inhaled and said, "David OrmsTONE-MeeTONE..."

"No!" David barked. "That'sss not it! It'sss OrmsTONE-MeeTONE."

Hallee would have laughed had she not felt so uncomfortable. She tried again, "OrmsTONE-MeeTONE."

"Hallee," David's tone revealed growing impatience. "I'm sssure you can do better. Try again."

"Maybe I should say the whole name of the company?" Hallee offered, trying to buy time. She wasn't sure what David was after. Obviously, saying his name properly was important (she, too, was often the victim of mispronunciation—"Hallee, rhymes with valley"—so she sympathized), but she honestly heard no difference between how she spoke and how he was "ssspeaking." She took a deep breath and repeated, "David Ormston-Meighton Architects Company, Incorporated. How may I direct your call?" She immediately felt stupid for including the second sentence, but by now it was so ingrained into her head that she had begun answering the home phone the same way. On the handful of times it had actually rung, that is, and she actually had been there to answer it.

Whether she had passed the test or not, David told her that he wanted to check his voice mail. Her hands were shaking as she pressed the transfer button. Fortunately, she transferred him correctly.

Hallee replayed the incident in her head. Perhaps she had a slight northern California accent of which she was unaware? She mouthed the company name again and again. Which must have cut a ridiculous figure to the petite old woman now standing at her desk.

"Don't fret, lovey," the mild mannered octogenarian (or possibly nonagenarian; she looked ancient and frail enough to blow over in a stiff breeze) said gently. "You look positively nonplussed!"

Hallee stared blankly at the woman in front of her. Perhaps Hallee *was* "positively nonplussed" because she had no idea who the woman was, what she wanted from Hallee, or what Hallee was supposed to say in greeting.

"Isn't this a wonderful company to be working for?" the elderly woman continued, and Hallee couldn't determine if the question was rhetorical. At last the woman introduced herself. "I'm Alison." Still no recognition from Hallee. "David's assistant?"

"Oh, of course," Hallee felt some sense knocked into her. "Lauren told me about you. I hope you're feeling better."

"Why thank you, lovey," Alison smiled. There was a glint in her eye that belied the fatigue expressed by her body. "I'm well enough, I suppose."

Fortunately, Lauren was making her way through the front entrance, laden with groceries for the office kitchen. Lately Lauren had been taking advantage of the extra help on the front desk and coming in closer to 9 a.m. As Hallee was expected to be in the office by 8 a.m., she tried to suppress the thought that Lauren was also taking advantage of her.

THE TRUTH

"Welcome back, Alison," Lauren interjected before turning to the coat closet with a somewhat dismissive, "We're glad to have you back." Lauren seemed all business with Alison, but Hallee detected something off-putting in the way Lauren was addressing the old woman. Of course, maybe Hallee was being ageist to think that Alison should be treated any differently than anyone else in the office. However, Hallee was trying to determine who was more senior: Alison by virtue of her age and position with the company or Lauren owing to having been with David since he launched his firm.

Lauren quickly scooped up the clipboard that held David's master schedule. "I have the updates to David's calendar for you. Do you want to start with that?" Maybe what Hallee had detected was something oddly condescending to Lauren's tone. She spoke more than gently; the tone was one Hallee often heard on the playground from nannies speaking to their charges. It was a tone she had never used with the boys, as she had preferred to talk to them in a natural voice. "Oh, Hallee... can you put these away?" Lauren nodded to the two canvas bags over-flowing with coffee, milk, fresh fruit, bread and peanut butter. Snacks to encourage the staff to remain at their desks rather than venturing out for sustenance.

Lauren ushered Alison off, holding a clipboard in one hand and Alison's elbow in the other. They disappeared around the corner towards David's office. Through the glass, Hallee could barely glimpse Alison slowly lowering herself into her desk chair and booting up her computer screen. Hallee off-loaded the groceries, per Lauren's command.

They say things come in threes, and the strange encounters were yet to end for Hallee. The phone rang once again, and with Lauren busy going over David's schedule with Alison, Hallee answered. She had barely begun the salutation when an irate voice interrupted.

"Who the hell is this?" the woman's voice demanded.

"Hallee Thompson?" she answered with doubt in her voice. The person on the other line could be anyone from a prized client to a deranged prank caller.

"Put Lauren on the line!" the angry voice was now screaming.

"I'm sorry," Hallee tried not to stutter. "Lauren is away from her desk."

"Oh, well, fine," the voice continued. "There's an ice cream truck parked on the sidewalk outside the apartment. I need you to call 911."

Hallee was dumbfounded. She would joke to her mother in Florida during their weekly phone calls (yes, it was her own mom whom she'd asked how to direct the call) that living in New York City was like falling through the looking glass. Now Hallee was sure she had encountered none other than the Jabberwock him(her)self.

"May I ask who's calling?" Hallee managed at last.

"It's Janine!" the creature on the other end of the line thrashed her jaws. "Are you new?"

"Um, yes, ma'am. I just started last week." Hallee was shaking again. She hated this inability to control her body when her emotions were out of whack. She didn't have that trouble when she was with Jeremy, but she had noticed it happening since moving here. She wasn't sure why she was so on edge in general, although she thought it might be some form of PTSD.

"Oh, Jesus Christ!" the angry voice hissed. "Janine *Ormston-Meighton*!"

Suddenly the cogs in Hallee's brain began to spin and make sense of the situation. Lauren had mentioned that if David's wife called to forward the call to her, but if she wasn't available, Hallee should do whatever was asked of her.

Hallee grabbed a small lined notebook pad and a pen. She wrote, "ice cream" and "911."

"I'm so sorry, Janine. Yes, an ice cream truck?" Hallee felt like an idiot, but she was more afraid of this woman's temper than of looking the fool.

"Yes," Janine continued, a bit calmer but obviously exasperated. "The truck is parked up on the curb, which is *illegal*. And it's idling right underneath my window, which is *illegal*."

"Um, are you sure it's idling?" Hallee asked, suspecting that the refrigerator unit was what Janine was hearing. And considering the weather, Hallee doubted it was there selling ice cream; it was more likely a delivery truck dropping off groceries to one of the resident's in David's building.

THE TRUTH

"Of course I'm sure. Don't talk back to me! I know an idling truck when I hear it!" Janine had barely stopped to catch her breath. "I want you to call 911 and report it. It's on the street right in front of my building."

"Okay," Hallee agreed, thinking this woman might actually be psychotic. How on earth was Hallee going to call the emergency hotline about an idling truck? Maybe the truck driver was on the Megan's Law list? That would be the only reason why the police would come and do anything. Perhaps she could flag down a traffic cop on the street? But if she could, would the cop even bother driving all that way to Janine and David's house (it was across town from the office)? And would the truck even still be there by then?

What was Hallee thinking? There was no way in hell a cop would do anything about this. Simply calling from the office would probably result in some kind of nuisance fine. Nine-one-one would track the call the minute she dialed through. Surely Janine knew how 911 worked.

"And be sure to report it anonymously!" With that, Janine hung up.

I guess she doesn't know how 911 works, Hallee thought to herself.

By this point, Lauren had returned to her desk. Hallee quickly sought her out for advice.

"No, you're right," Lauren agreed, after Hallee related the whole tale. "We can't call 911." The co-workers quietly considered their options. At least 40 minutes had been wasted and neither of them had done any work actually pertaining to her job.

"I know what to do," Lauren said. "Call 311. That would at least get the information to someone in the city government. That's something."

The 311 call line was for New Yorkers to report everything from downed power lines to unsafe construction practices. Hallee called and after another 45 minutes on "hold" listening to announcements about alternate side parking rules, various power outages and Muzak, Hallee finally was able to speak to a representative. Hallee said she wanted to remain anonymous in her complaint, after being asked three times to identify herself. The woman on the line was obviously irritated by the call, first doubting a roving ice cream truck in late winter and then proceeding to lecture Hallee in the mechanics of refrigerator units on ice cream trucks. Hallee listened patiently to what she already knew. What other choice did she have?

When she got off the phone, Lauren rolled her desk chair close by.

"I know Janine can be a bit demanding," she began, and Hallee snorted before she could stop herself. "You have to do what she asks, and you can't put it off. No matter what, even if it's for David, you stop what you're doing and work on what she wants. That's just how it goes here."

Hallee was processing this new dictum. Lauren had been with David Ormston-Meighton Architects Company, Incorporated, (*How may I direct your call?*) for almost 10 years. Hallee hadn't yet managed 10 days. Yet Hallee was to believe that the needs of David's wife outweighed the needs of David's company? It didn't make sense.

Suddenly Hallee had an epiphany. "Is she disabled?" she asked Lauren.

"No, no," Lauren quickly explained. "She is just rather particular."

"And in charge, obviously," Hallee added.

Lauren whispered, "Just be careful saying that. And do what she asks. Exactly what she asks."

Apparently Lauren didn't appreciate the irony of Hallee having just spent the last hour doing what Janine asked *in*exactly. Three-one-one instead of 911.

What Hallee wanted to say: "So we don't have to do what she says, so long as we don't get caught."

What she said: "Got it. Do what she says." Then Hallee added, "She's a bit like Miranda Priestly, isn't she, only without any talent or ability?" Lauren showed no recognition to the reference.

"Who?"

"Miranda Priestly," Hallee said. "You know? From *The Devil Wears Prada*?"

"Oh," Lauren answered and flushed slightly. "Janine actually bought me that DVD last year for a Christmas present. Said it was the funniest movie she'd ever seen. I never could bring myself to watch it."

Hallee nodded, absorbing the lunacy and dreading the possibility of getting to know Janine better.

And so it went, Hallee embracing the monotony of one day being pretty much like any other. Her work experiences all morphed together, her home life the proverbial silver lining. As winter progressed into spring, the boys settled into their new surroundings, and Hallee found some kind of strange comfort in the routine. Every day was the same, excepting the weekend, which was the same as every other weekend. On Saturdays, she ran her errands as early as New York City shops would allow (Hallee was convinced that it was easier to shop at 2 a.m. than 7 a.m., when she was up and looking for milk and Cinnamon Toast Crunch). Mid-morning, she and the boys together would clean the apartment and go to the Laundromat. Late afternoon and evening were spent doing something "fun" before Mary dropped off her kids. Usually this meant going to a nearby park where the boys ran her ragged. When the band of brothers gathered, Hallee would pop in a DVD while the boys ate hot dogs or pizza or some other kid comfort food. She would generally drift off within five minutes of getting the five boys to bed.

By the time Sunday morning rolled around, Hallee was mentally getting ready for work. She tried to adopt the mindset of not wasting her precious weekend by dwelling on the next days' activities, but escaping the notion that she was an automaton—sent home merely to recharge her batteries for work—was nearly impossible. Her one indulgence (other than regular glasses of wine in the evening) was the Sunday *New York Times*. After dropping Mary's kids, Hallee would scramble downstairs to the bodega for a paper and a stale croissant. She would stretch out over the boys' bedroom floor, propped against the wall with a couple of pillows. The boys would have taken over her "bedroom" space by now, immersed in their video games (Hallee remembered a time when she swore she would never get a gaming system, that it was an indication of lazy parenting; now she praised the Wizard of Wii, the Poseidon of PS2). In the *Times* she lost all sense of time. She knew it would have been more economical simply to read the paper online, but to lose that tactile interaction—the ink smudged into her skin, the flimsy newsprint flopping and scattering as she skipped over death notices and relished the surreal wedding announcements—would be to reenter the world of her reality, which was banal at best and desperate at worst. Let her have her $3 paper once a week. She would only look up when the boys' yammering for dinner (quickly approaching bedtime) could no longer be ignored. At that point, she would relegate the paper to the recycle bin; regardless of how much or little she had managed to read, she knew she would not be able to return to her idyll.

The boys fed and bathed, she would press her outfit for the next day's journey into vocation. And the predictable routine would continue.

Why she bothered with a wardrobe she had no idea. Lauren had warned her that nice clothes would only get ruined at David Ormston-Meighton Architects Company, Incorporated, and Lauren had not lied. Between sorting through dust-filled storage areas looking for back files and climbing around under desks to reroute computer cables, Hallee had mangled two blouses and a pair of tweed slacks. Fortunately, most of the damage had been superficial and was repaired with needle and thread or cleaned in the weekly trip to the Laundromat. This dirt was manageable. However, other "dirty" aspects of the job were less tangible and, thus, more difficult to wash away. A numbing sadness seemed to be all she felt day-in, day-out.

Hallee had admitted to having few expectations in her new life. After years of praying for better with Jeremy, she saw no point in setting herself up for disappointment again. Better to hope for nothing and be pleasantly surprised if something good came along. Which was probably why the banal routine of kids, work, kids, wine, sleep, do-it-again was lulling her into apathy.

Hallee hardly had time to consider her emotional well-being. Lately, everything was about paying for the basics: food, shelter, electricity. It was a new state for her, this vague sense of panic that she would fall off the treadmill if she stopped running and land in a vat of molten lava and perish. She had been somewhat insulated from the tech bubble burst out in Silicon Valley; as an academic, Jeremy had provided a comfortable, albeit low-key lifestyle. In San Francisco, Hallee had lived a strictly middle class life, with a small house on the outskirts of Oakland and access to a car that could get to Costco or the beach. She had never before seen the pace of extreme employment that was everywhere in NYC. Whereas "full time" in project management during the boom years of the late-1990s had generally meant she was working upwards of 45-50 hours per week, NYC in the late aughts meant a minimum 55-hour work week. And that was for admin. Many of the architects in the firm would work until the wee hours of the morning, return to their homes to shower (Hallee could vouch for the time based on the taxi receipts David would reimburse—the Supreme Leader did care that his employees traveled safely late at night), and maybe grab three hours of sleep before returning to work. With the exception of weekends, most of the junior associates were pulling 20-hour days. In comparison, Hallee's 60-hour workweek seemed almost reasonable.

As work was her one "grown up" outlet, Hallee found herself building vague alliances at the office, which seemed a more honest and apt description than calling them "friendships." Her lunch break being only 15 minutes (she had abandoned eating out as being too time consuming, not to mention unaffordable), she would tuck into the kitchen to heat a can of soup or gobble down a sandwich. These were the snippets of her day where she could chat with her co-workers (they were hardly "colleagues," being far younger and perhaps subconsciously giving off the vibe that they considered themselves far superior to Hallee). In truth, many of them had that idealism she once had felt herself. She didn't envy them; the odds were that life would come crashing down on their dreams and the 20-hour days would amount to little. Or maybe Hallee *was* jealous of their youth and optimism and the thought that they would get to have it all: a great career, financial security, love...

At first, Hallee was surprised that the few women in the office weren't dating their co-workers. However, between the long hours and the fact that these women were swimming upstream in a testosterone filled river, she realized that they were far more interested in their male supervisors' respect than in any form of romantic attention. It appeared that the architects broke down in two lines: married with kids (typically with stay-at-home wives) and utterly single. Hallee was the only divorced person on staff; Alison was the only widow.

Hallee hadn't considered the thought that she might want to start dating again, but seeing all these young junior architects who outwardly had zero desire to date shocked her. The senior architects that were her age or older could pay for nice vacations (and took them) and had somewhat saner hours, but they, too, seemed more invested in their careers than their wives. Hallee wondered if their wives cheated on them. She had recently read an article in *Time Out New York* that mentioned "Casual Connections" on Craigslist and was mortified by what she read—not to mention the eyeful she received when she clicked on a posting!—when her curiosity got the better of her and she had visited the site late one night. From that experience, however, she had gleaned the fact that a lot of married people were cheating on their spouses from work (or home when the other spouse was working). This drive to be everything at work seemed to dictate dating protocol. Hallee doubted ever having an opportunity to meet anyone organically in this city.

Unfortunately, her present work hardly felt like a career in which she could be invested. For the first time in her life, Hallee feared she was depressed. Her life force seemed MIA. She wanted to feel good about leaving Jeremy, but everything around her appeared no better, no worse. Just a different view. Even longer daylight hours as summer approached couldn't snap her out of it. She felt adrift and alone. She had even given up her nightly prayers with the boys. What was the point?

It was the first week of June when she felt the paradoxical hand of God reach out from the most unlikely source. The time was 2:17 p.m. on Friday, and the office was unusually quiet. From Memorial Day through Labor Day, David ostensibly offered "summer Fridays," which meant the senior staff left early. Although Hallee didn't get the afternoon off, it did mean the work was far less stressful. The afternoon had been so quiet, in fact, when the phone rang Hallee startled. She went through the routine greeting.

"Who is this?" a gentle baritone asked. "Oh, wait, it's Hallee, right?" The voice on the line was easily recognizable. Arnie Jacobs was Principle of the office, second only to David. While it would have been preferable to say Arnie's imprint was on David's designs, what his job title really meant was a great many frequent flyer miles. He was taking meetings all over the world and generally breezed in and out of the office without so much as a "Hi, how are you?" to the administrative staff before jetting off again. His demeanor was more harried than brusque, and Hallee had yet to form any concrete opinion about him, their interactions to date having been few.

"Yes, Arnie," she answered, vaguely aware she was pleased to hear his voice. "Back from London?"

"Finally, yes," he said and paused.

"Are you still there?"

"Yes, yes I am." Arnie cleared his throat and continued. "You know, Hallee, I never recognize your voice when I call. For some reason." He added the afterthought awkwardly as if he wanted to say something more.

What Hallee wanted to say: "Yes, I know. I really missed my calling as a phone sex operator."

What she said: "Yes, I know. I really missed my calling as a phone sex operator."

Arnie chortled. Hallee envisioned him coughing up through his nose some liquid he had just swallowed. When he calmed himself, he admitted, "You do have a really sexy voice. Uh, I hope you aren't going to sue me for harassment for saying that."

"Well..." Hallee's smile could—no doubt—be heard in her voice. "I said sex first, so I guess I should worry about *you* suing *me*." They both laughed easily, and Hallee felt more relaxed than she had in a very long time.

Arnie was simply checking in at the end of a long week. He was back home (he lived in Brooklyn, same as Hallee, albeit at a much tonier address in Park Slope) and would be regrouping next week at the office, assuming no last-minute fires needed putting out that required him to repack his bags and head off again. There was nothing untoward about the interchange. It felt human, and non-creepy; less a flirtation than a feeling that they both had simply let their guard down. Something that no one ever seemed to do in New York City. However, later on Hallee realized the phone call was key to changing her status at David Ormston-Meighton Architects Company, Incorporated, which Hallee had now started to think of in acronymic terms: DOMACI. She pronounced it as "domicile" without the "L".

In fact, the first thing Arnie did when he arrived Monday morning was to pull Hallee out of the queue to get into the conference room for the bi-weekly associates' meeting. Hallee's job there was recording secretary: She took notes that would later be sent out from Alison's e-mail, as though Alison had taken them herself. Hallee long ago gave up wondering why they were perpetuating the illusion that Alison was involved in day-to-day business when she rarely was even in attendance. Everyone knew it was Hallee taking the notes and typing them, forwarding to Alison for dissemination. Just one more of the weird goings-on at the domicile.

"I'd like to talk to you," Arnie said, touching her upper arm in a non-menacing way. "Can you come into my office?" Sensing her nervousness about being late to the meeting, Arnie offered, "I'm here today. They won't start without me." His smile was genuine. He had a doughy face, but rather than having an aura of illness, it seemed more teddy-bear-like. Unlike David, Arnie wore glasses for near-sightedness, so his clunky black frames (now back in vogue, these were the type of frame that Hallee distinctly remembered from her youth that only the poor kids wore) made him more endearing than "boss like." Arnie was as disarming in his charms as David was off-putting. How on earth had the two men ever come to work so closely together? Yin and yang, Hallee supposed.

Hallee followed him into his glass cave (similar in structure to David's office but one-third the square footage), where he closed the door and motioned for her to sit. Hallee did so, but remained perched on the edge of the chair. She couldn't imagine why Arnie wanted to speak to her, so she prepared herself for the inevitable blow she was about to receive.

"I feel like we've barely had a chance to get to know one another, Hallee,"

Arnie stated in his usual friendly tone. "You've been here, what? Three months now?"

"Yes, just," Hallee answered.

"It must feel like ten years!" Arnie joked. He was a man apparently devoid of malice, because the look in his eyes showed no mischief. He simply read what she felt sometimes. The job did often seem interminable.

"Look," he exhaled. "I haven't had a proper executive assistant in a really long time. I interviewed a few people after my last EA quit—she finally got fed up with the hours and bullshit. I get it. There's a lot put on the admin staff, and you gals don't get nearly the credit you deserve." A part of Hallee wanted to take offense at Arnie's use of the word "gals," but—again—he was so mild mannered that it was nearly impossible for her to hold him in contempt. And, truth be told, the administrative staff was entirely made up of women.

"So, what do you think?" Arnie stopped abruptly.

"Think about what?" Hallee asked, completely perplexed.

"About being my new EA? I can get you a raise, maybe $5K?"

Hallee's heart started beating faster. Five-thousand dollars would mean she could afford to get a private sitter and wouldn't have to do the babysitting trade anymore; she could put the boys in day camp when they got out of school at the end of June. She could get some small piece of her life back.

"Of course," Arnie added, "You'll have to work longer hours, but I know you have kids and are juggling a lot." As with the other senior architects, Arnie's wife was a stay-at-home mom with two young girls. Hallee once overheard Arnie say that the only thing he hated about being on the road so much was missing his family. He was devoutly Catholic, so Hallee believed his admission to be genuine and not some subterfuge that hid a secret trashy life on the down low. Not that all Catholics were good Catholics, but Hallee felt that Arnie was among them. Plus, she wanted to believe such "happily ever after" stories between couples did exist out there.

"Tell you what," he said, as if she needed to be further enticed to take the promotion. "There are a few projects that are coming up that you could do from home. I can specify which jobs you need to do here—you'll still have front office duties, but I can probably get you off full-time phones—and what you can do from home. So?" Arnie drew out the "sooooo" as a lead-in for her to answer.

"Absolutely," Hallee stammered. "I'm really surprised. I was afraid you'd be calling me in to fire me."

"Ha!" Arnie barked. "Haven't you learned anything by now? We have Lauren fire everyone." Arnie winked, and Hallee wasn't sure if he was joking or not this time.

They walked together to the staff meeting, where Arnie made the announcement about her promotion. Hallee wondered two things: Had Arnie already discussed this with David or was it his decision alone to make? And was the fixed smile on Lauren's face one of pleasure or a mask to hide her disappointment in not being offered the position Hallee now filled?

III

> "Was she told when she was young
> that pain would lead to pleasure?"
> *Girl*, John Lennon and Paul McCartney

What do you want?

To meet a single exceptional human being... To know justice will prevail... To be filled...

Ryan-Claude has a girlfriend. He has turned into a fucking cliché. He's dating the nanny. Not our nanny (I never relinquished what was right for what was easy), but she did babysit for us a few times. Like the time I was in Italy with my mother and daughter and he was home with our son for a whopping seven days. He couldn't stay sober that long, so he called her over to tend our son while he slept off a drunk.

I remember what he told me she had said to him: "You seem to have it all. Why are you wasting it?" Did she have designs on him even then? Adding insult to injury: She's French. A green card from a former green card holder, perhaps? I'm pretty sure the French invented *Le Pere du Sucre*.

Or perhaps the wife truly is the last to know. How could I be so naïve as to believe he was the exception to the "dirty old man" rule? Of course pushing 50, he would choose the 21-year-old baby sitter. They say the truth shall set you free. Perhaps, ironically, it has. I am sickened by the whole affair. Literally.

But I digress...

I have plumbed the depths of my subconscious in an effort to understand why this relationship upsets me so. Am I merely jealous, pure and simple? Certainly the easiest thing in the world would be for me to admit that I'm angry that Ryan-Claude has a new woman in his life, a younger woman, a French woman.

Richie, in his infinite tactlessness, has the temerity to ask me if she's pretty. "She's 21!" I scream. "We were *all* pretty at 21!" A slight shadow flickers over

Richie's face; I guess we weren't all pretty at 21. Perhaps he is not the only one in this conversation who lacks tact. Nevertheless, I burn with rage knowing that Ryan-Claude has chosen a woman with whom I could never—at least not with anything less than 25 years in a time machine—compete.

Yet if I admit this, I must go a step further: He vowed he hated French women. He disparaged both his sisters as "manipulative whores" and swore up and down that he would never have anything to do with his native females because they were notorious philanderers who lied through their teeth and wanted only to be well kept, gold-diggers all.

Now I have proof that this was his biggest lie of all.

Ryan-Claude is the consummate liar. He lies the way other people pick their noses: discretely or not, as need arises, without much thought or deliberation. He will lie about the blatantly obvious. Perhaps this is an addict's *modus operandi* or just how he has been able to get what he wants whenever he wants it. Perhaps it is diversion. Perhaps he thinks if he tells enough lies, he will be able to control what is true.

Despite knowing he has a penchant for lying, I was certain at specific times that he was being honest, true to me at the very least. Now my trust is shattered. Whatever idealized remnant I had from our 20-year marriage has vaporized, not even a glistening thread remains. He lied about everything. That's what bleeds inside me. That is what is eating away at me. The sickness within that grows is consuming me, and I struggle to be rational.

How easily I could destroy it all for him! You cannot live with someone for 20 years without learning his weakest points. I struggle to keep from ruining this for him. Yet that would be playing into his Kafkaesque lunacy. Keeping the nanny as your mistress? I had assumed his lack of originality was limited to the bedroom. Perhaps that is the purpose his lies serve: "I have nothing original to offer, so I lie about everything to escape the banal predictability that is me."

Was there anything remarkable about my life with my husband? I suppose we all want to believe we are above the fray, that we are uniquely special. I remember when I was young that I wanted to stand out so badly, to be noticed in some significant way, that I begged to wear glasses. I thought by wearing glasses I would somehow be extraordinary à la victims of the Khmer Rouge.

I'm not sure when I came to realize that I am not, actually, anything special. This is not self-deprecation; it is fact. I believe that few of us are exceptional. You may be a genius, as in, "the Mensa membership is in the mail," but if you don't theorize about relativity at Princeton or blow up a few Princeton professors at the very least, no one will remember you as a genius (disturbed or otherwise).

I wanted to believe that in love, at the very least, I could achieve greatness. As a teen, I wanted to be married to Prince Andrew (he was the cute, interesting Brit du jour). I wanted to have the famous husband (behind whom stood the wife responsible for that greatness). I thought Ryan-Claude was the answer to the existential question. In the end, he has become a caricature. The best he could muster was the obvious: Aging male grabs woman of inferior education and intelligence roughly the age of his daughter. Can a red sports car and little blue pills be far behind? He wasn't special. Even a little. Ergo, neither am I.

If I am to be honest to myself, my hurt goes even beyond this.

Since the nanny moved in with him, he never sees his son anymore. He never sees *our* son anymore. He'll pick him up for a few hours now and again, but he parades around with the freedom of a man without responsibility. Of a man who has no child worth seeing, let alone raising.

I have told Ryan-Claude flat out that I don't care whom he fucks, but if he *ever* gets her pregnant, I will kill her while the miscreant offspring swims inside her. If you are going to "date" (she sees it as dating while he sees it as fucking) a woman almost 30 years your junior, you better be ready for her to "catch pregnant." My daughter thinks I'm joking about killing the bitch. Or off my cracker. It's neither. My conscientiousness is deliberate.

I don't know why, but I wanted a lot of kids. I remember as a child, longing to be part of a huge family (I'm an only child). Where this longing came from, I have no idea. Maybe it was deflection. When you are abused, the more the merrier. Perhaps it was biological.

Men do not truly appreciate the biological clock/imperative that women encounter. I'm not sure women truly appreciate the biological clock/ imperative we encounter. Certainly we don't appreciate it while we are young. We feel it. We are propelled by it. But appreciation comes after there is no more womb at the inn. Then a woman knows she will not be giving birth to Christ reincarnate, even if she managed to retain spinsterhood into menopause. The Virgin waiting to create something more lasting than herself, until she waits too long and all is wasted.

Let us pause for a moment to consider the ironic etymology of the word, "menopause." You don't need to score 800 on your verbal SAT to see why this stage of life would cause males to abandon their mates. Menopause: Men must stop; from the French (yes, my own personal irony is bitch slapping me as I type this) MÉNO- men- + PAUSE stop. Interestingly, there is a lesser known synonym *climacteric*, from the Greek (now the Greeks certainly knew a thing or two about sex!) from Greek KLIMAKTĒRIKOS from KLIMAKTĒR critical point, literally, rung of a ladder. Thus, a woman—Greek or otherwise—at this stage of life is of paramount importance; imagine perching precariously on a shoddy ladder and how you should cling to its most vital rung. Try shouting the word aloud: "Climacteric!" How suspect that in American society the word that has taken hold in our vocabulary is the one that portends a woman's frigidity. As opposed to the word that sounds like the woman is in an enhanced and extended period of ecstatic climaxing. Men run away from their menopausal wives because they cannot satisfy a climacteric spouse.

Of course, men never have to concern themselves with life's arc of life. Although they shouldn't, the simple fact that they can create a baby at 82 means they never have to worry about "too late." All the modern science in the world won't help a woman create an embryo (her own at any rate) after a certain age, and a sperm donor half her age won't make up for this inability.

I doubt that men even think about sperm in a procreative sense, unless they are actively trying to create life. Women who are engaged in sexual activity view each and every period as a (non-) procreative event. When you are 20-something, every late period is traumatic. When you are 30-something and single, every month rains crimson as if announcing your very own onset of autumn: "Winter is coming!" you are reminded every 28 days, give or take. By 40-something, the official countdown has begun; it is only a matter of weeks, months, a few precious (or tedious) years and the blood will stop forever. The perimenopausal woman knows that whatever issue she has begotten is all there is or ever will be.

Perhaps it is unfair to equate spermatozoa with menses, but a lack of one certainly leads to the presence of the other. What is that called? An inverse relationship?

Regardless, I wanted more children and Ryan-Claude wanted fewer. I was a good wife. Always the good wife. Always putting the needs of my husband ahead of myself. I forced sterility on my body and never caught pregnant, until the one day—feeling his age—my husband said he wanted to try for a son. Our daughter was in high school by then, so I laughed, assuming a 40-year-old uterus was not going to house an ovum from the home team. Well, you know what they say about those who assume? Turns out I was wrong, and we had our son within a year.

Yet the interim remains: all those baby souls that never came unto me. A half-dozen could have easily fit between two siblings that were more like mother and child than the relationship I had with my son. Those who don't know me often suspect my daughter is the real parent; those who do know me saw how unbelievably fat I got during the pregnancy (it's not easy to have a baby in the countdown-to-bloodless decade). My "baby fat" has been the constant reminder of nature having a mind of her own... insert the predictable body image tropes here.

Ryan-Claude had claimed he didn't want more children, but now I know he lied about everything. I am waiting for the day when the nanny climbs upon his drunken unsheathed cock and gets herself knocked up. Maybe he'll even be glad she did so. And because he's a man, he will be able to have children in the same graduating class as my grandchildren.

Rage fills me not because he chose her over me. I am enraged because he chose her over us. The starter family. The American family. "Those" people to whom he could lie and cheat and not lose a minute's rest. After a score-long investment on my part, he has moved on from us all.

And this is what is killing me.

Φ

Why is it that women will try to fix what someone else broke but men see "damaged goods" and divert their attention elsewhere? As a woman, perhaps it is in my nature to nurture, but if I am honest about my own damage, I am *persona non grata* in terms of a potential mate. I'm not talking about communicable diseases here, but Ryan-Claude broke me and although I don't expect anyone else to come along and fix me, it would be nice to think that I at least warrant "gently used" resale.

I find it odd that my dearest friends are able to support me when I'm down, going so far as to call me out on inappropriate (even ridiculous) behavior, and we remain dear friends. In fact, the friends I consider closest (and this includes my daughter away at college on the "left coast") are the ones that don't pull punches; they are the ones who will tell me when I've been a colossal fuck-up and bring me back to earth (admittedly after I lick my wounds a day or two). They are the friends who have helped me grow over the years (decades even) into a more reasonable and decent human being.

Yet they are all women. Is this a female trait? Is it possible that the male of our species is capable neither of giving nor receiving constructive advice? Do they lack an empathic gene? I think not, but it does seem to me that at some point (probably right around the time the woman says, "I do") the man—now husband—relegates the woman's—now wife's—emotional needs into some kind of compartment where he stores unwashed hockey socks, cigarette butts and toe jam. Might as well add the wife's input, too. She holds not a voice of reason; she is but a nag or shrew. Of course, the woman feeling that she has been dismissed out of hand shows who is more powerful by withholding "favor" (for many women, this is euphemistic for non-vaginal sex). The demise of the relationship starts at this point, and few couples ever correct course to get back on a path of mutual affection and respect.

Do not despair, dear dick among the va-jay-jays (considering Oprah is a victim of sexual abuse, you would think she'd have the common sense to know that coy pet names for sexual anatomical parts is really fucking stupid... but I digress...), no, do not despair that I hold my own sex with greater regard. It is not only men who are to blame for a lack of love in long-term liaisons. Women are known to double down on their ill-thought choices and end up pushing the cart further along said path of no relationship return. Despite my woman-scorned tirade, I truly believe that men are not bad. Rather, society leaves them few options to be "real" men. Neither are women bad, but somewhere along the way we—as a gender in general—decided it is better to be right than to be happy.

Richie once told me something extraordinarily profound with regards to this dynamic. He said a woman should either tell a man to *do* something or *how* to do it, not both. I call this the *dishwasher dilemma*. In the dishwasher dilemma, the woman asks (fair enough, male reader, *demands*) the man load the dishwasher; she is tired of cleaning up after him and deems this a reasonable request. The man, whether wanting to please or desiring the woman to shut the fuck up, condescends to load the dishwasher.

However, the woman is not satisfied, and she then proceeds to instruct the man on *how* to load the dishwasher. This is the moment where right and happy go their separate ways for her. The man has complied; he has loaded the dishwasher. Yet the woman continues to be dissatisfied because he didn't do it the "right" way, i.e. *her* way.

What purpose does it serve the woman to tell a man to do something and then instruct him in how to do it? She is effectively dismissing him as incompetent. In truth, what would be sacrificed? A few pieces of meaningless Tupperware or a slightly more valuable wood-handled knife (it is true, men are incapable of differentiating "dishwasher safe" from its opposite; probably because unlike with—say—metal in a microwave, melting is not nearly as dramatic as combustive explosions).

Sadly, the "dishwasher dilemma" spills over into all aspects of a couple's life together. Now when a woman initiates sex, which most men claim they want, she creates an untenable situation by telling her partner *how* to make love to her. The man is too obtuse to differentiate kitchen from bedroom, viewing both as chore chambers. Once again, his wife/partner/girlfriend is telling him what to do and how to do it. He suffers from the pressure of never being good enough for her, and he starts to consider his options (usually by posting on Craigslist for a lover that won't drive him crazy).

Unfortunately, American society further exasperates the situation by emasculating men. There was a time when a man knew who he was and what he was supposed to do. It was simple and straightforward with no room for nuance or speculation. In other words, the ways of old were ideally established—true, by men—for a male mind that flounders in the details. Keeping it simple stupid was what worked for men for millennia, whether it was killing the beast and bringing it back or making the money over multi-martini meals.

In the 21st Century, men are superfluous. Women bring home their own bacon and fry it up in their own pans. They don't have to worry about some guy who makes less money, works fewer hours, pays less attention to the kids, and who, statistically speaking, will likely leave them at some point with nothing beyond a government-mandated 50 percent cash-out of both of their 401Ks. With in-vitro fertilization and looser adoption rules, women don't even need men to have babies anymore. Plus, with all those Craigslist posts a click away, women can easily host a honey if nature calls. Women now have bested men at their own game.

But at what cost to ourselves (assuming heterosexuality)? It's a self-fulfilling prophecy: By not needing a man, women make men feel unneeded. Men no longer feel compelled to serve and protect their families, who easily get taken away by independent females no longer compelled to look the other way when the male behaves badly.

I see Elise struggle with the lessons I've learned so harshly. She is fifteen years younger than I, her husband born a mere 20 hours after she met the world. She is here in New York City, trying to survive on her own while he is stationed with the Marines' 2nd Battalion in Afghanistan, trying simply to survive. After his last stateside visit, she felt isolated on base, so she up and moved to New York. While Elise misses him and frets, she also is creating an independent life for herself: She pays her bills from her job as a librarian; she's considering buying a dog; she has a whole new set of friends, myself included, that her husband has never met personally. He has been in Afghanistan for almost two years, and she has been faithful to him for almost two years. She has been celibate for so long that it is now her state of being.

Which isn't to say she doesn't long for affection. It is Valentine's Day, and we are eating at my place. It's cheaper, avoids us having to make a reservation, and ends our jokes about being a "lesbian cougar couple." We have opened a second bottle of wine, my son long since gone to bed, our dinner dishes still on the dining room table (I have a dining room table with no actual dining room to house it; welcome to New York).

"I would like to have sex with a woman one day," she announces abruptly.

"With or without your husband?" I ask.

"I don't know," she admits. "I haven't really thought a lot about it, but I would probably just want to try it. For myself alone. To have that experience."

I have probably had too much wine tonight and too little sex of late for this conversation. Elise has had an equal amount of wine tonight and even less sex of late for this conversation.

"Well," I smile, not sure if I'm serious or not, "I'd fuck you. But I'd worry it would ruin our friendship."

"I don't think it would ruin our friendship," she smiles back, and I'm not sure if she's serious or not. "I think it would just be one of those things where we sit around," she hiccoughs, "drinking wine ten years from now, saying," hiccough. "'You remember that time we slept together? What were we thinking?!'"

I'm not sure if I should continue down this path, but I admit I miss affection. "I wish I had someone to touch, you know? To kiss. I miss kissing."

"Well, I'd kiss you," she leans in, "but your lips are so thin, I'm afraid I'd get a paper cut."

Ignoring both the humor and cruelty in this remark, I lean in as well and my thin lips caress her mouth, my tongue gently parts her fuller lips, and I know I've made her wet. She pulls back in shock. I am sure she's not repulsed, just surprised. Her hiccoughs are gone.

"Wow," she declares. "You are an amazing kisser."

"You have no idea!" I boast. We both end up laughing and pour ourselves another glass of wine. In the end, that kiss is the extent of our dalliance. We fall asleep in each other's arms on the couch, but it is a chaste embrace. Somehow I realize, despite a drunken haze, that Elise is more lonely than lesbian. Goddess willing—it's a Sapphic moment—her husband will return in summer, and she will try to figure out how he fits in the life she has created here in New York without him. She will try to figure out which she dreads more: fitting him in or having him return to another tour of duty. I know she will struggle and feel guilt over her own version of the dishwasher dilemma, because in her situation, pushing her husband away could very likely lead to his demise in a country as remote as any on Earth with values as foreign to ours as any can possibly be.

The Man

Xavier Sebastiani was considered something of a buckaroo. Famous for his daring (some would say, recklessly insane) exploits, he had recently returned from a three-month stint in Afghanistan where he had been embedded with the 2nd Battalion of American Marines, carrying not an M240 machine gun but a Sony F23 digital camera. His documentary film coverage was already being touted as Oscar bait.

To the staff of David Ormston-Meighton Architects Company, Incorporated, however "X" was simply thought of as Arnie Jacobs' college roommate. X didn't call New York home—"home" being as transient as he was—but when he wasn't dodging IEDs or slipping off ship decks into the Pacific (his book, *Kyokuyo: A Whaling Pirate's Tale*, won the Kiriyama Prize and was a finalist for the National Book Award: Among the harrowing details, X relayed a not-so-funny-yet-amusingly-writ anecdote about the night he washed off the boat in high waves and nearly drowned), he would sleep in the three-story brownstone he owned in Carroll Gardens, Brooklyn.

Hallee had heard some stories about Xavier. The office was not prone to gossip, but X's reputation was known through Arnie, who would occasionally regale the staff with outrageous reports dating back to their Harvard days. From these accounts, Hallee had a picture in her mind how she imagined Xavier Sebastiani to look (she hadn't been curious enough to google him). As she was keeper of Arnie's schedule, she was hardly surprised when X arrived in the office with Arnie one Thursday morning. What did stun Hallee was his physical appearance, since she had imagined him as dark, grizzled, battle-scarred, stocky, possibly missing an appendage or two. In reality, X bore no resemblance to the creature her imagination had conjured.

First off, Xavier was fair, with naturally white-blonde hair reminiscent of her twins (in fact, her first thought on seeing X was that maybe her boys would keep their light hair into adulthood). His gray eyes were clear and exuded kindness rather than some steely resolve. His eyes also betrayed a sobriety: Despite being in his mid-40s, Xavier looked a good 10 years younger; Hallee doubted he drank or used drugs of any kind. His skin was tanned but unlined. He stood well over six feet with a lean figure and broad shoulders (Hallee's weakness for men was nice shoulders). When he smiled, his teeth were white and perfect. Standing next to bespectacled and average-looking Arnie brought Xavier's beauty into even greater relief. He could have passed for a Hollywood star, and Hallee couldn't take her eyes off him.

Nor did she feel any compulsion to look away. She had not felt lustful towards anyone in what seemed at least a decade (since all three of her boys were born within the past 10 years, she was undoubtedly repressing a memory or two), so it was a nice sensation to gaze upon Adonis. Plus, Hallee simply felt no shame in Xavier's presence. She was not brazen; she simply understood that a man like Xavier Sebastiani would never even see a woman like Hallee, a woman past her prime, a secretary in non-descript attire, wearing no makeup, *still* answering the phones in the office of his college roommate's employer (despite Arnie's promises, she was frequently back in the trenches of telephone purgatory, risking Janine roulette). Thus, she stared at X the way a homeless man stares through a restaurant's tinted glass at the $100 steak being eaten by patrons completely oblivious to him. Hallee coveted what she could never have, and the sensation was so unique to her that it never even crossed her mind to use caution, be discrete or show embarrassment.

Perhaps it was the intensity of her stare that prompted him to take notice of her. In retrospect, she probably should have contemplated that Xavier had literally been in the trenches and as a result was probably more aware of his surroundings than most men. He was at her desk before Hallee could think to divert her eyes, and by then she realized that any sheepishness on her part would look contrived. Thus, she inhaled slowly and braced herself to make the acquaintance of the beguiling Mr. X.

"Hi," he began simply.

THE TRUTH

What Hallee wanted to say: "May I help you? Are you looking for the restroom key?"

What she said: "Hello. I'm Hallee Thompson. You're quite lovely."

Xavier laughed. It was a masculine laugh, full bodied, and Hallee saw from her periphery that Lauren was shifting in her chair, probably uncomfortable with the lack of professionalism in the exchange. X held Hallee's gaze. For a moment, she had the sensation of engaging in a staring contest (Drake loved to play this game with his mother, and invariably she would stare him into blinking); she didn't blink first now.

Xavier broke the eye lock and smiled his perfect teeth. Maybe they were veneers? "I guess you know who I am." It was a statement, not a question. Arnie hadn't even waited for his friend, having wandered off in the direction of the kitchen for coffee. I guess this was all the introduction she would receive.

"I've heard the stories," Hallee admitted. She was intoxicated, feeling reckless in his presence. She had no idea what was happening to her; she totally was not acting like her normal self. Perhaps this is what it felt like to be washed off the deck of a ship in the dead of night. "I don't really care about any of that."

"You don't?" X asked, his tone somewhere between amused and disbelieving.

"No, I don't," Hallee continued. Her mind was numb, as though she had just done a shot of tequila. Her hands were shaking, but she grasped her knees under the desk so her nervousness didn't betray her.

"So you don't find my exploits diverting?" he mocked.

"Mr. Sebasitani," she leaned forward, secretly thankful that she had worn a low-cut top. Standing above, he now would see straight down her shirt to her ample chest barely contained in a blue lace bra. "I'm very interested in your *future* exploits." With this the phone rang, and she quickly answered it.

Hallee forced herself to ignore X from that point on, but her panties were soaked. Yet another foreign sensation; she honestly couldn't remember the last time she had felt "wet." In fact, had you asked her—medically speaking—she would have assumed that particular part of her anatomy broke down sometime during her first pregnancy. Apparently the switch wasn't broken but rather had been in the "off" position. This brief encounter should have left Hallee flushed with embarrassment, but she had so thoroughly enjoyed the exchange that the warmth she presently felt was exclusive to her erogenous zones.

Hallee recited the domicile mantra into the receiver.

"Who is this?" the cold tone of Janine was immediately recognizable and Hallee felt it penetrate her and sop up the remaining warmth of the morning's interaction with Xavier.

"It's Hallee, Janine," she answered.

"What did you say?"

"It's Hallee?"

There was a pause. An almost audible hissing. "You called me 'Jane'."

"Um," Hallee wasn't sure what to say. "I called you 'Janine'."

"No you didn't!" Janine protested. "You called me 'Jane'. Never *ever* call me that! My name is Janine!"

Knowing there was no point in arguing the truth with her, Hallee simply said, "Okay. Janine," she added with particular emphasis on the second syllable.

"Let me talk to Lauren. At least she's not brainless."

Hallee transferred the call with an audible sigh. Xavier hadn't lingered, and she tried to recapture the feeling from her pleasant encounter with him. At least he hadn't smacked her down; in fact, he had indulged her. Hallee held onto this notion as the wave of antipathy towards Janine came crashing over her. *This* is what being swept to sea really felt like.

At noon Archie left for lunch with X in tow. This time around, his eyes didn't return Hallee's stare, and she was neither disappointed nor relieved that he took no further notice of her. Lauren seemed agitated by her coworker's behavior but apparently had the good sense not to confront Hallee on this particular issue. Or perhaps Lauren felt sympathy for her old friend, understanding that longing for something doesn't necessarily go away simply when the opportunity to obtain it ceases to exist. She ducked into the kitchen for her 15 minutes of Campbell's Chunky.

Working as Arnie's assistant had proven to be much more challenging than run-of-the-mill administrative work. Aside from keeping his calendar (overbooked) and travel arrangements (too many indirect flights, which Hallee fought to avoid at any cost when she could), Arnie already had her doing ad hoc project management work. He didn't even ask her qualifications; he simply kept giving her harder tasks to accomplish. Hallee was a quick learner, and she planned to take full advantage of being able to work some hours from home by working twice as hard regardless of location. She finally felt that she was performing work that was worthy of her effort and intellect. When she came to this realization, she immediately felt guilty. Guilty towards Lauren. Even guilty towards poor Alison, who was a life-long administrator. The office couldn't run without them, but Hallee needed the validation that her new standing seemed to present.

Mostly though, Hallee just really liked working with Arnie. He rarely got angry, and when he did, it was a slow burn "disappointment" type of anger. This reminded Hallee of her own mom, who never yelled at her growing up, but often gave her a silent treatment that was far worse a form of punishment. When Arnie was tired, especially after having traveled to more than one location in a week's time, he could go into what Hallee best would describe as a "funk." Not depressed, exactly, but close enough to it that Hallee felt on edge around him. Fortunately, it was not in his nature to be moody, and he soon snapped out of these episodes. It also helped her ease out of her own depression, much to her relief. His excitement for the job was why Hallee started looking forward to coming to work. That he felt Hallee was part of his team meant more to her than any paycheck.

It was already mid-afternoon when Arnie finally returned from his lunch (sadly, Xavier was not with him). Arnie immediately asked both Hallee and Lauren to follow him into the conference room. Hallee was buoyant with anticipation until she rounded the entryway and saw David Ormston-

Meighton, the man himself, sitting at the head of the conference room table. Hallee hadn't even seen him enter the office. Lauren seemed less surprised by his presence or why they were being called before him. In front of David were several stacks of proposals, some professionally bound so as to look like a book, others held together with binder clips.

David slouched in his chair, his hand mindlessly stroking the stack of booklets closest to him. Arnie sat near David and motioned for Hallee and Lauren to sit down. Hallee stole a sideways glance at Lauren to discern if her co-worker was as disconcerted as herself. Perhaps the years of working with David had inured her to his presence, which offered an odd marriage of aloof indifference and a certain condescension that always made Hallee feel small and vulnerable. Lauren had an indecipherable little smile on her face, thereby making it impossible for Hallee to know what she was thinking.

"Asssss you know," David began, "this company has submitted my application for the Pritzker prize these past three years." Hallee didn't know. Hallee had no earthly idea what a "pritsssgurrpryssse" was. David looked up with his green eyes piercing—the pupil was a small black dot—like a snake about to strike a field mouse. He emphasized, "All to no avail."

Arnie interjected at this point. "We think that we need a fresh perspective on the application materials. Now, Lauren, you were instrumental in assembling everything last year, so we want you to take the lead on establishing a timeline and specific materials that should be submitted as part of the nomination."

David motioned with his hand towards the stacks of books as though he were casually swooshing a fly. "I'm sssure these look familiar, Lauren, asss you worked on them before." Hallee couldn't tell if David was making some kind of cloistered insult or was simply stating a fact. Regardless, Lauren reached out with her bony hands and pulled the stacks towards their side of the table. "And you!" David set his sights on Hallee and she flinched. He smirked and said, "Arnie speaks so highly of you, that I'm taking a chance that you can put together a winning application. I'll be watching you closely." Hallee didn't like the sound of that, and Lauren's fixed grin was long gone.

THE TRUTH

Hallee hadn't the slightest notion what David expected of her. She looked frantically from Lauren (who didn't meet her gaze) to David (still a piercing stare) to Arnie, whose soft glance and slight nod indicated he would fill in the information gaps once they were back in his office. Hallee exhaled in relief. Audibly.

"So, I think that's about it," Arnie said. "Everything must be submitted by October first. It's a hard and fast deadline. We can't have any last-minute snafus because they won't grant us an extension on this."

"Oh, I don't think there'll be any sssssnafoosss," David said, looking from Arnie back to Hallee and Lauren. "Not with Laurel and Hardy on the team." David snorted a laugh that Hallee would define as halfway between a cough and a cackle. His alliterative allusion-slash-insult appeared to delight him. Arnie looked down ashamedly. Lauren's gaunt cheeks (obviously she was Laurel) were flushed. Hallee was simply livid.

What Hallee wanted to say: "Wow! So she's thin and I'm fat and that's the most original insult you could hurl? No wonder your creativity hasn't warranted your fucking award."

What she said: "I'm really looking forward to the challenge."

She scooped up half the books in front of Lauren and stormed out of the conference room.

About an hour short of quitting time, Hallee found Lauren hunched over her desk with a migraine. Instead of feeling sympathy for her friend, she immediately worried that she would be handed a lengthy Janine "to do" list. Nevertheless, Hallee called a car service for her old friend—who had occasionally had disabling migraines in college, too—to drive her home. After Lauren was safely in a cab, Hallee went to clear her coworker's desk. She was hardly surprised to find a stack of forms Lauren had been filling out on Janine's behalf. Apparently Janine was thinking about traveling to China (heaven only knew why—or perhaps Lauren was privy to the intel) and was incapable of completing a passport and visa application without Lauren's help. As Hallee shuffled the paperwork, she saw one corner of Janine's face peeking out. It was a copy of the woman's driver's license. Curious, Hallee

63

took a closer look.

It turned out that Janine was not as young as Hallee had assumed; she was collecting social security, meaning she was a good ten years older than David. In addition, her name wasn't Janine Ormston-Meighton, not legally anyhow. It was Jane Weaver. *Jane*. Not Janine. The nasty bitch with an elitist name was just plain Jane, descended from working class who probably toiled at a spinning wheel in generations past. The hubris! The hypocrisy! And she held herself up as something so grandiose. Empress Weaver has no clothes.; long live the Queen!

The fucking phone.

Slightly shaken, she answered, "David Ormston-Meighton Architects Company, Incorporated. How may I direct your call?"

"I think you already have," a man's voice replied. Hallee felt a tingling sensation. Archie had left for the day. Surely she was mistaking the voice. After a pause, he continued, "It's Xavier."

Hallee exhaled—not realizing she had been holding her breath—and then smiled. In fact, she blushed, a delayed red that should have found its way to her cheeks when he had met her earlier. She felt completely lost yet more confident than she had in a very, very long time.

"This is pleasantly unexpected," she said.

"I don't believe you."

"Which part?" she toyed with him. She had picked up a pen and began doodling on a post-it pad. She made little "X's" and then realizing the significance converted them to asterisks.

"I don't think you're surprised I called," he sighed. His voice was as sexy as hers, although he looked the part. "I mean, this morning you were practically inviting me to fuck you right there on the desk."

Hallee laughed. She was truly happy that there would be no coy courtship. She now felt so desperately horny, and his intimation was all she needed to acknowledge her hunger.

"Really?" she purred. "And I thought I was being subtle."

"So, are you busy tonight?"

Hallee's confidence wavered. The boys. The cramped apartment. The stressful week. Now this. It felt overwhelming.

"I'm not busy," she said, either in acquiescence or simple defeat.

"Would you like to have dinner?" Xavier offered.

Hallee felt a certain impatience with him. "To what end?"

"Well," he hesitated. Hallee didn't know his intention, but she was not naïve enough to think he didn't have women from which to pick and choose. "To the end of sharing a meal."

"Look," Hallee tried not to sound like a total bitch, "I'm a single mom of three kids, and I sleep in the living room on a futon. I can barely afford childcare during the day on what I make here. Most of the time, I feel like I'm back in my 20s, but with only the bad, and none of the good. I'm overworked and underpaid. To be honest, I don't give a shit about dinner because I have it seven nights a week."

Hallee didn't know what to say next. The line was so quiet for a moment she feared Xavier had hung up on her.

"What time do your kids go to bed?"

"Nine."

Again, silence. Finally, Xavier said, "I'll stop by at 10."

Hallee was surprised. She had been abrasive, truthful, scared, and a little (okay, a lot) desperate. Yet, in a few short hours, Xavier Sebastiani was going to be in her bed, never mind that it was a futon. She gave him the address and her home number.

"Call if you change your mind," she told him.

"It's not my nature to change my mind. See you at 10."

Hallee was elated but terrified. She now had started on the strange journey of 21st Century dating. She wasn't even sure how to prep. There were all these new-fangled rituals in body hair and lubricants. Hallee was completely clueless.

Her biggest fear was practical: What if the boys didn't go to bed without a fuss? What if they didn't stay in bed (it wasn't like she could lock them in)? Fate was kind for once in its intervention, however, and the boys piled into bed on time and fell asleep within minutes of "lights out."

Hallee's trepidation was palpable, but she enjoyed her bath. Afterward, she applied a light lotion to her freshly shaved body and enjoyed the touch of her own skin. She dug a satin negligée from the bottom of her pajama drawer (she chose the pink nylon as opposed to the black satin cami), but she dared to add black thigh-highs and shiny leather pumps. She sat upon the flattened futon behind a seven-foot-high paper divider (one of the few luxuries she had afforded herself in decorating the apartment; she wanted some privacy and she drew the line—pun intended—at stringing a curtain the length of her living room). She had brought out clean sheets and the nicest comforter she had to cover the "bed." She felt awkward and stupid, so she added a short robe to cover up the ensemble while she waited.

She tried not to look at the digital clock on the side table. She tried not to count down the minutes. At 9:58 p.m., the intercom rang. Hallee tried to answer calmly.

"Are the kids asleep?" the echoing voice asked without introduction. Her reply? She buzzed him in. She fumbled with the robe, not sure whether she should keep it on or take it off. She compromised by undoing the tassel so that it hung open. She hoped she looked more sexy than ridiculous.

A knock on the door. She awkwardly checked the peephole before letting Xavier in. He stepped through the doorway, barely glancing at her. He had a wet umbrella (lately the weather had been more San Francisco than New York, with cold dreary rain almost daily); he held it out tentatively, not knowing where to place it. Hallee took it from him and set it on the kitchen linoleum, away from the wood floors of the entryway. In New York fashion, Xavier removed his shoes.

He had yet to look at her or say anything when he swiftly turned, grabbed her hair roughly and pulled back her head so that she was staring straight up at him. Even wearing heels, she was half-a-head shorter. He pulled her hair more while his free hand found its way inside the negligée and pinched a nipple so hard she gasped. If he was gauging her arousal, he didn't take long to determine she liked how he played. Hallee really had no idea why his actions felt "so right," but soon he was kissing her, and the harder he pinched or pulled, the more lightly he kissed her. He wouldn't force himself into her in any manner; he seemed to prefer that she fight against him (pulling at her own scalp as a result) in order to get closer to his mouth. She was hungry for him, but mostly she wanted him to devour her.

Before she was fully aware it had happened, she was naked in front of him, her secret à la Victoria scattered on the floor. He had left the hose and shoes, but the rest he'd peeled off while kissing, pinching and biting various parts of her anatomy. Whenever she had tried to remove his belt or shirt, he had smacked her hand away, one time with such force that he'd left a welt. Now that she was nude and he was fully dressed, he looked at her body. It was as though he was studying her, every blemish, every stretch mark, every ripple of cellulite. She could feel herself growing hot with shame; she was afraid she might start to cry. Didn't 21st Century men still like lingerie? Why was he doing this?

He scooped her up and carried her behind the screen to the futon. As he began undressing himself, he spoke his first words since entering the apartment.

"I like you just fine, Hallee," he smiled. "Cover up or don't. I've seen all of you, and you have nothing to hide from me." Hallee felt a bizarre wave of relief overcome her. She relaxed as though she'd taken a drug. Completely naked himself, and pretty much as beautiful as Hallee had anticipated, he said, "Now I'd like to taste all of you."

His mouth was no longer reluctant as he buried his face between her thighs. Hallee couldn't remember the last time Jeremy had "gone down" on her. He had always wanted to receive but not give in that department. X was both enthusiastic and talented. She came so quickly that she felt embarrassed. X just laughed and assured her it wouldn't be the only time she came that evening.

Despite a wish to remain quiet, Hallee failed at keeping her desire subdued. As promised, Xavier made her come repeatedly. He alternated being rough with extreme gentleness to the point of teasing, essentially requiring her to make him continue with his efforts to please her. When he finally slipped on a condom and was inside her, he, too, came very quickly, and once again Hallee felt that she was a disappointment.

"Why do you do that?" he asked, leaning back on the extra pillow. At least the futon was large enough to hold his frame. "Why would you think if I explode after nearly two hours of foreplay that that's a bad thing?"

"Please don't think I'm pathetic," she stammered.

"Now," he was kissing her fingers, but looking at her eyes, "why would I ever think that?"

"Well," she blurted without thinking, "I'm old, fat, stressed out, and in a dead end job that leaves me broke every month when I pay the rent."

"Only one of those can't be changed," he smiled, "and you're not old." He was caressing her hands now, somewhat carelessly, playing with her fingers the way a cat might bat a string. Somehow, all Hallee could hear was that he did think she was fat. What was the attraction, then?

"Let me ask you something. It's a serious question." He paused before asking, "What rocks your world?"

"It doesn't sound like a serious question phrased like that." In truth, Hallee didn't know how to begin to answer. She couldn't even be sure that Xavier was interested in truly getting to know her. She had no reason to expect that he was, so giving up revelations could be treacherous. Some vague admonition about milk and a cow flitted through her thoughts. Thus, she decided to choose her words carefully, allowing a bit of light into a small, dark corner of her world. If he wasn't scared off or outright dismissive, perhaps she would reveal more.

"I was married," she began.

"I gathered," he kissed the "scar" on her ring finger. After 16 years of marriage and only a few months ring-free, the ring's implant could still be seen on Hallee's skin.

"He was mean." Her brevity spoke volumes. Xavier sat up, looked at her with severity as though he were probing her mind for more details, then he pulled her close and just hugged her tightly. He said nothing and suddenly

THE TRUTH

Hallee was crying; she didn't sob, but tears streamed down.

"It's okay," he whispered. "It's okay to cry."

This approbation was all Hallee needed to let loose what was literally a lifetime's worth of tears. All the regret and fear and anger and pain burst forth and Xavier did nothing to quiet her. When she was spent (and probably looking hideous), he finally let her go. She instinctively went for the tissue box and only met his gaze after wiping her cheeks and ingloriously blowing her nose.

"You know," Xavier said quietly, "I don't think you're pathetic at all. If there's one thing I've learned in all my travels, it's that one man's pinnacle is another's rock bottom."

Hallee smiled weakly. "Even so, it's a bit much emotion for a one-night stand, don't you think?"

For the first time since she met him, there was a flicker across that lovely face. He blinked a few times, opened his mouth, shut it and blinked again.

"I guess I don't know what to say to that," he managed at last. He pivoted and his feet were on the floor. Without bothering to look at the clock or his watch, he said, "It's late. I should go."

Hallee's mind was reeling. A moment ago she had felt closer to Xavier than she had ever felt toward anyone in adult memory. Probably when she had been small, her mother had held her in a similar way and let her cry herself out. In a matter of a minute, that connection had dissolved into estrangement.

Xavier was putting on his pants. Hallee didn't want this awkwardness between them. She didn't want him to leave. She didn't want the silence between them, which wasn't even much of a silence because of the street traffic noise coming through her window.

"Please, Xavier," she was up on her knees leaning towards him. "Please don't go."

Xavier sighed and pulled on his T-shirt.

"Look, Hallee," he said, "I like you, but if you aren't that into me..."

"What? What are you talking about?" She was struggling to make sense of the conversation, but all she could do was blurt out her most immediate thought. "How can I not be into you? You're so fucking yummy!"

Xavier laughed, possibly in spite of himself. He sat beside her. Still on her hands and knees, she leaned in and kissed him. "I don't want you to go."

"Hallee, if you just need a hook-up, I did that and we're done," he said with a light tone that belied his words.

Hallee was stumped. She was trying to give Xavier an easy out, and he seemed offended. Maybe he felt it inappropriate that a "fat woman" like Hallee would dismiss a man like him.

"I wasn't trying to get rid of you, Xavier," she explained tentatively. "I just didn't want you to think I thought this was going somewhere?"

"Going somewhere?"

"I mean, look at me. I'm sure you have your pick of women..."

"Oh, please," Xavier said with disgust. "I don't feel sorry for you, Hallee, and I'm not here to make you feel better about yourself. I'm not here to boost you up. Whatever has happened to you in the past, all I know is who you are right now. I *like* you for fuck's sake. I'm not even going to talk about what I could pick or not because that's just stupid."

Hallee wasn't sure if there was a compliment somewhere in what he said. What she did feel was a harshness that she hadn't detected before.

"I didn't cry all over you because I thought you'd boost me up. The truth is it's been so long since I was treated decently by anyone—look at my work, for God's sake, you've been Arnie's friend long enough to know what goes on there—and I just... I just felt safe with you," Hallee tried to explain but she was uncertain of her motivation in sleeping with Xavier. Was it only a one-night stand in her mind? Did she even want to risk attempting a new relationship when her emotions were still so raw after Jeremy? Wouldn't he just be a transition man regardless?

Xavier tried to speak but Hallee interrupted. "You asked me what rocks my world. I haven't thought about what I want in so long, I don't even know how to answer that question." She looked at him earnestly. "I don't know what I want, so how do I ask you for it?"

THE TRUTH

Xavier was thoughtful and took his time forming a response, during which he held her forearm and etched doodle-ish figures along the underside. "You know, I've seen men blown up. I've literally had their bits of flesh on me. I've seen hell. I'm not trying to say what you feel isn't real. I'm guessing you've witnessed your own kind of hell. I'm just saying I'm not afraid of a few tears. I'm not at fault for your pain." He said this conscientiously, before letting out a small laugh, "I don't know where this might go—you and me—but I like you as is. And you fuck great." Hallee laughed as well. "It's a start, don't you think?"

Hallee shook her head in a way that signified neither yes nor no. "I'm a bit old fashioned," she said. "I always thought you dated and then you had sex." She was smiling and half-joking, but whatever tension there had been appeared to have wafted away.

"Hey, no blaming me on the dating-before-sex trope," X teased. "I did ask you to dinner, an activity that you participate in *seven nights a week.*" He sarcastically added exasperation that mimicked her tone from earlier. She laughed again, feeling truly relaxed for the first time since moving to New York.

"Do you want a drink?" Hallee asked.

"I don't drink. I mean, maybe on New Year's Eve I'll toast with Champagne," X admitted, adding a drawn out, "but..." He reached across to his jacket and pulled a small metal vial from his pocket. He extracted a device from the tube that appeared to be a tiny, metal spyglass, like the kind a pirate would use. If said pirate were four inches high. High being the operative word. Xavier patted the spyglass into the vial, bringing it up packed with a tobacco-like substance that Hallee assumed was weed. He also fished out a lighter. "Do you mind if I smoke?"

"Is that pot?" Hallee asked, somewhat affronted.

"Oh, please," X mocked her. "You aren't going to preach temperance after offering me a drink, now, are you?"

"Well, drinking isn't illegal," she countered, honestly not sure how she felt about the knowledge he used drugs.

"Look, if you don't want me to toke up here, fine, I won't," he stated and began to put away the weird little pipe. Hallee's hand was on his, stopping him.

"Nah, it's alright," she said. "Do you mind doing it closer to the window?" She jutted her chin towards the cracked window that overlooked the noisy street below. "So the smoke doesn't permeate the apartment?"

"Permeate the apartment," he mimicked again. His teasing somehow was endearing, although the pessimistic voice in Hallee's head wondered if she'd feel the same six months from now. Assuming he was still in her life six months from now. The futon butted up against the wall, so Xavier scooted over and opened the window fully, propping himself against it. Hallee crawled over beside him. Despite his comments that he liked her just as she was, she pulled the top sheet along to wrap around her midsection.

The rain had subsided for the most part; only an occasional drop splashed through the screen-less opening. X inhaled his toke slowly, held his breath, and exhaled through his nostrils. Hallee found this incredibly attractive and had the urge to lick his nose. Instead, she held out her hand for the pipe.

"You want some?" X asked with genuine surprise.

"What? You weren't going to share?"

"I thought you disapproved," he said, repacking the pipe. Apparently miniature pirate spyglasses only hold one serving. He held it out to her, and she gingerly held the pipe between her fingers. She had tried pot once in college, and vaguely remembered how it worked. Which probably had more to do with the fact Gavin used an asthma inhaler, and she had demonstrated it for him a time or two. She inhaled deeply and felt an immediate buzzing in her fore-brain. She held her breath and the room spun slightly. As she exhaled, she tried not to cough.

"Holy shit," she choked. "I don't remember pot being that strong."

"Yeah, well," Xavier put one arm around her as he took another drag for himself, "this came from Afghanistan. I probably should have warned you before I gave it to you."

"Will I become an addict?" she asked, starting to nod off on his bare chest. He put the pipe up to her mouth as she inhaled a second time.

"No," X smiled. "But that doesn't mean you won't like it one hell of a lot."

Hallee felt fuzzy. First the great sex, now the great marijuana. She heard her voice rather than felt it as she spoke. "I think I'm going to like everything about you one hell of a lot."

When she woke, a pillow was propped under her head. She lay with her feet where her head normally would be, her head beneath the window, now only open a crack. The rain had resumed. It was dawn, and Xavier was gone. Hallee pulled herself from bed to get ready for work.

IV

What do you want?

A lover who won't drive me crazy... To be understood... To get lucky...

I have decided to grab the horns of the bull, in a manner of speaking. I have decided to stop waiting for fate to intervene. I have decided to start dating again.

What exactly does it mean? To date?

I would argue that the act of going on a date is at best superfluous and at worst irrelevant in the Internet age. Once upon a time, two people would meet and society would dictate a protocol. These two people would follow said protocol, often ending up married while just as often ending up not. Dating was to the 20th Century what ballroom dancing was to the 19th. It was a required effort one had to put forth in order to mate.

In the 21st Century, however, everyone comes with a laundry list custom tailored to what he or she believes would make a perfect match. After all, what is an online profile if not a list of dos and don'ts? I am supposed to summarize the essence of my being in euphemistic metaphors. My potential mate writes in code as well, and I am supposed to discern his (or her, remember, I'm breaking free of heteronormative constraints; thank you, Elise!) personality in a few quirky sentences. To cast as wide a net as possible, I subscribe to many different "dating" sites. I also hedge my bets by finding real world activities to augment my potential dating pool.

Marilynn and I, once on a whim, decided to test our theory that all men were "Nefarious Creatures" when it came to sex. To wit, she wrote the following personal ad on Craigslist:

"Adult Ex-Catholic Schoolgirl Seeks Adult Naughty Altar Boy!"

THE TRUTH

We received 80 responses in 15 minutes before the ad was flagged for "inappropriate" content. No doubt some well-intentioned priest trolling for his own altar boy on an adult website ratted us out (competition, be *damned*!). The funniest part of the entire episode was that all 80 men sent along photos of themselves in various states of (un)dress.

I should have learned my lesson from this experience. Sadly, I have always been slow to face reality.

I think I have a handle on my situation and the general environment of New York City. Men complain that all women here are out for a free lunch (or dinner), so I decide that meeting for coffee is the appropriate way to show I'm no gold digger. Women know that men are looking for the easy lay, so I decide that meeting for coffee is the appropriate way to limit the amount of time I have to spend with a total creeper. Everyone in this city is on overdrive, working long hours and generally overcomplicating his/her life whether intentionally or not, so I decide that meeting for coffee is the appropriate way to deal with the time crunch. I double down on being appropriate with results predictable to all but me.

Date #1: Found through adultfriendfinder.com.

An older man who agrees to meet for coffee in SoHo. Let us call him Daniel. Daniel is perfect in that—as he is older—he knows exactly how to behave: Don't grab the girl (he's respectful); pay for her coffee (he's not cheap); slip the homeless guy a $20 (in fact, he's generous); give a nicely placed French kiss upon bidding adieu (not too much tongue shows he's patient); send off an e-mail within the next hour or so saying how much the evening was enjoyed (he's not going to cut and run). However, as he is older, he also isn't going to waste too much time on a "coffee date." Two days after coffee I receive an e-mail that Daniel is off to his cabin in the Poconos with a nice man for a bit of fun and hopes to see me again when he returns.

Daniel, this lioness is not gonna invite you into her den. Hey, I'm embracing my own eschewal of heteronormativity. I've a ways to go on embracing the efforts of others.

Date #2: Found through OkCupid.com.

After signing up, I receive multiple inquiries from men of all stripes and sizes and one woman whose size is indeterminate because she didn't complete her profile (red flag). Roughly half of the men don't have photos on their profiles either. I move on to the messages from suitors that appear to have, in fact, read my profile. I am able to eliminate another 50 percent. I'm now down to two fellas, one of whom is more likely to date my daughter (so I have an expected aversion to meeting up). The winner by elimination is a pleasant-looking, "everyman" guy who lives fairly close by. I message him back.

We exchange e-mail for several days, and he's witty, smart, single, thoughtful in his responses. I agree we should meet. For coffee.

He then tells me he has recently watched some online porn where a woman was taking a shit on a man's cock. Would something like that interest me? Maybe I could start by pissing on him? *Quelle sigh.* I guess he missed the memo about it being Ok *Cupid.* Romance is dead. I politely decline his kind invitation to use him as a toilet.

Date #3: Moving on to eHarmony!

So much for the stings of Cupid's arrow. I fill out an extensive application that was more rigorous than the INS interview Ryan-Claude and I underwent two-plus decades ago, back when there still was an INS. Surely this website that boasts of more marriages and serious coupling than any other dating website—not to mention the thorough questioning—will separate the wheat from the chaff and provide me with the quintessential romance I seek.

Going on their recommended match, I end up with a younger man who agrees to meet for coffee in Chelsea. Let us call him Fahrid. As a younger man, Fahrid does *not* know exactly how to behave. He shows up clad in sweats with a three-day growth of beard. He doesn't pay for my (or his) coffee. He admits he is recently unemployed. He admits he has six roommates in a loft nearby. He goes to the restroom and doesn't emerge for 20 minutes (was he hoping I'd bail?). He steels away after a single good night kiss and then waits six weeks to call for a second date.

Needless to say, even if I hadn't moved on, I had moved on from Fahrid.

Date #4: Met through work.

THE TRUTH

I decide to get offline and meet a man from the tangible world. Let us call him Jose. Jose is a man my age who, upon learning I am single, begins to pursue me with a serious but disciplined effort. He is sweet. He is thoughtful. I neither encourage nor discourage him, owing to the whole "shitting where you eat" thing. When his contract is complete, I call him and give him my number, saying, "Now that we're not working together, maybe we could get together."

Jose is very happy to hear from me, telling me how much he wants to spend time with me, but he is swamped and could I call him back the next day. I do, but he is out of the office. I leave a voicemail. A few hours later, I receive a call from "Anonymous." Jose is returning my call, happy to hear from me, telling me how much he wants to spend time with me, but he is swamped at the moment.

After three more rounds of phone tag, I finally ask him for his cell number. He tells me he has lost his cell and had the number turned off. As soon as he gets a new number, he will let me know. If he were unemployed, I might believe that he can't afford a cell phone. So I ask him for his home phone. He tells me he has a meeting to run off to, but he really wants to spend some time with me. When he's less swamped.

I get the memo on this guy. Adios Jose! So much for real world, face-to-face, intimate connections.

Date #5: Contacted me after I signed up for match.com.

Let us call him Byron. An only slightly younger man (I've dipped my toe in the pool of 50-something, 20-something, 40-something... he's 30-something) agrees to meet me for coffee in Cobble Hill. As we are meeting before twilight, I suggest we venture down to the DUMBO waterfront and take in the sunset. He holds my hand, he knows how to behave. I think to myself, a man who appears to be normal, has a good job, attractive, smart, seemingly interested in me. Have I found a diamond amongst the lumps of coal?

We make polite conversation, and all seems to be going well. Then I mention that I am looking for a "best friend." Byron stops cold. He drops my hand. He becomes agitated, even belligerent. Waving his hands violently through the air, he shouts, "I have plenty of female friends. I don't need any more!" I say,

"Well, how can you have a long-term relationship"—which he has claimed he is seeking—"and not be friends?" He screams, "I am looking for a partner who will be there for me, who will accept all of me, who will love me from the very first date!" I say, "We don't even know each other. I'm sorry I upset you. I thought we were having a nice time." He asks through gritted teeth, "Is this a date?" Byron now has a crazy look in his eye, he's nearly apoplectic. I'm not sure how to respond. I say, "I thought it was." He says, "And will it end in sex?" Flabbergasted (I should remind you that we haven't even made it to the coffee shop) I blurt, "Of course not!" He says, "Fine. See ya," and storms off into the night.

On the way home, I walk right past the barista and into the liquor store.

Date #6: Met in my writers' group.

I view this as the blame-it-on-Elise date. I take a totally different tact, and I ask out a woman from my writers' group. Let's call her Debra. She's rather butch, but I figure nothing ventured nothing gained at this point. We agree to go out for coffee after two hours of discussing some really awful poetry. Each of us pays for her own java. We stay out late, discussing our prose (she's writing a comedic take on being a lesbian from the Lower East Side), politics (we are both leftward leaning), passions (we both love foreign films), pet peeves (irony alert: people who don't clean up after their dogs), and plans (she's spending the Passover holiday with a sister she hates but her parents are ailing and she feels compelled to visit). This is the best date I've had, well, since I can remember dating.

We walk to her apartment, and I hint about coming up. Debra tells me she has a roommate and it would be impolite. I lean in to kiss her, but she flinches. She exhales. Audibly. "I'm really sorry," she tells me. "I thought we were just going out as friends." I tell her I'd like to be more than friends. She exhales again. "I like you, but I don't date bisexuals." With that, she offers me a handshake. I take it half-heartedly and head home to my empty bed.

Φ

Despite being in a hot bath, I awkwardly reach for the ringing phone. The caller ID merely confirms what I already know. I knew she would call me back if she could. With no perfunctory introduction, I say, "I just did the stupid, most reckless thing in my whole life!"

"You let a gay guy fuck you in the ass?" Ah, that's classic Marilynn for you. She is perfect in every way, except for her disability: She lives in San Francisco. She is also on disability, which means we don't get to see each other as often as we should.

"No!" I exclaim in feigned disgust. "He was *straight!*"

She is howling with laughter, as am I. I struggle to hold the phone in my sweaty, sudsy paw. I am happy. I now know the last time I had sex: it was tonight, a few hours before this call.

My thoughts about Ryan-Claude had been eating me for weeks, but after I accepted what was eating away at me, I sensed a different kind of hunger swelling inside me. It has been here for months, simmering, spitting like an angry cobra. Elusive, dark but ever present. I know if I don't get laid right here and now, I will rape someone. Literally. I simply cannot risk this: If I'm going to jail for something, it had better be murder. I'm keeping a list of possible victims for that potentiality.

Owing to my lack of fuckable dating prospects, I make a decision, throw caution to the wind, and text Richie. I don't tell him my plan, which is to jump him the minute he shows his face; instead I just say, "Come over and we'll watch pay-per-view." I half expect him to blurt out, "Porn?" in which case I will have to come clean and admit I cannot take celibacy a moment longer. But he doesn't joke. He just agrees to meet me at six.

It is a perfect storm. Ryan-Claude picked up our son for the first time in months for a sleep-over (the appropriate term for a play-date that extends to the next day; Ryan-Claude is no longer our son's father, but rather a friendly acquaintance our son meets in the park on occasion). Our daughter is home from college but decided to go clubbing with her friends and won't return before 2 a.m. I have the apartment to myself and am as horny as Rip Van Winkle after the 20-year snoozefest.

So, I lie in wait for Richie to reap what he has not sown but has long coveted. It is, in short, a moment of Biblical proportions. I'm bathed and shaved, and I

. I wait. I have waited.

: becomes obvious that Richie has stood me up, I laugh with a bitterness and relief. All for the best, I suppose.

Every now and again—particularly if I want to stop feeling sorry for my sorry state—I read the "Casual Connections" posts on Craigslist, admittedly not the best place to go for a "date." However, some of them are hysterically funny: like the man who wants to watch a woman wearing only a garter and stockings clean his kitchen (sounds like he ran short on money for his housekeeper this week). I read for diversion more than titillation. Occasionally, I will get drunk and even answer a post, only to wonder the next morning, *What was I thinking?* Tonight, however, I am sober and just looking for the Eleanor Rigbys of the world to know however lonely I am I am not alone.

I click through a few, but mostly look at the lead-ins:

> There have to be some horny honeys out there... – m4w – 28 (Staten Island)
>
> Looking to eat a squirting pussy – m4w – 55 (Upper West Side)
>
> Hey Lady? Wanna get off hard? Apply here – no timewasters – m4w – 42 (Jersey City)

I don't know why, but I feel the urge to read more about Mr. New Jersey. I click on the heading. In his post, he promises to use me and throw me out when he is done. That sounds about my speed, so I send off a picture (face only, thank you very much, deeply disturbed dear reader) and this note:

> I've attached a pic. Please send one back. I am not sure how I feel about a casual CL pick up. If you like how I look and write back and if you can get to Manhattan tonight, maybe we can do something. Not going to write a tome here. Let's exchange pics and see if we're worth a few hours to each other. I haven't had sex in a while, so I'm not looking for more than a good (safe) time.
>
> Let me know. Thanks.

Minutes later, I receive a slightly pixilated photo of a very attractive man along with this response:

> Believe it or not, this would be the first random hookup for me

> through CL too. I totally get you about the uncertainty, and can only
> assure you that I would be more than willing to meet somewhere
> open and public for you to decide if you want to go ahead. Coffee?
> And I promise not to be too pissed if you bottle out.

He boasts he'll get me off hard and doesn't want to waste time, yet he offers me coffee? I have had it up to *here* with coffee! Plus, it's almost 8 p.m. for fuck's sake. I answer:

> I don't need coffee; I need to be ravaged. I'm serious about tonight.
> I separated over a year ago and haven't been fucked since. I figure
> if I wait to meet the right guy, I'll never get laid.
> I'm being kinda reckless and stupid here, but I do have a doorman
> building. So if you're planning on killing me and throwing my body in
> the Hudson, you'll have witnesses.

Within an hour, "Kevin" is at my door. I told him my real name, but I suspect an alias at work on his side. That's okay; it may mean he doesn't do this particularly often. Perhaps he even has told the truth about this being his first Craigslist hookup.

He has a lovely accent. What is it with me and European men? I find the hyperlink in a haystack that leads me down the path of destruction every time. It's a bizarre fate that I cannot shake. I ask him if he wants a drink.

"I don't drink."

Well that's a new one; perhaps fate is being less fastidious than usual.

I'm nervous and the sex is tentative; we fumble with condoms and all those encumbrances that society tells us we must when sleeping with strangers. Do I even care at this point? I no longer fear death. I dispense with what is appropriate and he's hard inside me.

This feels familiar. I look in his bright blue eyes. "Is your name really Kevin?"

He smiles gently. It's a sad smile. He's intelligent. He shakes his head and says, "Frank."

"I like that better than Kevin." He chuckles.

For the first time in a long time, the sex is good. Frank is, shall we say, very talented. I wonder if he does this to every strange woman he meets. I wonder if he put multiple posts on Craigslist and he was also looking for a squirting pussy to eat? Oh, no, that was an older man on the Upper West Side. Frank delivers on his promise to get me off hard.

He's a gentleman, as well, and doesn't jump out of bed. We chat quietly about Obama and the economy. Is the worst over? Will the democrats manage to get their act together and push through the health care bill? We talk a bit longer. He mentions being a vegetarian.

I put two and two together; he doesn't drink, doesn't eat meat. "Are you a Buddhist?"

He nods and tells me about his time living in Asia, that he's a martial arts expert, that he works in international trade.

Oh, Lord. It's a good thing this is only a one-night stand. He's got "my type" written all over him. The martial arts explains the lean, muscular physique. I could so fuck him again.

"I didn't really expect to be having an intellectual conversation this evening," Frank smirks, his accent making the statement more ironical.

"Well, what then?" I lean on one elbow and smile back. "You just thought you were going to come over here, fuck me in the 'arse', and then go without pillow talk? What kind of woman do you take me for?"

"You're... just not what I expected," he admits.

"Well, you know that old joke," I'm joking about the joke, making it up on the fly. "A Buddhist and a submissive walk into a bar..."

"Wait," he interrupts. "Is this the one that ends, 'How did you enjoy your foray into BDS-Zen?'" I find this to be one of the funniest punch lines to a made-up joke I've ever heard. I laugh until he pinches my nipple with his nail, practically piercing it. I cry out, wincing, and then I shudder. "Do you think that might be you? Because I have a bit of experience in that."

I withdraw from him, admittedly too timid to explore this path further, "Since this is a 'one and done,' I guess you'll never find out."

A little while later, Frank is dressed to leave, but he lingers by my piano. "Do you mind?" he gestures towards it.

"No. I hardly ever play anymore."

For the better part of an hour he plays. He tells me that he composes on the side, but he only has a keyboard in his apartment. It's a treat to play an actual piano. *Yes, handsome: You played my piano and you play my piano. Works for me!*

It's getting late, and I don't want to risk my daughter coming home early and finding him here. I tell him he needs to go. He kisses me.

"You know," he says seriously, "you really should be more careful. This was a dangerous, stupid thing you did tonight. I mean, me too, but..." His voice trails off.

Something just happened here, between us, in this moment, but I cannot grasp what it is. I shake off this enigmatic tugging.

He kisses me again and says goodnight.

Φ

I recount it all for Marilynn. She is truly happy for me. I almost feel like it isn't real until I tell her, as if she is my aural historian. Of course, it helps that she lives in San Francisco, because nothing I say can shock her. She's seen it all and managed to do quite a bit herself in her younger days. Now, she's happy to live vicariously through me.

My tale told, my bath drained, I luxuriate in my post-orgasmic glow. I go to my whoMi datebook and I circle the date. I put little stars around the numeral as if I am back in sixth grade and had just laid eyes on Tony Simons, that boy we all crush on when we're 12, doodling his name in bubble letters and accenting with hearts and artistic ephemera. I am giddy and gloriously satisfied. I have asterixed the calendar box, and I will never have to worry that I don't know the date of my last fuck. It is starred and red-lettered for me to reference. In a week or a month or—if I manage—a year, I will be able to return to this page and know when was the last time.

The next day, Frank texts me. He would like to see me again.

The Wife

Whether because she had drunk the Kool-Aid of David Ormston-Meighton Architects Company, Incorporated, or because of her newly rekindled lovelife, Hallee found herself excited to go to work. She also found a growing respect and admiration of her many co-workers' efforts; their passion was infectious. As she was also becoming educated in the esthetics of architecture, she saw them as true professionals who were pouring so much time, sweat and inspiration into their work. It was uplifting to work with people who truly cared about what they were doing with their lives. She tried to harken back to a point in her life where she felt that passionate about anything. In truth, even caring for her kids could sometimes feel like a "must do" rather than an undertaking in which to be fully engaged. Hallee wanted to be embracing her life the way her co-workers embraced the creation of a new building. She felt herself uplifted by the energy around her, and it made her contemplate the possibility of a higher purpose in her own life. Despite lingering misgivings about her job title and status, she finally had begun to feel that she was contributing to something lasting and larger than herself.

Unfortunately, she was still subject to the rules of the fiefdom, meaning these positive feelings were not allowed to linger for long. Invariably some action would result in a reaction where Hallee would be harshly reminded of where she ranked therein. Not coincidentally, these harshly real moments mostly came courtesy of Janine.

None of the architects liked being at Janine's beck and call, but they generally were only solicited for minor construction projects, of which there were a finite number (Janine had already redesigned the Ormston-Meighton kitchen two times in Hallee's short tenure, and a junior architect was currently cursing his bad luck for being selected to design an interior powder room). When it came to the administrators and interns, however, the level of vocational skill was deemed so low that any deviation from Janine's edicts could potentially result in David terminating the go-fer. Among the more demeaning tasks was doing personal shopping for Janine, and the requirements were always overly specific, meaning the better part of a day could be wasted on a single errand. Hallee was often on the verge of a panic attack when she was unable—after spending half a day visiting 10 different farmers markets—to find garlic scapes or some other random fruit or vegetable without which Janine's cook's recipe would be ruined *ruined RUINED!* David often would cook on the weekends, but there was a hired cook during the week; Janine apparently lacked the gift to boil water. The cook and maid were present at the apartment Monday through Thursday, meaning daily shopping adventures. Janine felt it below her cook's dignity to shop for his own ingredients, but apparently it wasn't thus for the administrative team of Lauren and Hallee.

Lauren did her best to take on Janine's myriad activities, including scheduling doctors' appointments and outings to the beauty salon. For the most part, Hallee handled the groceries and random trips to department stores around the city in search of the perfect skillet or drapery. Hallee tried to find the humor (usually of the highly absurdist variety) in these assignments. She would often make jokes in moments of extreme pain or anxiety, her thought being that humor was literally the last thing to go. When life completely ceased being funny, Hallee assumed her internal clock would simply shut off and she would die on the spot.

On one occasion, for example, she had had a particularly onerous time at the farmers market (looking for fennel or heirloom tomatoes out of season? Hallee honestly had forgotten the details). On the way back to Janine's kitchen, she had seen a group of bikers revving their motorcycles outside the farmers market. One was wearing a T-shirt that said he'd "lost his bitch." Momentarily forgetting Xavier and their somewhat vaguely defined romance, Hallee imagined herself climbing on the back of the bike and roaring away. She felt a longing to disappear completely. Where did they go this time of year? Sturgis, maybe? She decided the fantasy was impractical.

Aside from X and the job, she had her sons to consider, not to mention these past few months spent establishing a new life for herself (and them). Plus, she suspected that most of these bikers were in gangs, meaning her romantic sensibility would soon give way to a reality of continued abuse and degradation. She'd been there, done that. Had her own T-shirt. But these moments of distraction helped get her through the drudgery of doing another person's household errands before being dismissed to go home to do her own.

One particular event that brought Hallee a twisted kind of joy was her weekly schlep to deliver bread to the apartment, an activity that she would be doing again today. Rather than buy from a local bakery or even—heaven forbid!—a grocery store, Janine bought her bread from a west coast baker at the price of $12 per loaf. She always purchased two loaves, so when you added on handling and overnight shipping, the weekly tally came to just shy of $100. That worked out to $50 per loaf, or approximately two dollars for a slice of bread. Maybe Hallee's kids ate crap, but she paid less than that for an entire package of Wonderbread. The inherent lunacy of the bread quest always kept her smiling.

Thus it was, after two hours of schlepping around in the rain, Hallee finally made it up to the apartment. Janine greeted her with a fluffy towel and an old T-shirt with a Van Gogh painting on the front, urging Hallee to "change out of those wet clothes." Apparently today was a day when Janine had taken all her meds (unable to make a simple phone call to the pharmacy, Janine had the front office call in scripts for Zyprexa and Clozaril—Hallee googled the names from home and discovered they were common antipsychotics). Janine was in a happy and sunny mood, having made lemonade "From real lemons!" she shouted with the glee of a child opening a summer curbside stand to raise money for Muscular Dystrophy or maybe a new pair of skates. Hallee followed her into the kitchen to off-load the groceries. She put the produce in the bins, carefully separating the food for tonight's planned meal from the rest of the groceries. As Hallee finished putting everything away, Janine thrust a glass into her face. Hallee flinched, but Janine was still smiling at her.

"You have to try some," Janine insisted, pouring a small quantity of the pulp-filled liquid onto an inordinate amount of ice (custom-made from bottled water; Janine had tap water issues). Hallee sipped with trepidation and was surprised that Janine's concoction tasted pretty good. It was overly sour because the kind of organic sugar Hallee was drafted to buy from Whole Foods had settled into the bottom of the pitcher, not mixing with the lemon juice and—what Hallee assumed was—distilled water. Nonetheless, the tang of the lemonade was refreshing.

Hallee had been granted permission to enter the apartment for the past month. Prior to that, she had to leave everything with the doorman (there were three of them, all immigrants: Jose, Pavel and Jiri; Hallee liked their accents). When she finally was allowed inside, she was struck by the aesthetic, which was identical to the office: white walls, clear fixtures, the only discernible color the silver spigots in the kitchen and bath. It felt like being in a hospital, and Hallee just didn't understand the literal white-washing of the place. Of course, the Ormston-Meightons had neither children nor pets, so the likelihood of stains was less. But Hallee always felt uneasy whenever she had to visit, even if Janine wasn't home. The walls were too blank, too antiseptic. Each room held a buzzing air purifier, and Hallee felt a bit like she was surrounded by static, as if she had been sucked into some parallel universe à la the movie *Poltergeist*.

Hallee remembered her shock the first time she had met Janine. Her initial interactions with the boss's wife had been over the phone. It turned out the mental image she had conjured was far from the real thing. Janine could be mean, unpredictable, unrealistic in her demands, and often inhumane. However, her appearance was not one of the trophy wife but of a hag. Her age was indeterminate, as was her general weight. She wore baggy clothes and over-applied garish make-up (blue eye shadow? red lipstick?). She simply appeared unwell, and given her mental state, undoubtedly she was. While Hallee could avert malicious feelings for the woman, she could not summon any compassion. Who hadn't had a rough go of things? Certainly Hallee understood mental illness and how it must be to feel pretty fucking awful most of the time, but most people didn't have an entire team of workers to call on to do their bidding. In fact, instead of sympathy, Hallee simply wondered if she failed to appear with the regular grocery delivery, would Janine simply starve to death, incapable of making her way to a deli.

As if reading her mind, Janine pushed the box in her direction. "Hurry up," she encouraged in a tone less menacing than euphoric. "I want to see my bread!"

Hallee pretty much had the lay of the kitchen down, and she found the exact pair of scissors Janine preferred for her to use to open packages. Hallee never really understood why these packages couldn't be sent directly to the apartment building, but she often considered that Janine was so lonely that these daily trips were all she had to look forward to. Other than David and Lauren and herself, Janine was alone with the exception of the chef (who never chatted on the few occasions Hallee had tried to engage him) and the maid, for whom Janine had a great distrust (her cleaning lady was a young Russian who reminded Hallee of Tatiana, meaning Hallee and Janine had a bit of a bonding moment over their mutual suspicion that the girl was guilty of some as-yet-undetermined crime). Despite never knowing how these visits would go, Hallee truly didn't mind delivering the mail and opening it for Janine when she was in a rare good mood like she was today.

As the FedEx box gave way to the cutting blade, copious amounts of bubble wrap were evident. Janine gasped. Clicking her tongue in that way a proverbial English school mistresses might, she "tsk tsked" her disapproval.

"This is just awful," she scolded, and Hallee prepared herself to take the blame for whatever was "awful" to Janine. Janine was scooping out rolled and scrunched up bubble wrap. Hallee couldn't help thinking that the boys would be enthralled by it, wanting to squish each dome until it popped. Finally, Janine had reached the center of the box where two loaves of bread, shipped directly from Portland, Oregon, were wrapped in "more plastic!" Her tongue clicked again.

"I want you to call them, Hallee," Janine explained slowly, either because of her medication or because she felt Hallee was incapable of comprehending had she spoken more quickly. "You need to tell them that they are destroying the environment by using so much plastic. Tell them to pack the bread in a smaller box next time. This is incorrigible."

Hallee beheld the woman as she overlooked her loaves. Obviously Janine missed the irony in worrying about saving the planet when she was having fresh food shipped 3,000 miles. However, she seemed so happy with her stupid bread, that Hallee couldn't even muster a feeling of antipathy.

Janine was trying unsuccessfully to assemble a sandwich. Hallee reached out cautiously for the knife. "Here, let me do it." Janine put several gourmet condiment jars on the counter, a block of cheese, the three-quarters-of-a-pound (who the hell orders three-quarters of anything?) of Spanish prosciutto Halle had just purchased, a tear from a head of farmers market lettuce. Hallee stacked the ingredients and topped the pile off with a second $2 slice of toast.

"Cut it diagonally," Janine motioned to Hallee to put the sandwich supplies back in the refrigerator, as she brought out two plates. She placed one triangle on her own plate and pushed the remaining half towards Hallee. Hallee was nonplussed. Breaking bread with Janine, literally, did not sit easily on her stomach. She supposed she'd have to settle for $30 per pound ham, $20 per pound Jarlsberg, and the aforementioned Portland pumpernickel. If she couldn't summon any pity for the old woman, the least she could do was enjoy a $10 sandwich.

Of course, even a good encounter with Janine meant Hallee was forced into working longer hours. The Pritzker submission (Hallee had googled the name resulting in "Nobel Prize of Architecture" immediately after receiving the daunting assignment) should be taking up the bulk of her time, but Arnie hadn't let up on her when he was in the office (happily, he was in East Asia for the rest of June). Her time with Xavier had been limited, as well. They had managed only one daytime assignation since the night he spent in her apartment. Finding time for him was proving a challenge.

And although Hallee couldn't be certain, she felt that Lauren was punishing her for her rise at the domicile. Her old friend—a term that seemed more dubious by the day—appeared to be shirking her duties more and more, leaving Hallee even further stretched than usual. Aside from working shorter days than Hallee, her headaches would come on a little too frequently. She also seemed to wait for Hallee to answer the phone rather than picking it up herself. Lauren knew that Hallee didn't want to answer, if she could avoid it. Aside from the possibility the caller was Janine, constant phone interruptions sucked away precious time that Hallee could put towards the Pritzker application. Maybe she was being paranoid, but she sometimes got the sense that Lauren wanted her to fail at helping David to win his coveted prize.

Of course the inevitable finally happened: Janine called when Lauren was out, reciting her perfunctory "to do" list, which Hallee transcribed word-for-word. So much for working on the Pritzker this afternoon. Instead, Hallee would be negotiating an umbrella in the pouring rain. She sometimes wondered if Janine sat at the window waiting for a downpour before calling the office to order up her errands.

Janine's edict du jour: She needed 1,500-count, pure cotton white sheets, two fitted for twin, two flat for twin, one fitted for a double, one flat for a double, four standard pillow cases. They were to have no additives or flame retardant chemicals. They should have no identifiable trim such as lace or satin. Hallee was to deliver them to the apartment today. And while she was out, Hallee needed to pick up Indian curry chutney—fresh, not processed commercially—along with Zaatar spice (in glass, not plastic), and Hallee was to bring these items to the apartment by 5:30 but no earlier than 5:15.

By 5 p.m., Hallee was in tears. The 1,500-count cotton sheets were a special order item. Hallee opted for the 1,200-count sheets, hoping that Janine wouldn't remember the extra 300 threads on the order. The even less possible item to find was fresh chutney. No one at the seven Indian grocery stores she visited sold fresh curry chutney. Janine would be furious if Hallee arrived with nothing, and she was at least 20 minutes away from the apartment. In desperation, she called the office to see if Lauren had returned. Fortunately, she answered and Hallee quickly relayed the conundrum.

"I think you should go ahead and buy the jar of pre-made," Lauren advised.

"Great, thanks," Hallee closed her cell, grabbed the processed chutney, and checked out at the deli. She briefly contemplated getting a cab. David and Janine's place was a good 35 blocks away, and it was rush hour. Hallee gathered up her various packages and ran to the subway.

Soaked in sweat (what was the point of the umbrella?), she arrived at the fancy brownstone lobby at 5:29 p.m. Today it was the Russian, Pavel, who was manning the desk and at present helping an elderly woman into the elevator.

"Pavel," Hallee gasped for breath.

"Miss Hallee," Pavel smiled. "How are you?" His Russian accent was generally charming, but Hallee was nearly apoplectic.

"Please let Janine know I'm here," Hallee pleaded, grasping his arm. "It's urgent."

Pavel patted her hand and went to the house phone.

Hallee held her breath. *Please answer*, she willed. *Please answer.*

"Mrs. Ormston-Meighton?" Pavel's voice acted as a sedative as Hallee felt her blood pressure lowering. Pavel turned to Hallee and motioned for her to go upstairs. The elevator light indicated the old lady was still on her ascent, so Hallee headed for the stairwell. Hallee leapt stairs two at a time. Fortunately, the apartment was on the third floor.

She rang the bell. She waited. Sweat dripped down her back. She tried to muster a smile. She tried to hold impending dread at bay. Despite her best effort, she had not followed Janine's instructions to a "t", and she anticipated ramifications.

Janine opened the door. Hallee hesitated, unsure whether she should enter the apartment. Janine blocked the way, partially shielded by the door.

Janine's cold stare bore through Hallee, causing her heart to beat faster, her pulse to reverberate in her temples.

"Here are the sheets," Hallee handed them over in one bag, despite the fact that they had been purchased at two different stores. Janine placed the bag behind the half-opened door.

"My food?" she snarled.

"Well, here's the Zaatar," Hallee said, handing over a jar that she had purchased and into which she had poured the packed-in-plastic Zaatar. She now felt ridiculous. Why hadn't she purchased another unmarked jar for the chutney?

"There was a problem with the chutney," Hallee stammered. She didn't think it possible, but Janine's grimace grew tighter, her thin lips almost one dimensional. "Um, well, no one had fresh chutney. Lauren thought this would be okay."

Hallee tentatively held out the jar. The purple label screamed out, *Commercially made! Not fresh!* To her surprise, Janine snatched the jar from her hand. She retreated into the apartment.

Suddenly a shot went off. Hallee jumped. Janine had dropped the jar from four feet, and it had shattered all over the stone entryway, splattering chutney on the door, across the foyer, and all over Hallee's shoes and slacks. Protected behind the door, Janine was unscathed. Hallee stood in shock. Her stupor was interrupted by a large, rag-like towel hitting her in the face.

"Clean this mess up!" Janine ordered. "And don't bother Lauren anymore. My husband pays you to think for yourself!"

With this reprimand, Janine slammed the door.

Hallee stood there stupidly. Stupidity morphed quickly into obscenity, as she carefully mopped up the chutney.

What Hallee wanted to say: "You fucking bitch! Who do you think you are?"

What she said: "I hate my husband more than I hate this job. I hate my husband more than I hate this job. I hate my husband..." She had nowhere else to go.

THE TRUTH

She left the entry cleaner than it had been before her errant delivery.

The next day, an e-mail was sent out to the entire office:

> From: David Ormston-Meighton
>
> To: Office_All
>
> Subject: How to Run Errands
>
> To all staff:
>
> If you run an errand, you should take your cell phone. If you do not have one, borrow one from a friend.
>
> If you cannot find what you were asked to buy, you must call the person who requested the errand in the first place! Never make a substitution unless you have been given the prerogative to do so. The more personal the errand, the higher the need that you vet changes with the originator of the errand.
>
> Honestly, people, I am embarrassed to have to write this. Were you raised in a terrarium? You really don't have the brains you were born with.
>
> David

Hallee suspected that Janine had written this and forced David to send it out. This actually gave Hallee a slight, perverse pleasure (she imagined the old woman in a corset wielding a whip, David beneath her replete with dog collar). Of course, the e-mail itself was degrading and belittling. Not to mention ridiculous. What friend would be loaning a cell phone during work hours? How many times had both David and Janine chastised her (and, granted, most everyone in the office) because she was "too stupid" to think for herself? Perhaps *his* days in a terrarium had impacted David's ability to communicate on a human level.

Not to mention, David was documenting how he wasted company resources on his personal errands. Hallee's transition through the looking glass was irrefutable. Kafka himself was probably spinning in his grave. Of course, in Hallee's mind, there was no grave spinning. Hallee's belief in God precluded it (it was also why Janine's taking the Lord's Name in vain irked her more than it should have). But God obviously wasn't going to rescue her from this Purgatory.

Two days after David had fired off the "errand from the terrarium" decree, as Hallee was calling it, she snuck off to see Xavier during another errand run. She knew she should be spending time on the Pritzker, but Hallee felt so dejected that she hoped an hour or two with X would make up for all the shit at work.

After more great sex (despite the fact that she barely knew the guy, she loved his bedroom technique), she felt that desperate longing once again simply to disappear from her life. Would it be wrong to ask to stay with him forever? Not as a wife, but something more secretive. She would hide out there and be protected from all the pain that reality kept throwing at her.

Without actually admitting this desire, she did say to him, "Sometimes I just wish that there was a way to control it, you know? A way to make the pain just stop, without the pot." He had brought out his little pipe and she had smoked a bit. Now she had to get dressed and go back to work. She thought about how much she had been drinking at night. About how she never felt the need to drink on the weekends. The stress of the job was getting to her, and she'd barely been there four months. She was turning into a complete wimp.

"I just wish there were some kind of training program that could prepare me for all that this life throws at me," Hallee continued as she slipped on her pants and shoes. "I try to be resilient. I pray. I still end up feeling, well, terrified."

Xavier had barely spoken since she'd arrived, which wasn't all that unusual. He was a "good listener" as they say, but he only weighed in when he really felt the need. Finally he said to her, "Sounds like you need a vacation."

"Well, I don't get paid time off until I've been there a year."

"You get July 5th, right?" He looked at the calendar on his desk. Independence Day was a week from Sunday. "Because the holiday falls on the weekend, you get Monday, right?"

"Well, sure," Hallee admitted, not knowing where the conversation was headed.

"Three-day weekend," X was smiling, trying to pull her back towards the bed. Hallee was tempted, but she knew the pile of work on her desk would only increase. "We could do something with that."

"My kids..."

"Get a sitter," X was biting gently at her neck.

Now Hallee was losing patience. Despite the slight pot-buzz, she was lucid. "Do you really think I could get a sitter for three days?" She pulled away from him and started down the hallway away from his bedroom. He quickly came after her and grabbed her hand. He didn't hold it roughly, but he did stop her from progressing.

"Look," he said, "we never get to see each other. I think there's something here, Hallee, but you won't make time for me."

"How can you say..."

"I know you're swamped with this job," he interrupted. "I get it." Now they were walking together towards his living room. He still held her hand and as he sat on the sofa, he pulled her to sit beside him. "All I'm saying is if we don't get some time alone together, I don't see us having a friendship."

Hallee wasn't sure what to make of his comment. "Is that how you think of us, as friends?"

"Hallee, honestly, I don't know what to think," X admitted. "I want to get to know you better. Three days is a lot of time to see how we click and if this is worth pursuing."

"But I'm a parent..."

"I'm not stupid. I know that." He paused, and Hallee could tell he was thinking about potential options. "What about their dad?"

"No, they're not ready for that," Hallee stated before adding, "and he hasn't even called them since we moved out here." Xavier squeezed her hand. Hallee blinked back tears. She didn't want to think about Jeremy while she was here with X.

"What about Mary? That's her name, right? The woman you said watched them sometimes?"

"Yes, but I'd have to pay her," Hallee reasoned. "That's way too big a favor to ask."

"I'll pay for it," X offered.

"No, I wouldn't feel comfortable with that."

Now it was X losing his patience. He launched himself from the couch and walked towards his window. They were on the second floor, so there were trees that gave a much lusher view than the actual street provided. "Look, Hallee. You either want to make time for me or you don't."

"Of course I want to," Hallee felt like she was pleading.

"Then stop making excuses! Either take me up on my offer to pay for a sitter, or ask Mary." X was crossing back towards her, more frustrated than angry. "Sometimes if you ask for help, people can surprise you."

"Alright," Hallee reluctantly agreed. "I'll ask her, and if she wants money, I'll let you pay."

That evening, Hallee invited herself over to her neighbor's, a bottle of wine in tow. As the five boys all played together, Mary and her husband Tyler broke out some wine glasses and listened to Hallee relaying her story of meeting X and him wanting them to go away together.

Then Hallee asked if they would be willing to take her three sons for the holiday weekend. She offered to pay without mentioning the money would come by way of Xavier.

"The only problem is we are going to Cape May," Tyler explained. "We'd love to have the boys but we can't fit all five of them in the car."

"What if," Mary suggested, "rather than you paying us, you rent us a big SUV? Then we could take all of them, right Ty?"

"Sure, but that would probably cost Hallee at least $300," Tyler said, "and I don't know if you have that kind of money. We could maybe split the cost of the car?"

Hallee was tearing up again. Xavier had been right. All she had to do was ask. And for $150, she wouldn't even have to get the money from him to pay for the car rental. She was so unbelievable grateful to her neighbors, and she couldn't even begin to thank them.

THE TRUTH

"Oh, don't worry," Tyler said. "You pretty much had us when you said you wanted to get away for a weekend of sex!" They all laughed, finishing the end of the wine. Hallee retrieved her kids and returned to her apartment.

After the boys were in bed, she called Xavier to give him the good news.

"See? I told you that people want to help when they can. You just have to let them." She hadn't told him about the car expense. It would be enough that he was paying for a hotel somewhere. Hopefully not Cape May. "So…" he said, drawing out the word. "Do you have a passport?"

V

"Plutôt cent morsures, plutôt le fouet, le vitriol, que
cette souffrance de tête, ce fantôme de souffrance, qui
frôle, qui caresse et qui ne fait jamais assez mal."
Huis Clos, Jean Paul Sartre

What do you want?

A world where my survival is equal to or greater than being a survivor...
A different outcome... To handle my pain in a socially acceptable
manner...

I recently came across an article (apologies for lack of citation, but I cannot
find it to reference) that pretty much smashed the foundation of the Laws
of Attraction. For those uninitiated amongst you: According to the Laws of
Attraction, negative thoughts bring forth negative change, whereas positive
thoughts bring about positive change. There's something distasteful in the
"blame the victim" principles of this philosophy, but there's a "drink the Kool-
Aid" impulse that makes me want to believe that I have some control over my
own destiny. Surely it cannot be that easy? If per the theory Brooke Shields
could suicide over knee socks, how is the power of positive thinking supposed
to save those of us who face far worse setbacks? Leaving aside for the moment
that Karma or Kabala or whatever rhythms of the Universe may be affecting us
at any given time, I argue that some of us are outliers who are tousled about
on these rhythms because we are neither projecting nor manifesting intention.
The article I mention speaks to this condition of being neither. The author
posits that while victims abound, not everyone is a survivor; that, in fact, some
of us are too busy *surviving* to be counted among those who are survivors.

Because of the resonance this idea holds for me, allow me to impart a
grammar lesson on the native English speakers still wading through this text
at the half-way mark. I think it may help clarify this notion of being in a state
of surviving but never graduating to a different plane.

THE TRUTH

When it comes to verb tenses, English is not at all intuitive. I remember learning my French and the idea of the *plus que parfait* tense was utterly beyond my grasp; it wasn't due to an absence of intellectualism on my part or the ability to frame thoughts abstractly. No, rather it was a combination of the truth that no one thinks of her first language grammatically (I don't know if it's a good or a bad idea that the elementary school curriculum has abandoned diagramming sentences... I simply remember the task being heinously discharged by my first-grade teacher) and the fact that English has non-transparent declension and conjugation systems. No one thinks about the dative in English: Whether you throw *him* a ball or throw the ball *to him*, the grammatical case appears objective (yet is neither!).

But I digress...

This notion of surviving v. survivor is easiest to understand from a grammatical perspective if illustrated by perfect and imperfect (not to mention the past perfect) tense. Consider an action taking place (I am running a marathon) versus an action that took place (I ran a marathon) versus an action that occurred prior to the past action (I had trained for months prior to having run a marathon). These various states of completion are helpful in understanding why this idea of survivorship can be unattainable for many people. If you are still surviving (imperfect tense) then you aren't a survivor (perfect tense), not to mention you possibly will never *have survived* the hardships that are now behind you (pluperfect tense).

The author of the article I mention neatly summed this up for me, and it was a relief. I feel as though the mantel of blame has been lifted. *I am surviving*, but I may never get to the point of being a *survivor*. All my strength and energy and coping skills go into this daily battle of surviving. I cannot simply look out and see the rainbow for the storm, believing that all the world is aright (even if only in my point of view). I don't understand survivors—the Oprah Winfreys of the world who overcame their abuse to attain the pinnacle of success (at least from my point of view)—any more than they can comprehend why my getting through the day without suicidal ideation is an achievement of import. That my glass will never be half-full, or even 90-percent-full. What is missing *is* the center of my focus. Because what I'm missing is *important to me*. I cannot let go of what I don't have when it's what I most need. Aside from those who would tell me to relinquish that tenth percentile and dismiss me out of hand, there are others who decree my needs are twisted and perverted and misunderstood...

Take, for example, my perfect Sabbath.

My perfect Sunday starts with a cock in my ass. No, really! Being awoken to intense anal penetration ranks really high for me. I tend to rise early—no pun intended—so being fucked into consciousness in the most intense way possible seems just fine by my whacked sensibilities. I know there are many women (probably all the sane ones) who would argue that this would be tantamount to rape, and when I stop to dissect my perfect day, yes, I'm forced to concur (it seems being forced is my raison d'être). But I never claimed to be linear in my sensibilities. In fact, I have to admit just the opposite: I am a feminist who craves domination; I am determined to seize power from my captivity.

Returning to my day of masochistic empowerment...

Sex is followed by coffee with heavy cream, which he brings to me just the way I like it. I used to add sugar, but managed to bugger off the sweet—pun intended—so just cream... but the good stuff, from a local farm, clotting at the mouth of the bottle. The plug drops in and foams at the rim, eager to be lapped. Maybe we do the *NY Times* crossword together in bed; no cheats allowed. Then we grab a couple of canvas bags and head off to the New Amsterdam Market where we eat samples from the Nordic bread guys. We drink Kombucha. We nosh on meat tacos from Jimmy's No. 43 and crab sliders from the seafood folks. Sour Puss Pickles lend tang. To take away, we pack up freshly churned artisan pasta, cheese, and local wine from Brooklyn Oenology.

Back at home, sweaty from the walk, we settle into a two-person Jacuzzi tub (yes, I live in NYC, but this is a fantasy! I get a tub with a greater capacity than my entire current bathroom). We bathe and chat and pumice each other's feet. Back to bed for some major league fucking. Then snack on Painted Farm goat cheese (accompanied by the wine). We snuggle on the couch with a DVD playing, fast-forwarding, only watching the best parts of *Lord of the Rings* (i.e. all the segments featuring Sean Bean, Miranda Otto or Viggo Mortensen; and we masturbate ourselves and each other when any of the three appears on screen; sadly, not all three appear together, so my fantastical ménage à trois can never happen in a linear timeline). Sleepy and sated, we nap.

Napping is followed by donning sweats and going for a brisk evening walk: lots of waterfronts in NYC, so we pick one. Maybe I feel up for a jog; no doubt my lover will cajole me to push myself harder than I think I'm capable. Dinner is pickles washed down with Sixpoint cans. We fuck again for good measure.

The rest of the week is devoted to work and deadlines and pressure and dysfunctional family and catching up on the world news and pain and suffering and everything that is real but meaningless. We only have one day of bliss—when the cacophony is shut out—but it's all we need. It's all I'm looking for. This fantasy world of one day's respite.

My ideal Sabbath is perfect. Except that it isn't. No man wants to wake me by shoving his cock in my ass (it doesn't help that I'm an early riser, typically up before dawn). None of my clients patiently overlooks a deadline just because Sunday is supposedly a day of leisure. The New Amsterdam Market might be there to fill my canvas bag, but pretty much everything else in this fantasy is as tangible as a fart: You think you smell it, but then it's gone and you're not quite sure where to point the finger. Only that you aren't to blame.

Perhaps I never am happy with that 10-percent-empty glass, because I'm fixated on what isn't there: What has been missing is what I covet most.

Φ

Being single again has given me time for contemplation. Why I am so diverted by the question of coupling drives my daughter to distraction, but Elise is a willing conversant in my Socratic methodology.

"Why are there no honest men?" I begin with ironic earnestness.

Elise rolls her eyes. She believes her husband to be honest, her brother, too. I think she is myopic. However, she is clever and tries to circumvent answering.

"Isn't it more accurate that *people* are not honest?" For what was Socrates' point if not to follow up a question with a question?

"I do think," and I am thinking as I formulate an idea... it's just behind the curtain and I fear its revelation will be both obvious and a disappointment. "I do think that people tend to take the shortest route to get to where they're going. For many that's through deception. But I'm an honest person."

"I am, too," Elise protests, "and I think honest people attract honest people." Ah, the Law of Attraction rears its lofty antlers, ready to impale me.

"People are hell," I quote, but Elise doesn't catch the allusion. She merely rolls her eyes. I don't bother to delve further into French philosophy.

For many years, I never told a lie. Not in the George Washington mythological sense, but just because when I was young I never viewed the world in shades of gray: You were either good or bad, true or false, right or wrong. I considered myself to be a good person so I spoke the truth... and I most assuredly attracted liars. So why am I the anomaly?

"I guess I'm just a square peg trying to get into a round hole," I devise a cliché to avoid further introspection. Better to look without for answers.

"Look, I get it," Elise tries to hold her exasperation at bay. "You've been hurt. Deeply hurt. Maybe by more than one guy." I nod and want to interrupt but she silences me with one fierce glance. "I'm not going to let you disparage all men because of your lousy track record."

Does she think I'm at fault? Have I invited my own destiny?

"Fine," I acquiesce. "People are hell and everyone lies."

"Thanks, so much, Dr. House," she mocks me, referencing the television show wherein a medical specialist insists that everyone lies. Oh, and it's never lupus. But I digress...

"Maybe," I begin again, "The truth is that women lie to other people, but men lie to themselves." I haven't considered this argument before. It is new ground I tread.

"Well, I don't..."

"No, no, no!" I demonstrate. "Hear me out! I think I'm on to something."

Elise excuses herself to pee. She says she cannot pay full attention to me with a bursting bladder. When she returns, I've formulated my thesis.

"Women do lie. They lie to get something, to fulfill an agenda... sometimes? Just to be polite. In fact!" I'm getting excited now. "It is *women* who first instruct men to lie. I mean that whole, 'Do I look fat?' or 'Are you attracted to that woman?' is a trap that men refuse to fall into. If they are honest, answering to the affirmative in both cases, they know they're screwed. Minus the actual screwing of course."

"So if men lie, it's their wife or girlfriend's fault?"

"No, but I think boys see their mothers for what they are: manipulators. Maybe they see their dads as survivalists. Anyway," I shake my head, gulping my wine, "it doesn't matter. That's not my point." I should drink more carefully. I have the hiccoughs.

"Oh, do please share your point with the class," Elise mocks me. I disregard her. I am rabidly coming to an epiphany.

"Men don't become liars to survive us; they become liars to survive themselves!"

Elise lets out a sound that is a mix of a snort and a raspberry. I fear I won't get this thought out there into the open, I won't be able to distill it, and it will evaporate before I'm clear in understanding.

"Please, Elise, please," I'm begging. She cocks her head like my cat sometimes does. I don't know if she's capable of hearing me, but she seems willing to listen.

I continue. "Think about what most men complain about their wives: She nags him and doesn't fuck him enough, or well enough." Elise nods to that. Score one point for the obvious analysis.

"Yet, all the advice columns..."

"Advice columns written by women..." she interrupts.

"Not necessarily," I reclaim the conversation. "Even in interviews with men, the one thing everyone agrees upon is that if you fuck a guy on the first date, he'll never be serious about you or want you for anything but sex." I hiccough twice while trying to get this out.

"Well, of course," Elise agrees.

"But why?" I'm shouting, but I don't care. "Why? When men claim to want women who love to fuck? Why on earth would they dismiss a woman who enjoys sex enough, enjoys *them* enough, to fuck on a first date?"

"Because they assume that a woman who does that is a total whore! She's bound to cheat on him at some point."

I shake my head so hard I feel dizzy. "The problem with monogamy is it's a false paradigm," I lecture. "Let me explain how monogamy between two people really works." Elise reaches forward for her wine glass, cupping it into her left hand, then in a graceful countermotion swings her feet up, folding them in mid-air before settling into a corner of the sofa, legs crossed, her eyebrows raised and face held in faux rapture. I know she finds me amusing at this point, and I'm not entirely sure it's in a flattering way. Nonetheless, I'm on the verge of an epiphany and her sweet mockery will not be a barrier to my sermon.

"Look, let's say you and I make a deal that all we're ever going to do is eat pie…"

> You tell me: "Great! I love dessert!"
> I tell you: "But it's not all desserts. It's just pie."
> You: "Okay, there are tons of pies. Lots of variety. I can have coconut cream, pumpkin, apple, cherry, mincemeat…"
> Me: "Sure, you can have all those."
> You: "Well, speaking of meat. There are meat pies: Shepherd's pie, chicken pot pie."
> Me: "But that's not…"

"Now all of a sudden, you have stretched the notion of what a pie is. This is not what I meant when I said we are going to be on an all-pie diet, but me—wanting to maintain the peace and make you happy—I say, 'Sure, I guess chicken pot pie counts.'

"And now within the context of our agreement *my* mind is going off on tangents. I'm no longer thinking about how to make the best Boston cream pie you ever tried. Nope. I'm thinking how I really miss the eggs I used to have for breakfast every morning before we agreed only to eat pie…

> Me: "Whoa! Quiche is kinda like a pie. I mean, it has a crust! Right?"
> You: "Pizza! A pizza pie."

THE TRUTH

"And I think, sure, why not pizza? Only I like Napolitan or Margherita style pizza, and you prefer fancy pizzas with goat cheese and arugula. So, now we are not only no longer eating what we originally defined as pie, we're not even eating the same kind of pie. Hell, we're not even sharing the same damn pizza! And then one day, I look at the arugula pizza with all that uncooked greenery on top of the melted cheese, and I realize: You aren't just eating pizza, *you have a salad.* You are eating a fucking salad on top of your fucking pizza!" Elise is laughing so hard now she has tears in her eyes, but I keep going. "And I start screaming hysterically, because I finally see the connection: You've cheated! And I see the truth: I let it happen. Or maybe I encouraged it when you ventured from mincemeat to meat pies and I looked the other way. Maybe it started when I couldn't deny myself quiche. Regardless, now there's blame and recrimination and anger. And maybe we can come back from that. Maybe you can give up arugula pizza, and I can give up quiche. Or maybe we can't. Maybe you start to resent me for making you give up your salad-on-a-pizza ways. And all I can think is, but we promised each other to eat only pie for the rest of our lives. Why did we agree to that without defining what that meant to you? To me?"

Elise has finished her glass of wine. She stares at me for about 30 seconds without saying anything. Then she explodes with laughter again. I mean literally: The sound emanating from her mouth is plosive, and I feel the vibration through my core. It takes her a good two minutes to stop snorting. I probably am smiling slightly, but it's not enough to keep her buoyant mood aloft.

"What?" she asks.

"Nothing," I answer.

"Pie? Pizza? That's a euphemism for sex, right?"

"It's euphemistic, but I think you missed the point."

Elise is holding the glass out for more wine. I fill her glass half-way and top off my neglected glass. She holds her goblet out at an angle, offering to "clink" glasses in a toast. I lean forward to meet her half way.

"I get it," Elise says before taking another sip of $10 Chardonnay. "A pie-only diet is boring and people aren't meant to eat only pie."

"Sure," I draw out the word, trying to make sense of my own metaphor. As I said, I am in the process of an epiphany; it's foggy, almost tangible.

"The problem with pie—monogamy—is that it means different things to different people. It's not just about how your junk fits into my junk and no one else gets to touch each other's junk. Even the act of loosening the bond of monogamy alters it forever. Thus, if I'm bored in my marriage and I start fantasizing about Henrik Lundqvist, I'm loosening that knot that ties us together."

"Oh, come on," Elise's voice is loud, but it's the wine as opposed to any offense taken from my supposition. "Everyone wants to do it with King Henrik!"

"But that's the point!" I desperately want Elise to understand me, because if I cannot relate to her, I'm pretty sure I stand no chance ever to connect to anyone else. "Monogamy puts us in this confinement. *It's a false paradigm.* It just doesn't exist except in theory. As soon as I think about Lundqvist, it comes undone. And that's just a thought. Only a crazy person would call thinking about having sex with Henrik Lundqvist as 'cheating'."

"So, what is cheating?"

"I don't know," I admit.

If I think about Ryan-Claude and his girlfriend, I burn with jealousy. When I think about longing to be touched by someone who isn't my husband, I'm wracked with guilt.

"Maybe cheating is lying." I say at last.

"Too bad people lie," Elise smiles. She's drunk, and sleepy. And I don't know if she believes what she's saying or is just trying to please.

Will what I have to say ever be heard? Will I ever find my way to the exit into understanding?

Φ

Frank may turn into the regular lover I've been missing. I am trying not to begrudge my gift horse: He's beautiful, he's smart, he's talented in the sex department. There's one problem, however: He claims to have no time for a relationship. It's a recurring theme in this *commedia dell'arte* that we're playing out. In fact, it is only our second liaison when he pronounces the death sentence.

"This is the last time I can see you," he says.

"Frank," I respond with a mixture of bewilderment and impatience, "this is the second time you've seen me."

"I know," he admits, his fingers back inside me after a sweaty sex session. "Look, I just can't do a relationship. My job is too taxing. I'm too busy with my music, my passions. I just cannot be passionate about you, too."

Well, gee, thanks, I don't say to him. Whatever. When he leaves, I asterix a new date for the final fuck.

I check my e-mail, and there's one from Frank. That didn't take long. He's rethinking tonight's proclamation of it being our last time together. I'm losing my patience.

> Hon, you really aren't extraordinary. In fact, I have a long line of lovers who didn't know what to do with me. You're in a formidable queue.

He responds seconds later.

> I know what to do with you.

He's nothing if not succinct.

> I don't believe you. And you obviously don't care to try to do anything with me.

I click send.

> I've known women like you. I have some experience with submissives. If you have finally accepted that's what you are, I could show you what you are capable of.

I sense I'm crossing a line here that might be best left uncrossed.

> How do you plan on doing that if tonight was the last time?

The gauntlet is thrown. Will he pick it up?

> I will show you, but it has to be the last time.

I hesitate. I wonder why should I relinquish my control to a man who has zero interest in a relationship with me? Of course, I could ponder why he has zero interest. Is it about me? Is it about him? Is it about both of us?

I'll think about it.

Thus ends our second "date."

The Vacation

The cabbie was smart; he took all the back roads to John F. Kennedy International Airport, avoiding the clusterfuck of traffic that inevitably forms on the Brooklyn Queens Expressway on holiday weekends. Having seen how few people remained in the city over Memorial Day, Hallee was convinced that the best time to be a New Yorker was when everyone was out of town. However, her heart was racing today in anticipation of her trip with Xavier. Aside from finally getting some quality time with him, this would be Hallee's first trip away since she had moved to NYC (after the first month in Brooklyn, she had sold the car that she had driven across the country; it was too hard avoiding on-street vandalism or parking tickets and too expensive to park long-term in a garage). The entire way to the airport, Hallee begged X to tell her where they were going. Aside from her packing list—sturdy shoes, one dressy outfit and a bathing suit, plus her passport, of course—she had no clue as to their destination.

For most of the trip, X did nothing more than smile, and the more Hallee pleaded for answers, the wider his grin became. Hallee loved Xavier's teeth, so she enjoyed his pleasure in keeping her uninformed. She was also strangely aroused, although far too reserved to act out her impulses in the back of the cab.

"I'll find out when we get to the airport," she said at last.

"Well," X was toying with her, "Maybe I'll just blindfold you and walk you through security." His smile seemed slightly devious, and for the briefest of moments, Hallee wasn't sure if he was joking.

The Friday night exodus out of the city finally caught up with them at Terminal 7, where the queue for the sidewalk check-in was extensive. Xavier pushed through the line with his roll-aboard (he had Hallee repack when he'd picked her up, noting a weekend trip didn't require checked luggage). He had checked them both in online, so he wended his way through the travelers heading to various destinations. There were too many flights in and out of this terminal for Hallee to deduce their own destination. She briefly considered snatching the boarding pass from his travel portfolio—an experienced traveler, X had a specific satchel for his most important documents—which now included Hallee's passport. Without an explicit agreement, Hallee had determined that part of this trip was about the suspense, about her trusting X, about him having complete control. She doubted very much that he would abandon their mini-vacation if she didn't play along, but she sensed that he would immediately be disappointed in her if she revolted in the slightest degree against him. An added benefit was that for the first time in nearly six months, Hallee wasn't calling the shots, and she felt a tremendous release as she let go and let Xavier make the decisions for her.

She thought she might find out their itinerary at the security check-in, but the male TSA agent (had X chosen a male guard intentionally?) took both passports from Xavier, only asking Hallee to confirm her name. When the guard handed her boarding pass back to her, it was enclosed inside the passport, which she handed back to X without much more than a glance at the documentation. Hallee slipped off her shoes, purse and hoodie (despite the order to pack a swimsuit, Hallee opted for a zippered sweater both in the event of air conditioning or cooler temps; her San Francisco summers taught her to expect any kind of weather in July) and placed them in the plastic bin. Xavier allowed her to cross through security first, and he easily scooped up their two bags on the other side.

Hallee assumed the suspense would end, but X didn't take her to the gate. Rather, he pulled what looked like a credit card from his document pouch and led them into the Priority Club. Hallee had never been a frequent flyer, so she tried not to gawk at the amenities of the lounge: wide, comfortable chairs positioned around cocktail tables; a full bar; a sideboard with snacks ranging from quesadillas to cold shrimp. Suddenly Hallee felt under dressed; she had opted for comfy jeans, a T-shirt and tennis shoes, but nearly everyone in the lounge was wearing business attire. Xavier led her to a corner chair, setting down their belongings before kissing her cheek with a whisper, "I'll be right back."

Hallee seated herself facing towards the room as X headed to the bar. Right in front of her the document pouch taunted her. She smiled, knowing that X had left it there intentionally; it took all her restraint not to check the boarding passes that extended roughly an inch beyond the passports that were tucked into a front pocket of the folio. All she had to do was lean forward and she likely would be able to see the destination, or at least the gate number. Xavier probably wouldn't even see her do it. However, the anticipation was now a game, and she again felt strangely aroused by not knowing what he had in store for them.

When he returned with two glasses—Champagne for her, Perrier for himself—X barely glanced at the documents. Had he memorized their position on the table? If so, Hallee had passed the test, because she remained ignorant of his plans. X handed her a flute, and they clinked.

"What are we toasting to?" Hallee asked as she sipped the wine. It was a superior vintage, but she felt it inappropriate to ask him what kind of Champagne it was.

"To getting to know each other better, I suppose."

"This is actually the first time I've ever been in one of these," Hallee admitted. "The club lounge, I mean."

"It's better than waiting at the gate, that's for sure," Xavier replied, but Hallee sensed he was teasing her; if they were sitting at the gate, she'd know where they were heading.

"You're enjoying this, aren't you?" she asked.

"Yes," X winked. "The Priority Club is very good."

Hallee looked out the glass windows, watching the holiday travelers trying to negotiate security. She made a few comments about how there always seem to be those people who forget to pull their electronics out for separate screening, making delays for everyone else. After a little while, her voice trailed off. X was being even more reserved than usual.

"Does it bother you that I talk so much?" she asked him. He shook his head. Hallee sighed. "It might help if you were a bit more communicative."

"Help what?" X asked.

"I don't know," she admitted. "I just feel like I'm doing all the talking, and you aren't saying anything."

"Well," X hesitated slightly, "You aren't really saying anything either, Hallee. You're just filling the silence with chatter. I always feel that some of the best moments are quiet ones."

"Oh, I'm sorry," Hallee flushed.

"Don't be," X admonished. "I hope one day you'll be okay with the quiet between us, but if it makes you feel better, it's time to go."

Hallee smiled widely, excited at last to discover where they were headed. She had already guessed it would be somewhere in the Caribbean, simply because the weekend precluded a long flight, although maybe Xavier would pull the romance card and take them as far as Paris. When they arrived at the gate, however, Hallee caught her breath. Perhaps she should have considered Xavier's penchant for danger zones.

"Reykjavik? Are you joking?" Hallee stopped short, not sure she wanted to enter the first class preferred lane with him.

"What?" X feigned ignorance. Or, at least, Hallee assumed he was faking that he had no knowledge of the recent travel blackouts over Iceland owing to a still-erupting volcano.

"Oh," X smiled slyly, "you mean Eyjafjallajökull? That's under control." He grabbed her hand and pulled her through the final check-in before boarding. Had someone put a gun to one of the boy's heads, Hallee wouldn't have remembered the name of the volcano that had erupted earlier in spring, not to mention she wouldn't be able to pronounce its name even if she could recall it.

"Enjoy your journey," the Icelandair representative said.

"Takk fyrir," Xavier replied.

"You know Icelandic?" Hallee asked, impressed.

"A little," X admitted. "But pretty much everyone there speaks English, so you won't need me to interpret. Much." With this he laughed and led her on to the plane.

The series of "firsts" continued as Hallee settled herself into first class. Of course the seats were more spacious, but they also allowed the two of them privacy. After settling in, X raised the arm divider between them and took Hallee's hand (he had given her the window seat). Soon the attendant came by to offer hot towels, which Hallee took more out of courtesy than need. It was a red-eye flight, so Hallee wiped her face and hands while Xavier requested pillows, white wine for Hallee, light hors d'ouevres, and a fluffy Scandinavian style duvet, which X strategically placed over both of them. Within minutes of the lights being dimmed, X was unbuttoning her jeans and putting his hand down her pants. She was already buzzed from the wine, but he leaned closer to her and whispered for her to be very quiet. She glanced beyond Xavier to the passengers across the aisle. Xavier had positioned himself sideways, so she had to lean up to see over him. Fortunately, the traveler in the aisle seat had donned a blindfold; the passenger next to him was completely obscured from her view. She relaxed completely as X fingered her until she came, almost crying out before he covered her mouth with his own.

He smiled before whispering, "I guess this is as close to the mile-high club as you're getting."

"We could sneak into the bathroom," Hallee offered.

"That's not as easy as it sounds," X admitted, and Hallee immediately felt angry that he obviously had tried—and possibly succeeded—in having sex in an airplane bathroom. Were there any "firsts" left for them to explore together?

Hallee was already drifting off, so she wasn't sure if she simply imagined Xavier's next comment: "Don't worry, Hallee. I think you're the one I've been waiting a long time to find."

When she next woke, it was with a start. They were landing. She hadn't even felt their descent, although her ears were slightly clogged and some drool had crusted in the corner of her mouth. She felt mortified, but Xavier had held onto one of the hot towels (obviously, the attendant had come around again). He wiped her face gently, and kissed her lightly. "Good morning. Velkomin til Íslands."

Hallee desperately longed to brush her teeth, so she excused herself to use the restroom inside the airport. Despite the early hour, the day was bright. It was the height of the "White Nights," and Hallee immediately felt wide awake despite the few hours of sleep she had managed on the flight.

Xavier obtained a taxi for them, and the fare into Reykjavik seemed hefty even by NYC standards. He pointed out sites along the way, including Blue Lagoon, where they would be checking in early tomorrow. First, however, he wanted to show her as much of Iceland as they could visit in a day. The first stop was to Centerhotel Arnarhvoll, where Hallee had just enough time to unpack, shower and change ("Wear your walking shoes," X advised, "And bring along your swimsuit.") before they were loaded onto a bus tour that would take them to the continental rift. As they drew closer to the volcano, the tour guide explained how this group of tourists were "lucky," because tourism numbers were down for the summer, and the crowds were less dense owing to the still active Eyjafjallajökull. Somehow, despite having Xavier's hand to hold, Hallee didn't feel particularly lucky.

The landscape was, however, some of the most beautiful she had ever seen. She felt a certain thrill as the bus crossed over into Europe and then back into North America again. Hallee had never thought about this island as bridging both continents. Their hike through Skaftafell National Park made her aware of just how small human beings were. This was possibly the closest she had felt to God ever. It was both a religious experience and utterly thrilling.

"You think this is thrilling?" Xavier raised his eyebrows a bit deviously. "Just wait until the way back."

The "Golden Circle" tour continued with stops at Gullfoss, its roaring waterfall attacking all her senses (her ears—no longer clogged—now rang from the deafening cascade of water). They stopped briefly in Geysir, where Hallee literally gasped in wonder at the regular spouts of steam and the bubbling ground. The final leg of the trip back to the country's capital included a side journey to Thingvellir Lake, where Xavier explained they would be SCUBA diving into the crack between the continents.

Hallee was terrified. "Xavier, I've never SCUBAed. Ever."

"Well, you can wimp out and snorkel, if you like," X said, and Hallee wasn't sure if he was teasing her or truly disappointed by the notion that she wouldn't risk her life alongside him. Fortunately, there was a brief "refresher" class for those who hadn't used a regulator in a while. Xavier signed them both up, and handed her sweatpants and thick socks to change into. Hallee was confused, but did as he commanded. When she joined him with the dive instructor, he was already suited up in a drysuit. He helped her don her own. They then joined the class in a shallow pool off to the side of the main dive era, although X certainly needed no tutorial. As the instructor glossed over diving technique, Xavier gave Hallee the extra attention she required to feel confident enough to go on this adventure with him.

"The most important thing is to control your breathing," X advised. "If you feel panicked, take a long, deep breath and hold it briefly. This isn't a deep dive, but you shouldn't ascend while holding your breath. Just hold it until you can hear your heart beat. And then exhale. If you trust me, Hallee, I will protect you."

There was something slightly ominous about his assurance. Hallee had no reason *not* to trust Xavier, but the fact that he was commanding her *to* trust him made her want to resist. It was as if he instantly detected this, because he took her a little farther from the crowd and away from where the instructor could monitor her.

"I want you to try something with me," he said. "Try not to be scared. I need to you trust me implicitly."

"That's not something I'm very good at," Hallee admitted.

"I know," X said calmly. "I will teach you how to be better, if you'll let me."

Hallee nodded.

"Okay, here's what is going to happen," X began matter-of-factly. "I'm going to hold you underwater, and I want you not to panic." Hallee's heart began to race; she was pretty sure she was already starting to panic.

"Hallee, listen to me," X commanded. He was cupping her chin in his hand, but he held her face up indelicately, his fingers wrapped more around her neck than truly supporting her head. Despite being in a drysuit, Hallee began to sweat. Xavier kissed her gently, his body was now blocking her view to the rest of the group. "Just breathe. Relax."

"Are you ready?" he asked. Hallee nodded, but she wasn't ready at all. "Remember, Hallee, you need to trust me. The water will be very cold on your face, so get ready. Now, take a deep breath."

Before she knew what had happened, Xavier's right hand covered her mouth and nose while his left hand forced her head underwater. At first, the terror grabbed her as she fought against him. She was unable to gulp for air because he was blocking her mouth and nose. Of course, there was no air to gulp for, and she quickly became aware that he was preventing her from swallowing water or expelling the deep breath of air that she did have in her lungs. How long had she been underwater? Mere seconds. Even at worst, she could probably stay under for up to a minute. If she would just calm down and stop fighting him. Calm down. Listen for her own heartbeat.

It was racing. She had no SCUBA mask, so she hesitated opening her eyes underwater. How far under was she? She was on her knees, and X continued to apply pressure to the top of her head. She briefly opened her eyes and in the moment before the sting of the water forced them closed again, she realized that X had pressed her face up to his groin. Through the thick drysuit, she couldn't be sure, but she had the unwavering sensation that he had an erection. Now she was even more panicked than before; she simply couldn't calm herself. She reached a hand up to tap his hand on the top of her head. She assumed that if she tapped him, like she had seen wrestlers do in fights, that he would let her go. She assumed incorrectly.

Now she was fighting against him, both hands pulling at his. She dug in her fingers and he let go of her mouth and nose. This made matters worse for Hallee, as she exhaled and tried to shout. How long had she been under? It felt like she was about to drown; she began to choke, aware she was sobbing underwater. Then suddenly it was there: the regulator was pushed roughly into her mouth and she could breathe again. She released her hands from the back of Xavier's and held the regulator in place. She grew less scared, despite the fact that X still held her under. She breathed more carefully and with deliberation, no longer thinking that she was drowning, no longer afraid of him holding her under. After what felt like an eternity, he released her. They returned to the group lesson where no one seemed aware of their side interaction.

"I'll be right back," X told her. "I have to attend to this." He held up his left hand, which was bleeding. She could see the indentations in the back of his hand and felt the need to apologize, but he abandoned her so quickly that she didn't even have the time to utter a response. When he returned, he had the drysuit glove on his left hand; she assumed it was bandaged.

He helped her out of the water. As she turned to speak to him, he interrupted her by saying, "We'll talk about it later. I want you to enjoy the dive. Remember," and with this he smiled, and it was genuine, not forced. "Try not to panic."

In fact, she didn't panic. Despite the warning that only experienced divers should be in the water, she was never far from Xavier who made sure she navigated the chasm without nicking her suit or banging one of her air tanks. In fact, compared to the incident during her brief "training" session, the dive was gloriously uneventful. And spectacular. Hallee was practically giddy when she joined X in the geothermal pool, finally being allowed to take advantage of the swimsuit she had packed.

It took them less than an hour on the bus to get back to their hotel. The entire return trip Hallee was aware of the bandage that covered Xavier's left hand. The one time she tried to speak to him, he shook his head emphatically as if to say, "Not here. Not now." Back at the hotel, Xavier still refused to discuss what had happened in the pool, instead telling Hallee to dress for dinner. In fact, Hallee had completely lost track of time. The bedside clock read 19:10, but the day was bright and the snacks they had eaten at their various stops had sustained her. Now, however, she felt a growling in her belly that reminded her how little she had eaten since they had left New York.

Dinner was one more spectacle, as Xavier had managed reservations to Perlan, the rotating restaurant that looked over the entire city. Hallee didn't even realize that they were moving until she went to use the restroom and had trouble finding her way back to her table. For the briefest of moments, she thought that X had abandoned her there. She was flooded with relief when she finally found their table. Xavier laughed at her confusion, "You didn't think I'd just leave you here, now did you?"

"I wasn't sure," she admitted.

X hesitated, cocking his head slightly as if he was viewing her for the first time. "You need to stop thinking about what happened with my hand." That wasn't exactly how she would have phrased the incident, but his comment made her accept that he wasn't planning on addressing their earlier interaction. Or, if he was planning to, it would be on his own schedule. Instead, he surprised her with a fairly descriptive retelling of his time spent previously in northern Iceland. He was effusive in his conversation, which was a relief to Hallee. He seemed completely at ease with her, and happily recommended the lamb and salt cod dishes. The food was exquisite.

It was nearing 11 p.m. when they left the restaurant, but the sun was barely grazing the horizon. Instead of returning to the hotel, Xavier asked the driver to drop them at the edge of the city.

"Are you okay walking in those shoes?"

Hallee wasn't sure she would be okay walking in heels; it had been months since she had dressed in anything other than "sensible shoes." Nevertheless, she told X she was fine. Fortunately, every few blocks there was some kind of party pouring out of a pub and onto the narrow streets. Between the revelers and the occasional stop for a drink, the pacing was slow. Whenever Hallee's feet began to hurt, she would lean on Xavier and he would intuit that it was time to sit and rest a bit. At one point, they found themselves near a geese pond. He removed her shoes nonchalantly and began to massage her feet. Hallee suddenly realized that neither of them had spoken for many minutes. Had she found that "quiet space" X had mentioned to her yesterday? Probably not. The crowds were boisterous. Reykjavik could be as noisy as Manhattan.

"Do you mind if we go back to the hotel?" Hallee asked.

"Are you tired?"

"I don't honestly know," Hallee answered. "I might be. It's hard to tell with so much daylight."

"Alright," he said, helping her back into her shoes. They walked away from the din of the city's center. The streets were quieter closer to the hotel. Xavier didn't speak, but at one point he pulled her off into a doorway where he kissed her deeply. His body pressed her into the wall, as a hand reached under her dress and pulled at her panties.

Hallee hadn't much time to consider that—other than the brief dalliance on the plane—X had barely touched her in a sexual way since they started their trip. Suddenly she was famished for him. She was ready to let him strip her in this doorway, if necessary, simply to feel him hard inside her. She began to pull at his pants, but he stopped cold.

"Not yet, Hallee," he said with slight disdain. Had she done something wrong? As if he knew she was wondering precisely that, he held up his left hand in front of her face. "We need to discuss this first." They walked the rest of the way to the hotel and up to their room in silence.

When they entered the room, which was still aglow from the never-setting sun, Xavier surprised Hallee by grabbing her with intention, his mouth suddenly seemed everywhere as he easily stripped off the dress. She sighed with relief to be out of the shoes. She knew better than to force him to undress, but she was hungry for his cock. Every time her arousal peaked, however, he would stop short, wait for her breathing to regulate, and then begin again. What was he waiting for?

"I want you to fuck me," she whispered at last. This was like being underwater again; time had lost its meaning. He could have been teasing her for a minute or an hour. She looked over to the clock, but he had discarded her dress on top of it. Was it deliberate? He always wore a watch, but he had removed it at some point. The sun was up, but it meant nothing. "How long?" she asked at last.

"How long what?" he replied.

"What time is it?" she asked, clarifying.

"It's whatever time I say it is." Hallee suddenly became aware that X had pinned her arms down, and the one leg he had thrown across her spread thighs had pretty much immobilized her.

"What are you doing?" she asked, but this time she was unafraid. This seemed to placate him. He released the tension he had used to hold her down, but she didn't move a muscle. She remained his captive, even as he let go. He smiled genuinely.

He rose from the bed, but again, Hallee didn't move. She attempted to follow him with her eyes, but frequently only caught a glimpse of him peripherally. He was rummaging through his roll-aboard.

"Have you finally agreed to trust me?" he asked, but Hallee sensed it was rhetorical, so she didn't answer. He returned, holding what appeared to be a metallic case. He lay down beside her casually. She was desperate for his touch, but she remained motionless.

"I want to ask you about this," he said, holding up his still-bandaged hand.

"I was scared..."

"I know that. That's the obvious response." He apparently didn't want her to defend her actions. What did he want from her?

"How long do you think I held you under the water?" he asked, pausing. "Go ahead, take a guess."

"Two minutes?" Xavier shook his head. "Ninety seconds?"

"Twenty-five, actually," he said. Hallee was shocked.

"Twenty-five seconds?" Hallee moved her position now, but only slightly. Was it even possible that she had been held under water for such a brief period of time? If so, why had she panicked? "I don't understand," she admitted.

"Hallee, do you remember saying that you wanted to disappear?"

Hallee nodded slightly.

"I can make that happen," X said, and Hallee felt the flicker of panic return. What was that supposed to mean? She had visions of her body being buried somewhere here in Iceland. How well did she know this man? She was completely insane to have traveled to another country with a total stranger. She began to rise from the bed.

"You're so quick to run away?" Xavier asked, not even trying to stop her. Hallee hesitated. Mary and Ty knew she had gone off with him. Arnie was certainly aware of X's character or he wouldn't have been friends for all these years. Hallee was being ridiculous.

"What did you have in mind?"

"I want you to trust me," he said. "Implicitly."

Hallee didn't know what this meant. She was sitting naked on the bed, X still clothed. He revealed the contents of his hand: a DVD player. He switched it on, and immediately Hallee felt the color drain from her face. Pornography. Great. Just what she needed. She sighed. Audibly.

"I thought you were a little more original," she admitted. Xavier stilled the picture; fortunately it was not in the middle of a sex act.

"I can talk you through it," he said. "I'm actually not that in to porn."

"Oh, really?"

"Yes, really!" He seemed to be losing patience with her. He got up from the bed. He started to pace. In the small hotel room, he had the gait of a trapped animal. Which was a bit ironic since all Hallee wanted was for him to pounce.

"Look," he said at last. "I'm going for a walk. I'll be back in 30 minutes. Do me a favor and watch the video. That's all I'm asking."

With that, he grabbed his jacket and the room key and left her alone.

Hallee was nearing tears. There was something so indecipherable about men, and Xavier was the least transparent male she had ever known. As frustrated as she was with him at this point, she kept thinking about those 25 seconds in the pool. She wouldn't let go and trust him for even the briefest moment. Now he had left it up to her whether or not she would watch the DVD. She switched it to "on."

Almost immediately, Hallee was intrigued. Maybe it was the fact that this was the first time in her life that she was watching porn alone. Maybe it was because this video was like nothing she had ever seen with Jeremy. Maybe it was because she found herself incredibly turned on.

In a series of vignettes, one fully clothed man (and in one five-minute video, a couple) were variously torturing a naked and bound female. Although torturing was an inaccurate verb choice. The woman was obviously enjoying being forced into begging to be fucked, first through bondage, then through spankings and all other manner of pain induction. At the end, the woman subject to the ordeal was forced to orgasm, while Hallee was forced to turn down the volume on the player. Interestingly, only one of the videos showed any actual penetration with a penis; several of the videos showed penetration with a fist. Hallee was completely aroused, much as she would have preferred not to be. When she heard a knocking at the door, she startled and slammed shut the player.

"Who is it?" she asked.

"It's me. May I come in?" Hallee opened the door, not even remembering that she was still naked. Xavier looked at her with a tired smile. They'd both been up too long without sleep.

He closed the door, pulling her towards him with a hug.

"I watched," she started to explain.

"I know you did. And I know you liked it." He allowed her to pull away from him, but she buried her face in his chest rather than show her embarrassment. "I'd like to explore that with you. In a way that challenges you, but where you'll trust me. I can go as slow as you like. Or..."

"Or?" Hallee encouraged him to finish his thought.

"Or," he continued slowly, "Not at all. I won't make you do anything you don't want to."

Hallee wasn't sure what she was supposed to say to all of this. It was late. She was exhausted. Yet all she wanted was to feel him inside of her.

"Let's sleep on it, okay?" X said. Ending the conversation for the night.

THE TRUTH

Hallee pulled on panties, but they were immediately soaked. She wanted X to fuck her. Badly wanted it. He wrapped himself around her, and she rubbed her ass into him. He spanked her. Hard. He laughed, and then nibbled on her ear.

"So I guess you really did like what you saw?" She turned to face him. She hadn't bothered with a nightgown. Her bare breasts were erect. He grabbed them roughly, making her shriek before his bandaged hand came down quickly on her mouth to reduce her sound to a whimper. Her upper leg now straddled his thighs, pulling his groin towards her. Suddenly his hand was wrapped around her neck, choking her. Instead of fighting back as she had underwater, she relaxed. As her emotions waned from panic to acceptance, she raised her eyes to his. Those clear grey eyes were calm, kind. She began to lose focus, his face growing fuzzy, the room dimming at last. She was vaguely aware of putting her hands above her head, as if he had pinned them there, but his hands were still around her neck.

And then there was air. She was breathing again. The air was so clean, so life-renewing. She vaguely became aware of her surroundings. This was probably what birth felt like for a baby.

X was smiling. He was practically beatific. "How long do you think that was?" he asked. "Go ahead, take a guess."

Hallee's brain was a bit fuzzy. Time had literally stood still for her. He told her he had held her under water for 25 seconds. This was definitely longer than that had been.

"Forty-five seconds?" He shook his head, but he was smiling, so she guessed she had underestimated. "One minute?"

His beautiful smile took her in. Despite not having had sex, she felt the endorphin rush of an orgasm washing over her.

"I'm very pleased that you trusted me, Hallee," he whispered at last. "That was one-minute, 10 seconds."

Hallee was pretty sure she had misheard him. There was no way she had held her breath for that long, but she no longer cared about her performance. She melted into him and fell asleep.

The next morning, they headed to Blue Lagoon, where Hallee learned to trust Xavier completely.

VI

What do you want?

**Not to speculate about a future I cannot control... Not to sleepwalk my
way through my existence... Not to miss the ennui of daily life...**

Maybe I've been approaching this all wrong. Rather than wanting more,
perhaps I should want less. Eschew all that is out of my control, unknowable,
unattainable and—worst of all—unimaginative. Want nothing and desire no
more. Isn't that what they call Nirvana?

I am on a vacation, of sorts. In Iceland. Frank generously both paid for the
trip and allowed me an extension (I am paying for my expenses and hotel once
he's returns to the States). I arrive in a state of anticipation that both unnerves
and invigorates me. We are in first class, my first time sitting so near the exit.
There's nothing like being the first person off a plane in a country to which
you've never been before. I'm pretty savvy, but there's a foreignness to being a
foreigner. It's largely psychological—I certainly don't feel lost or incapacitated—
but being in a place where I don't know the language (despite his talented
tongue—hahaha—Icelandic isn't in Frank's repertoire) is off-putting. The trek
through the airport is easy, owing to Frank having traveled here many times
on business, and a couple times on vacation en route to the U.K. This airport
is odd; we have to clear security to get to Passport Control. When I am told to
remove my shoes, I forget to take off my watch and the sweater I was wearing
to shield me from the airplane's climate control (I covered myself with a blanket
while on the plane, half hoping that Frank would initiate me into the "Mile
High Club," but alas... he slept the entirety of the brief flight). Fortunately, I

do not trigger any security alarms, and we are off to get our passport stamps. I am briefly separated from Frank, who enters via the EU queue. I thrill at the stamp in my passport, and meet him on the other side to retrieve our bags.

We grab a cab to the Blue Lagoon resort. Frank likes its proximity to the airport (having been to Reykjavik before, he has no interest in "wasting time in the city"), not to mention the healing properties of the spa's waters. For the past four days, I have been schooled in ways I could neither fathom nor anticipate. It has been educational to say the least. My mind has been opened to possibilities I never before contemplated.

Let's just say I have taken full advantage of the soothing muds and salts that salved my skin when it needed it most, a fact that Frank apparently anticipated when picking this venue for my "training." However, within minutes of his departure, I am on the first bus out. The long days bring warmth and a clusterfuck of tourists—both from Europe and greater Iceland—to the opaque, whitish-gray waters that form inside the crater. The waters are fabulous; the crowds too reminiscent of home.

Now I find myself touring the countryside, and aside from my fellow bus mates, I am blissfully by myself. To be surprisingly honest, I am loving the solitude. I had forgotten how it feels to be alone, to be one, to be separate from everyone and everything. I feel complete in my loneliness and aware of my every sensation for the first time in what seems like forever. Maybe it is the first time, period. I am no longer conscious of my chronology. Or, at the very least, I am no longer self-conscious. Perhaps it is this unending daylight of the White Nights or the fact that I've barely slept since the plane landed. I've also failed to record the exact path of this week's narrative: I am no longer certain which came first in an unending blaze of sensory experiences I've enjoyed of late. (*Enjoyed* being an inexact word choice; I'm lacking for vocabulary to put a descriptor on all I've encountered on this latest leg of life's journey.)

It is entirely possible that this is the first time in my meager and lackluster existence that I am living the in the present. I am—startlingly—present tense. My mind is clear, almost a blank canvas. I am not devoid of thinking—in that way I can be when I'm drunk—but rather my mind is a conduit through which thoughts simply flow in and out without much consideration. Oh, hello, voice from the past... thank you for dropping by.

I appear to have found the "ends of the Earth," as it were. I am standing at the brink of two continents, straddling North America and Europe, as the continental drift expands and volcanoes rumble beneath my feet. I can see them all along the horizon, in every direction if I strain my eyes, the still-active Eyjafjallajökull choking out its weakened breath of ash. At "night" the sun circles around the periphery of this world, silhouetting these mountains of molten uncertainty.

Have you ever tried to meditate? Frank wakes every morning at 5 a.m.; he did so even here in Iceland. He meditates for 30 minutes before launching into yoga and tai chi. As I lay in bed, all I could hear was his carefully paced breath (no disgorged ash there). I loved waking to listen to him breathe: It was like a metronome, or like these waves I now hear breaking along the cliffs of North America only to drift back—the rate of the continental movement is two centimeters per year, the tour guide tells us—to land on the shores of Europe. A gentle swaying of breath that never allows his psyche to venture away from the present.

I don't caress the edges of the rift; I'm the message in a bottle: cast out to sea to journey for a very long time in search of a far-off shore. My peace is always beyond the maelstrom, yet to be discerned.

As such, I've never been able to meditate. Forget 30 minutes. I would be lucky to attend to the "now" for 30 seconds! My mind drifts away much farther than two centimeters from this moment, as I contemplate what's next on my agenda, the meals I will be making for lunch and dinner, the requisite grocery list that pairs to those meals, the errands I will run on the way to the grocery story, the people I may bump into on the way to do so—oh, yes, don't forget to return my mother's phone call. What was I thinking again?

However here, in the land of the Midnight Sun, where two continents meet, standing upon what is for Earth a relatively young landmass, I discover myself ever-present. I no longer drift into the future or reminisce about the past. The air I breathe in is the cleanest ever to meet my lungs. After drinking Icelandic water, I may never again be able to swallow water from the New York aqueduct system without wretching. I contemplate the thought of staying here forever. Perhaps I could meet a nice sheep farmer with a sadistic side who will take me in, bed me, set me up as a cheese monger. I won't slaughter the lambs, but I can milk their mothers.

I want to be of this earth, in this new place, a phoenix of the Atlantic, rising up from the ash. No wonder everything in Iceland feels so *now*.

How to explain the world that has been exposed to me? If you are capable of meditation, of taking quiet reverie and losing your sense of space and time, then perhaps you understand what true bliss is. It's less feeling than absorption. Every molecule of these two continents I traverse is sucked into my being as I become one with the now. Every person I see or whose arm brushes my own is a connection. The birds—oh does Iceland have birds!—soar and swoop and chirp and chatter and screech, and I am one in flight with the flock. The active volcanos threaten, but it is the dormant ones that have captured my imagination. I understand them; I know only too well what it is to be left alone for too long, what fury can be discharged if left untapped and forgotten. No one walks with caution along the dormant doormat. Only by gradual release can you avoid the sheer magnitude of destruction that occurs when the dormancy comes to its inevitable end.

I am learning about my tolerance for pain. I try to rationalize how ethereal I feel as compared with how helpless I have been the past 60 hours or so. I'm sore everywhere. No matter how I move—even if I remain as still as possible, holding my breath—something aches or burns. I love it. I cannot escape this moment even if I wanted to, and I most assuredly do not. I am in constant reference to here. I don't miss Frank. I don't miss home. I am missing nothing at all.

There is power in this feeling.

Only as point of reference (not as diversion), I recall a line from one of my guilty pleasure movies, *GI Jane*, when Viggo Mortensen's character is torturing his charges as part of their Navy Seal training and notes, "You know what the best thing about pain is? It tells you you're not dead yet!"

THE TRUTH

I'm not dead yet.

Φ

While I remain present, I am not completely insulated from the life to which I will shortly return. In fact, I am dealing with a "first world problem" that nearly caused me to be apoplectic. I am sitting in a coffee shop in Reykjavik after a scary but "successful" visit to an ATM. I have been nervous about burning through nearly all my Icelandic Krona; my budget is modest to begin with: roughly $150-worth to carry me through. The issue is that I keep messing up the exchange rate; unlike the Euro, which pairs slightly higher than the dollar, I keep missing the prices in Iceland by an entire decimal. While this is hardly uncommon when dealing with a foreign currency, my brain is malfunctioning due to over-stimulation, I suspect. In fact, I learned when studying linguistics that the brain can only learn one number system. Thus, no matter how fluent you become in a foreign language, you'll always revert to your native tongue to compute math. My American brain sees 5.400 and thinks, "Wow! What a deal!" Because my native language is the dollar, and I read $5.40 rather than nearly $54.00. I first discover my computational deficiency as I am buying a bottle of wine (while Frank was here, I didn't touch a drop) that I purchase for a buck-forty-five (i.e. $14.50), thinking it was a steal.

Anyhow... I mention my "successful" trip to the ATM because it was a bit too successful. While I admit that $150 will last me more than today, I want to do some shopping, bring back gifts for the kids, maybe something for Elise. So what I really need is an additional $100 in Krona (you who have slept recently probably know the O'Henry twist that is about to be revealed). It is with joy that I face an English-speaking ATM. However, when I choose $80-worth of currency, I am shocked when the unassuming ATM on Tryggvagata Street vomits out a wad of cash so fat I can no longer fold my wallet shut. Naturally, I have $800-worth of Krona, not $80. Note to Chase Bank: How is it I have a daily limit of $600 at home but can get $800 in Reykjavik? What if my card had been stolen? Or I am being held at gunpoint to withdraw the maximum amount? Or simply had a brain freeze and moved the decimal one digit to the left, which—apparently—did in fact just happen?

I instantly break out in tears! My rent is due in a few days, and I am 100 percent certain my landlord will balk at being paid partially in Kronas. As I sit here at one of the ubiquitous coffee shops that dot the city—no, not Starbucks, thank the Norse gods!—I am now pumped with enough caffeine to visualize a solution to my problem: I will simply change the money back into dollars once I get back to New York. I will probably lose $20 in the exchange, but that's a small price to pay for this lesson: Think before you exchange.

The streets of Reykjavik are crowded by local standards, but so very different from New York City. I am happy to be away from the stench and the inhumanity that rapes my metropolis of her inherent beauty. I am glad not to think about home.

As these things often go, now I have become the annoying tourist I hate so much, handing over a 5,000 krona note to pay for my coffee; even in overpriced Iceland, this action causes my barista to growl something I understand despite the foreign tongue! I hunker down with this notebook (purchased for $3.30— not 33¢—incidentally) because for the first time in what feels like forever, I actually want to remember where I am and what I am feeling. Gone are all the fantastical creatures who usually keep my mind in a near perpetual state of distraction. Even on the bus tour yesterday as I felt fantasy-du-jour sit beside me, his imprint on the seat next to mine, his hand on my thigh as we peered out the window, I thought, "No. Go away. I don't need you right now. I want to be here, feeling, remembering."

When was the last time I didn't feel sad to my core? The fantasies are pretty much all that have shielded me from the painful reality in which I've been living. However, today, in this new land, with these powerful sensations, I have to go back in time 20 years or more to remember this feeling. It's the whole *Burnt by the Sun* sensation, with days that stretch on and on: I took a picture at 4 a.m. this morning and it could have been taken this afternoon. It's all the same, and I am sublimely content to be here.

I am happy.

I do not want to sleep, even if I could. I want to live in this rare moment of bliss, where the pain has ended, only an echo of it remains in my psyche.

THE TRUTH

I don't need the fantasy to shield me anymore. I would like to return here in winter and see the opposite effect: all dark instead of light. Or perhaps I shall remain here indefinitely. Disappear into the timelessness of this place.

To get my bearings—or perhaps retain my scattered wits—I decide to go for a walk. My hotel is on the outskirts of town, not far from the beach, but after Blue Lagoon I am indifferent to going there. The domestic airport buzzes with regular flights, small planes, turboprops. The hotel is not particularly convenient to town, requiring a shuttle or the local bus to get back and forth. The Perlan power station sits high atop Öskjuhlíð hill; I have decided to dine there this evening (I have a wallet full of cash, afterall).

I set off along one of the walking trails, unsure of where it will lead me. I see several cyclists in the distance and pass another of the city's ubiquitous smokers (cigarettes and coffee seem to be the raisons d'être here), but considering the country's "green" ethos, the noxious cigarette clouds lurking outside nearly every building seem incongruous. I have walked probably four miles, encountering many people, few beasts (other than the birds—the partridge-like wrens my favorite thus far—which have found a bit of lake away from the humans bathing farther in). I marvel at the black sand beach, missing all the landmarks because of signs written exclusively in Icelandic. I end up walking along a highway before deciding to double back and look for a more scenic route.

I'm in luck. A cemetery is located just a bit off the path; I hadn't seen it from the direction I was walking. There's some strange quality about traversing through a foreign graveyard. I would think it odd to take photos of a grave in New York City (other than perhaps at some of the more historic sites no longer burying the recently dead), but here I feel free to photograph at will. This cemetery appears to be full, but the graves are not terribly old. Families still tend them, lighting lanterns, trimming grass, pulling weeds.

A thought occurs to me as I view these headstones. In Iceland, surnames are derived from the patronymic; thus, Olof's son is So-And-So Olofsson and Olof's daughter is So-And-So Olofsdóttir. While I instinctively find such patriarchal ties misogynistic, on this island of only 300,000, I suppose this is one way to narrow the chances of inbreeding. If you're both descendants of the original Olof, it's probably better to seek a Sigmundsson or a Dagsdóttir. Keep looking for a mate who isn't a distant relative.

At the top of the cemetery (I've been strolling a sloping hill), I come across a bloody stain. I assume it is from a critter of some kind and not human blood I see here. But the blood unnerves me for some reason. The evening—I check my watch to confirm that it is, in fact, evening—has grown chilly and the people who were tending the graves earlier all seem to have packed up their cars and left. I return to my hotel to change for dinner.

Φ

The Perlan overlooks the belching tanks of geothermal energy that powers this country from home electricity to cars to the burgeoning tourist trade. Ironically, the hand dryers in the restroom here are quite weak. It takes forever to dry my hands. I have a table for one at the Pearl, but I've lost track of where I was sitting. I was drinking wine, but only one glass. When did I last sleep? Am I hallucinating? A kind waiter saves me from my confusion and leads me back to where I had been sitting.

It suddenly dawns on me that my view has changed. We are rotating. I guess I missed this in the guidebook. I hadn't even realized I had slowly been moving. By the time dinner is completed, I will make it a full 180 degrees and be looking out over Reykjavik, away from my hotel.

For dinner I am having roast puffin. As an appetizer, I chose the whale Carpaccio. It is delectable. Rich and bloody, like ostrich, but with a definite sea saltiness to the flesh. I am not oblivious to the endangered status of my meal; I simply do not care. And I mean that in the best sense. In this moment of peaceful present, this is my last supper. I am the inmate on death row: *What would you like for your last meal, Prisoner 24601? Whale Carpaccio and roasted puffin, if you don't mind. We have chicken and mashed potatoes; will that do? Dead man walking…*

I'm not dead yet.

Perhaps if I remain in Iceland, find my sheep farmer, disappear into the white night, I will become so of this moment as to be immortal. I will live forever in the now and never die.

Sadly, this is the first fantasy to take hold of me since I arrived here, and it proves to be just as illusory. I am back at customs, and the agent is older and unattractive—almost ugly, in fact. He's scowling over my passport. Perhaps this is government mandated, his grimace, because it doesn't seem personal. I begin to flirt with him.

"I don't want to go, so you can deny my exit if you like," I say.

He looks up at me, no longer frowning. "Why's that?" His voice is soft, his English barely accented.

"Because I love it here," I tell him, just a faint pleading in my tone. "I want to find a nice sheep farmer, maybe a widower. I'll make cheese."

Instead of laughing at me, the customs agent smiles. "You'll be back," he says and hands over my document.

Yet somehow I know: I will never return to this place. I have been here a mere seven days, and I feel as though it's been two years. Or maybe a lifetime. I think of the word I hate to use, because it's never used correctly: Iceland is awesome. This week has been awesome. I have never before felt this awed and suspect I never will again.

As I take my first class seat, I almost immediately drift off into sleep. It is dark in the cabin when I feel someone sit beside me. I feel his presence on the seat next to mine, his hand at my waist. I force open an eyelid and see the chair remains empty.

"Oh, hello," I whisper subconsciously to Loneliness. He says nothing, just pulls himself closer until I am enveloped by him. I try not to choke as his fetid breath fills my lungs once more. Not Frank—not even Iceland—could wrest me permanently from his mangled bony grasp.

He reminds me: It's time to go home.

The Boys

Hallee returned to Brooklyn a new person. She didn't mean this romantically. In fact, there was little romanticism in her life at present. If anything, her relationship with Xavier made her realize how little sustenance her "princess fairy tale" fantasy had provided her over the first 40 years of her life. Nevertheless, the combined pains of working at the domicile and living in NYC seemed thoroughly endurable to her now. Learning to judge different types of "pain" had allowed Hallee's consciousness to expand in a way that was borderline transcendental. While she still wasn't completely comfortable with the basis of their relationship, Hallee was forced to admit that time with X had helped her reserve stores of what he liked to call "adaptation energy" when it came to the many challenges she was facing on a daily basis.

Probably the best claim she could make from her current circumstances was that her stretched funds and long, hectic work days were good for her physique: She had dropped almost 15 pounds in the last month and a half. Undoubtedly, some of that was due to the unbearably hot summer. Hallee had literally been sweating off the pounds as she made her regular errand haul for the Ormston-Meightons (she had resigned herself to the fact that whe was still regularly being pulled into their domestic realm, with Janine's edicts keeping Hallee working well past her dinner hour). The extreme heat bothered everyone, but having become accustomed to the cool foggy summers of the Bay Area, Hallee was physically overwhelmed by what the NYC weather forecasters were calling the hottest summer on record. And the heat did nothing to improve the ambiance: The filth of the city was truly breath taking. As in, it sucked up her fresh breath and exhaled a noxious mix from dog turd residue, litter and rats. And that was above ground. The subways added a fine vintage of vomit, human sweat (not to mention human piss) and homelessness, which her nose detected a good 20 yards before her eyes could see.

To be fair, however, the weight loss was not purely climate-related. Hallee also was trying to tone up a bit to match her boyfriend's physique. Boyfriend. The word still didn't come naturally, and her relationship with Xavier certainly would not be considered one of a traditional boyfriend/ girlfriend. Mostly they took the odd random lunch together and fucked at his Brooklyn home (yes, she now made time for him—when she didn't, he had very interesting methods to remind her that she was neglecting him). His place was much nicer and far more private than Hallee's apartment, and they both seemed to take delight in making sure Hallee made as much noise as possible. When she wasn't moaning from pleasure, X had a rare talent to make her cry out in other ways. X continued to be very careful to discuss limits and fantasies away from the bedroom (a striking change from Jeremy—had she mentioned that different was good?—who never even considered that Hallee might have a few kinks of her own to work through). It was refreshing and weird and troublesome and joyous all wrapped up together. She was a jumble of mixed emotions when she was with him, but her attention was hyper-focused now at work, excepting the few hours following their assignations.

Since they usually couldn't *liaise* more than twice a week, Hallee was somewhat surprised at how much she appreciated having the profound release when they were together. Not to mention still feeling Xavier's "presence" long after copulation had ceased; the post-"lunch" afternoon found her generally in too much discomfort to sit easily in the expensive office chair. For an as-yet-unknown reason, Hallee was aroused thinking about X while pressing her swollen bottom into David's office furniture. Maybe she was simply taking a perverse pleasure in defiling the office, but X had opened a window onto a world Hallee had never seen despite her years in San Francisco (obviously, she was aware of the BDSM movement, but it seemed as distant from her as comprehending Swahili). Knowing she was still "suffering" from their raunchy luncheon (and the fact that on more than one occasion Hallee would return to work high on Afghan weed) made life at the domicile just a bit less awful.

Of course, clarity would always come raging back, even though it was generally more surreal than the dope-induced breeziness Hallee felt whiling away the afternoon. Unlike alcohol, Xavier's pot didn't seem to prevent her from working efficiently. Hallee finally understood why musicians were so into the drug: You really could focus on one thing—multi-tasking be damned—and block out everything else. While the old, sensible Hallee would have been mortified to see the woman she'd become of late, Hallee actually liked the new her. She had a blooming confidence she had never known previously, and she felt good about her appearance and competence for the first time in years.

The only time she began to doubt her comfort in this new construct was when she stepped back and realized that her good mood was predicated on other people. And most of those people were men; all her strings seemed to be pulled by a man (even horrible Janine was only allowed access to her due to David). It shamed her to admit that when things with the men in her life went well, Hallee was sublimely happy.

She knew that letting her own happiness be determined by her boss or boyfriend was not an ideal pathway to feeling better about herself, but she was glad to feel better nonetheless. However, she wished she could empower herself instead of relying on some man to do it. Hallee sensed she was failing her own personal Bechdel test; her entire life revolved around men, from Arnie to David to Xavier back to Jeremy and her three sons. She couldn't remember the last time she had a conversation or even a random thought that didn't revolve around a male in her life.

What about Lauren? With Lauren it was *all* about David Ormston-Meighton Architects Company, Incorporated. In fact, Hallee's carefree attitude was often tempered by work, especially in the front office. Hallee had noticed a growing coldness in Lauren, which may have had to do with X (man at the center of it all alert!). Lauren was unmarried, having for many years worked the same 60-70 hours each week that Hallee now was. Whereas Hallee looked good minus a few pounds, Lauren had gone from thin to gaunt. Hallee didn't want to suppose her friend was jealous, but between being passed over as Arnie's assistant and then for the Pritzker lead, Lauren now watching her old roomie with a hot guy seemed to be causing a rift in whatever friendship remained between the two of them. (Hallee wasn't public about it, but Lauren more than suspected what was going on, and Hallee was fairly certain Arnie knew it, too.) The thought that Lauren was less than happy for her made Hallee forlorn, but whenever she would attempt to engage Lauren in personal topics, her co-worker would immediately shift to "all business," leaving Hallee little recourse in making whatever amends she could.

A more positive non-Xavier front was at home. The boys were enjoying their summer at day camp, and at least one evening a week was spent with Mary and Ty, playing board games or teaching the boys how to play Charades. Hallee occasionally would look around her, admittedly with a glass of wine in hand, and try to capture these moments like a memory photograph. Mary and Ty, their sons, her boys... this was her family now. And she was coming to love this family with a tenderness she hadn't felt in many years. Yet as much as she enjoyed spending time with Mary and Ty, even there she felt she had more in common with the husband than the wife. Hallee made a mental note to seek out more female relationships. If she ever found a minute to spare, that is.

The spare minutes she did have were pretty much reserved to her sons. She almost never saw Xavier when she was with them (only once had he snuck over late one night, and the sex was by necessity subdued and limited, as X would always leave after Hallee had fallen asleep). Not only could Hallee not figure out where X fit into her home life, she wasn't even sure that he fit in at all. Aside from their atypical sex life, Hallee always had this feeling in her gut that he viewed her as a summer fling. He never even asked her about her boys. He never asked her about her work. Everything was about sex; when a different topic surfaced, it was she leading the conversation. There were times when Hallee felt as if X wasn't even interested in her as a human being. Although she herself couldn't really figure out how to fit X into her "normal" life, she was starting to feel a slight resentment towards him for not making an effort to be included in her boys' lives.

One night in early August after a particularly rigorous "session," she decided to question him.

"Why are you with me?" she asked.

"Are you kidding me?" was Xavier's response. "I really hope this isn't about me 'being able to attract whomever I choose'. Because since I choose to attract you, that should be the end of it."

This comment should have resonated with Hallee, but mostly she was distracted by the larger picture.

"No," she admitted. "I guess I'm more interested in how you see us. Moving on. In the future."

X had untied her and was rubbing a salve onto her wrists and ankles. Hallee loved this part of their encounters the most, when he showed such intense tenderness. She never had to clean herself (X would bring warm washcloths to sooth her) or tidy his bedroom (he was quite adept at changing the sheets around her supine body). He would massage her and ensure her comfort without hesitation, as if the previous tortures had not been endured (or, possibly, she was being rewarded precisely because she had endured them). Hallee did her best to avoid any Dr. Jekyll/Mr. Hyde allusions, but there were times when she felt as though X was channeling two distinct personalities.

He sat next to her and seemed to be weighing what to say to her. "Well," he began slowly, pulling her up gently to sit beside him, fluffing a pillow for her to lean against. "Let's talk about that." The fact that he was completely naked and she was covered by the bed sheet should have made him appear more vulnerable. In fact, he seemed impervious, as if he needed no protection whatsoever from whatever this conversation might yield.

Hallee waited for him to begin the conversation, but he simply sat beside her, his eyes unblinking, saying nothing. Hallee blinked first.

"Maybe you should start…"

"It was your idea to broach the subject, Hal."

"So you don't have any opinions..."

X sighed, his chest raising visibly. He scratched his head slightly, as though he were trying to eek a thought from his brain. Finally, he said, "I'm not comfortable with this, Hallee, but it's probably not for the reasons you think."

Hallee felt her heart sink. He obviously wasn't comfortable discussing their future because he didn't see them as having a future together. She pulled away from him physically, but he caught her arm precisely where one of his inflictions had raised a welt. Hallee winced and immediately he released her wrist.

"I'm sorry," he said. "I don't want to hurt you."

Hallee had to smile at that, considering it was his actions that had created the bruise to begin with. "Sarcasm, much?"

"I can see how you might think that," Xavier admitted. "Look, Hallee, if you want to ask me a question, I wish you'd just ask it. I don't like games, and I don't like the feeling that you're testing me."

"Have you had a lot of girlfriends?" she managed, not quite sure the reason this question popped first into her mind.

X cocked his head and gave her "the look." His eyes were penetrating but kind, and she never liked this moment that the stare required. She could almost hear the synapses in his brain connecting.

"I've never been married," X said at last, and Hallee felt the implication was that since she had been she wasn't in the position to question him about his past. She tried another route to the information she desired knowing.

"What about this, what you do to me?"

"You mean what we do to each other?" X corrected.

"It doesn't feel like I'm doing anything to you," Hallee said. "You're the one in control."

"In a way, sure," X replied. "But I'm happy to change places with you, if you want." He smiled maliciously, and Hallee didn't know if he was joking, baiting her, or angry. It turned out he really was none of these.

"Hallee, do you really think I've had many partners in this kind of relationship?" X asked. "I don't want to talk about other women I've dated, but I understand your interest in my past. I've had a couple serious relationships in my life, and I've experimented with BDSM off and on, finding what works for me, learning not to injure my partner or not be injured by a partner."

The idea that he had shared something so precious with another person, weighed on Hallee. At the same time she was somewhat mortified by the activity she imagined him undertaking. "So you have been a bottom before?" Hallee asked sadly.

Xavier laughed so loudly, Hallee jumped slightly. "I wouldn't say that's exactly accurate," X said still chuckling. Hallee blushed, feeling like a virgin in the dragon's lair. What did she know about any of this? Other than witnessing some porn—which Hallee had viewed from a negative perspective simply because it was associated with her ex-husband's cruelty—Hallee had very little experience in anything kinky or sexually alternative. What the hell did she know about sexual terminology?

"Hallee," X explained, the laughter only in his eyes now, "I'm not that well versed in BDSM. What I'm saying is, I am comfortable with you, and if you want to try something different or take a break, all you have to do is communicate that to me."

"You seem to be taking the lead, so I don't really get much opportunity to communicate."

"Well, at the risk of sounding like a complete douchebag," X paused before continuing with what Hallee assumed would make him sound precisely that, "Your body communicates a lot to me."

What Hallee wanted to say: "Yuck."

What she said: Nothing, but the look on her face must have told Xavier that she didn't like the Rod Stewart-esque vibe he was giving off.

"Alright, look," X tried again. "I really love being with you, Hallee. And if you want to dial back and start again, we can do whatever makes you feel good. I won't make assumptions..."

"Yes, but that's just sex," Hallee felt a slight irritation growing. Also, she noted his use of the "L-word" and wondered if he chose to use that verb consciously or was he casually throwing it out there because love meant nothing to him. "Honestly, I feel like our entire relationship is predicated on the physical."

"And whose fault is that?" X's tone was accusatory. Hallee didn't want to feel that it was her fault, but she couldn't really blame work and family either. However, X obviously didn't want to start a fight, because he quickly added, "I know your work is intense. And I imagine being a single mom isn't easy either. But I don't like feeling that I have to compete for your attention, Hal."

Hallee considered this before saying, "I just need to know if you think we have a future together."

At this point, X rose from the bed and disappeared around the corner where a bend in the room lead to a walk-in closet beside a bathroom with a jacuzzi tub (she had used it once, and it was the best bath she'd had since coming to New York City, where all the tubs seemed designed for Lilliputians). When he returned, he was dressed in sweats and a T-shirt.

He sat on the edge of the bed, and began. "I won't talk specifics about us, but I can tell you in general terms my feelings about relationships. I owe you that much, and I hope you'll hear me out before you dump me altogether."

Uh, oh. This isn't going to be good, Hallee thought to herself.

"For much of my life," X explained, "I struggled to have what would be considered a 'normal' relationship, but that's mainly because I don't really have a normal life. I travel to crazy places, doing crazy things. I absolutely *love* the thrill of life. Maybe I transferred some of that into our sex life together, but I think I would be thrilled with you regardless of the particulars."

Again, Hallee wasn't sure X's implications, but he continued before she could ruminate further.

"That said, I honestly don't believe in making future plans, Hallee. I'm really a here-and-now, what-you-see-is-what-you-get kind of guy. I see how unhappy you are, and I want to take some of that away. Give you some kind of break from all that fear you face on a daily basis..."

"You do know that you scare me sometimes?" Hallee interrupted.

"Do I?" X wasn't mocking her. He seemed intent to make her understand something that was just beyond her vision, like he was when he went to get dressed a moment before. "You can make me stop whenever you like, Hallee. How is that scary? You really think I'm controlling you, forcing you to bend to my will? Because I don't really see it that way."

Hallee wanted to affirm or deny his supposition, but she honestly didn't know how he fit into her world view. She simply said, "So, you don't believe in a future regardless of me?"

"I just think that making plans for the future is wasting the present. And I think the whole paradigm of marriage and monogamy is false. I assume you said 'till death do us part' when you got married?"

"Well, it was a civil ceremony," Hallee said, "But I get your meaning." Nothing lasts, she supposed, and X was already looking for an out.

"I don't know," she continued. "Maybe it's different as a parent. I have to think about my kids..."

"Of course you do," X interrupted. "But putting money in a college savings account doesn't trump making sure they eat dinner and are safe today, right? If anything, you're probably more present when dealing with your kids than at any other point."

What Hallee wanted to say: "Any other point than when I'm tied up in your bed."

What she said: "You said you didn't believe in monogamy."

"Yeah," X sighed, "I figured that came through loud and clear. I'm not looking to cheat on you, just so you're aware."

"I'm not sure I believe you," Hallee admitted.

"My idea about being in an open relationship is not about anyone but you and me. I'm not asking for permission to be polyamorous. I don't want to 'share' you with anyone, nor do I expect you to be willing to 'share' me. I just don't want *either* of us to feel trapped. I just think that being open is more likely to lead to honesty. When—*if*—we don't enjoy each other anymore, I want us both to leave whole, intact." His gaze wasn't one of pleading or frustration; he simply needed her to understand, to trust him, to have faith. This was not something that was easy for her.

"I don't know, Xavier. I don't know if this is for me..."

"Well, you wouldn't be the first woman to say that to me," X confessed. "It's why I don't date a lot, to answer your earlier question. I try not to become emotionally entangled because when I finally explain myself, I end up feeling like a jerk."

"Why don't you ever ask about my sons?" Hallee questioned. "I need you to be in their life."

"So," X was drawing out the vowel as he so often did. "Are you asking me to be in their lives? Because that would be a huge step, Hallee. And it would no longer be about just you and me. Are you prepared to explain to them where I go when I'm not with you? Are you willing to bring me into their lives knowing that sooner or later, I will leave? Because I'm not getting that vibe from you. At least not yet."

Hallee felt utterly dejected. X was already talking about leaving her. Her mood had gone from ecstatic to devastated in a manner of minutes. Once again, she was being affected by the man in her life... by the *men* in her life (even though her sons were still boys, she felt their maleness even in her basic interactions with them—*Put down the toilet seat! Pick up your "floordrobe."*—and she longed for just one girlfriend who would "get her"). She now felt exhausted her to her core.

She looked into Xavier's gray eyes and saw so much sadness. She honestly didn't know if she cared that in some inexplicable way, she had injured him. He took her hand, examining it. It was an oddly charming quirk he had, and only in very specific moments would he strike this pose of vulnerability. Hallee was pretty sure it was a subconscious action on his part.

"You know, Hal," he said without looking up, "If you need to hear 'I love you', I can say that." His eyes raised slightly to her, and she thought she saw tears in them. Whiskey. Tango. Foxtrot.

Hallee had no idea what he was intimating. If he loved her, truly loved her, why not just come out and say it? Suddenly a cold sweat came over her; she could feel the dampness in the sheet she clung to as a garment. It was the dawning realization that if he told her that he loved her, she could not reply honestly that she loved him as well. She simply wasn't ready. What had she thought when they first met? That he would be her "transition man."

What Hallee wanted to say: "I think we should let sleeping dogs lie, as they say."

What she said: "Do you mind if I enjoy a bath before I go home?"

X's chin moved up and down just slightly, in what might have been the saddest nod of all time.

VII

"Love me as I am, sweet one,
for I shall never be better."
Wives and Daughters, Elizabeth Gaskell

What do you want?

A friend... A companion... A soulmate...

Squalid.

While not exactly *onomatopoeia*, there's a certain quality of "mouthfeel" in speaking the word "squalid": the tongue working through the linguistic equivalent of a sŭrya namaskâra with vinyâsa flow. Our oral sun salutation begins with a pursing of the lips but quickly the tongue arches into its own downward dog only to flick back to the teeth for that final plosive "d."

I return to NYC from Iceland to nearly 100 degree heat. The city is pure putrescence, visible vapors vibrating from the concrete of every sidewalk, the glass façade of every building. A mingling of blue and white with red differentiating the sweaty soccer fans who ooze out the doors of rank bars mid-day to watch the World Cup semis, blocking every other sidewalk with their shouting masses. At night the whir of air conditioning units humming louder than traffic on West End Avenue creates a kind of metallic mosquito medley. But even the vermin are hiding in this heat.

The worst part about leaving the island idyll is that I choke on the tap water: it's liquid toxin despite the local government agency's claim that ours is the best tasting H2O in the nation. I gag as I drink it, but I gave up buying bottled water when I learned that the major distributors were simply purifying municipal supplies from various locations, using clever branding and exotic names to fool consumers into believing this latest incarnation of snake oil will cure all our ills. Regardless, I cannot bring myself to lug jugs of water back from the grocery in this wretched weather. So I try to imbibe without puking: the stuff of life.

145

The best part about returning home is that my daughter is here. I sometimes feel that we are two lost souls always destined to be together but mismatched, at least on a romantic level. Perhaps she was a favorite pet in a previous lifetime. Or we were prisoners of war in separate cages, never allowed to see or touch but within hearing distance. She is more than just my pride and joy: She is my friend.

If you've never seen the film, *Love Actually,* well, you should. It's a film my daughter and I watch every year on Christmas Eve. The movie lays out several story arcs, each showing a different kind of love: parental, filial, romantic, lustful, unrequited, etc. My favorite storyline involves the recovering heroin addict, a musician who comes to realize the love of his life is, in fact, his roadie manager, the one who stuck with him in good times and bad, for better or worse, for richer or poorer... yadda yadda. But in all honesty, it's a profound message: that sometimes the love we get isn't what's in the storybooks.

I have always hungered for romantic love. I have fallen deeply in love several times in my life, and even when I didn't feel "love" per se, I would crush hard, and crumble in devastating ways when the inevitable end came. Because God likes to fuck with me, I finally found true love... in the form of my own daughter.

Hélène—named for Ryan-Claude's mother—is like no one I know. She is the Monster to my Doctor Frankenstein. With far less obscene results. When I found out I was pregnant with a girl, I was terrified. Mostly I worried she would grow up to be exactly like me. I did everything I could to ensure that she didn't, and the outcome was a bit too successful. She is independent to a fault, and she can be quite harsh in her judgments of others. That said, she is the wisest and most balanced human being I have ever met in my entire life. I sometimes joke that I wonder who her mother is.

She decided to spend this summer at home before going abroad to study in the fall. She'll be in Paris, where she will be staying with her namesake, whom she likes far more than she does her father. I've tried not to demonize Ryan-Claude to his children, but Hélène saw too much... and I concealed too little. How many tears does mommy have to shed before daddy becomes the bad guy?

I want to write a parenting book, illustrating how despite all my fucked-up-ness that I am raising these amazing kids. Especially Hélène—stick a fork in her—she's done. I'll include instructions on how to break the cycle and create hardy children that evolve into productive adults capable of having fulfilling lives. I would dedicate the book to all the world's children and title it, *You Don't Have to Grow Up to be Your Mother: The Dysfunctional Parent's Guide to Raising Functional Children.* Or maybe I'll call it, *I Broke the Cycle... Too Bad my Kids Don't Want Kids of their Own!*

And Hélène doesn't. Of course, by the time my son came along she was old enough to witness (and participate in) the rigors of parenting. Aside from her selfishness—in the best sense—Hélène knows that kids are a crapshoot: maybe they turn out great or maybe they become the Unibomber. Worst of all... maybe they just turn out to be average. Hélène is anything but average.

For example, she picked up her brother from daycare today, and he's crying. I immediately want to know what has happened, but she fires a warning glance across my bow not to interfere. I make a cup of tea, lingering in the kitchen as she sits on the futon that doubles as a guest bed in the living room. She has handed him a tissue, which he uses to blow his nose and wipe his eyes. He tries to hand it back to her—"Ew. Gross!"—which makes him laugh through his tears.

He explains to her that one of the kids at school was mean to him and no longer wants to be his friend. He's unhappy because he feels there are no kids in his class who like him. He's lonely and wonders why no one understands him. I feel a twinge in my stomach. My son is like me.

"Let me tell you something about happiness," Hélène begins to lecture her brother. "Think of all the things that make you happy: mom, me—sometimes [she makes a funny face]—video games—always [she feigns a snarl]—going to the beach, playing soccer..."

Her brother nods.

"Okay," she continues. "Pick up all those things, every last thing that makes you happy, and put it in your backpack." She pantomimes picking things up from the coffee table and loading them into his school backpack decorated with large cartoon penguins. "So, now you have your backpack of happiness, and you carry it around wherever you go.

"Then, a friend comes along, and you decide to take off your backpack of happiness and hand it over to him... or her," she quickly adds. She's nothing if not grammatically correct. "And you see what you've done?" Her brother shakes his head, not comprehending the moral of this story.

"Well, you've gone and given up your own happiness, expecting your friend to carry it around for you! What if he forgets? What if she gets tired of carrying your backpack of happiness? What if he or she decides that being responsible for your happiness is not something that is important?

"Never give *anyone* your backpack of happiness," she summarizes, and his five-year-old brain seems to be clicking, making sense of the metaphor. "You can care about others, even love them. But never *ever* let them carry your backpack. You'll be happy every day—good days and bad—if you don't give away your backpack thinking someone else will take better care of your happiness than you can."

He hugs her and runs off to play Club Penguin. She walks over to me, her eyebrow cocked à la Mr. Spock, and I already know that she is wondering where I've left *my* backpack this time. If only I'd had an older sister (or anyone from my childhood) to explain things so simply. I hand her the brewed tea, over ice, with milk and a ton of sugar, just the way she likes it. I drink mine straight.

As hot as it is—even with the a/c on there's warmth in the apartment—the iced tea is a comfort. The heat means I'm also wearing short sleeves. As I reach across the table to retrieve my tumbler, she notices the welt on my wrist. Ligature marks. I feel myself blush, as I attempt to hide the mark from her.

She touches my arm gently. "Does it hurt?" she asks simply. Considering the fact that she hates Frank—for no better reason than that she thinks men are a waste of time, and truly caring for them is forfeiting the backpack—and frequently lectures me about my mood swings relative to his attention, she's being remarkably restrained.

THE TRUTH

"No," I say, staring into my Chamomile, noticing the ice has melted; I should have poured it over ice in the teapot before putting it into a glass. I would like to avoid this discussion. While Hélène and I have a strangely transparent relationship, it's still awkward between parent and child to talk about sex, regardless of which party is copulating. Our mother-daughter friendship is one that few of her friends *or* mine truly understand. She's become my partner in life, oddly enough. It's very much a *Love Actually* relationship, where the love you make and so on. But there is so much that—despite maturity beyond her years—she cannot understand about what it feels like being middle-aged. And maybe she never will understand the loneliness I feel, the emptiness, the pain. Pain versus pain. How do I explain that to a person—not to mention my first-born—for whom pain is to be eschewed and those who inflict it avoided at all cost. *You don't have to grow up to be like me.*

"So..." she takes her time as I brace myself. You would think that considering she is always on me about letting others affect my emotions that she would be less likely to take aim. "Are you a submissive?"

My mouth drops open. How on earth does she even know what that is? "How on earth do you even know what that is? What are they teaching you at that west coast school of yours?"

"Come on, mom." Her tone borders on disgust. "It makes total sense. Look at your relationship with Dad!"

I hadn't considered how my self-deprecation might have been part of the dynamic of my relationship with Ryan-Claude. It's only since meeting Frank that the word "submissive" has entered my vocabulary. How do I identify? Am I a masochist? Do I seek out pain in one form or another? I try tentatively to explain, perhaps as much to myself as to my daughter.

"I guess it's my nature to put others first, so maybe that's a submissive mindset. I certainly know about self-sacrifice."

"But you let him hurt you," Hélène interrupts. "That's not cool, mom."

"It's less about the pain than the relief afterwards." I struggle to formulate my thoughts; I haven't taken time to analyze what I am doing with Frank. "Maybe your dad was all about the former and not the latter. In the end, our marriage was based on utter indifference. He wanted me to want nothing from him, and he got exactly that. I stopped wanting anything. I stopped feeling *anything*." I feel my eyes well up. I fear that God is messing with me again, playing on those unfounded fears that my daughter would grow up to be just like me. Giving me a son who is too sensitive, too longing to serve, too willing to pass along his backpack. My daughter will be fine, but what about my boy? "I'm very sad, you know?"

"Yeah, mom," and she's grown impatient with me. "You're always sad." She finishes off her tea, trying to tip into her mouth the remainder of the sweet syrup that has coagulated at the bottom of the glass. She looks at me, and there's a rare moment of quiet between us. Most of the time, we're interrupting each other's commentary, venturing off on tangents, whiling away the minutes until they are hours and procrastination morphs into a larger delay in living our lives. We would have enjoyed hanging out with Socrates in the garden... perhaps that was where our souls met, in men's bodies, debating the nature of truth... perhaps I played Plato (the apologist) to her more radical and independent Xenophon.

"I just don't understand why you think a man will make your life better," she lectures.

"Hélène, I don't want to justify myself again..."

"You're talented and capable and you have so much to offer," she says, shutting me up. I don't think she's ever praised me before. "But you think the Universe is just going to provide for you without investing in yourself."

Ah, yes, that damned Universe. Hélène isn't much for God, but she does believe that the Universe has its peculiar rhythms of destiny intertwined with intention. She will ride the quantum waves to great success, whereas I always feel that if there are universal surges, I'm either missing the influx altogether or being crashed against the rocks, struggling not to drown.

"That's not a fair summary of what I've invested, Hélène," I protest weakly. I am no match for her, despite the improved mood resulting from my relationship with Frank. "I am a very broken person. I'm doing the best I can day-in, day-out. And I hope from the bottom of my heart that you never ever have to suffer what I have."

She starts into the same diatribe about oppressed women in the middle east and impoverished women who are being beaten by their husbands and boyfriends and and and... I know she means well, but I've heard it all before. I block out everything she's saying, a buzzing in my head like white noise. When will she stop the narrative?

More and more lately, I find myself retreating into some compartment inside of my brain, where imaginary guards stand at the ready to protect me from the onslaught of life. I sometimes wonder if this isn't a direct result of life in New York City, I need a haven that is impenetrable to sound, where chaos is blocked, where I am protected from harm. The irony of my present sexual awakening notwithstanding.

"I wish I could explain it to you," I finally manage, as she has stopped speaking and stares at me waiting for a coherent reply. "I simply feel very present when I am with Frank. I'm not scared anymore. Maybe I'm just crazy."

"Maybe you are," she snarks back at me.

"Then this is my form of electro shock therapy. It sounds extreme and wrong, I know. But when I'm with him, I'm not depressed. I'm not worried. And I always feel more alive afterwards."

Hélène sighs. I know she's different from most young women, but she's also very different from me. Maybe it's our ages, our life experience. Or maybe it's that she never once doubted that she was loved. I have loved her every day since she was six weeks old and she uttered her first genuine giggle. I remember very few events in my life with extreme lucidity; call it the writer's curse to embellish or alter what has passed. I was sitting on the very same futon that we sit on now; it has traveled with me across many states and is lumpier now than it was then, obviously. I have replaced the cover, so the color is different. But 20 years ago I held her in my hands, cooing at her, and she began to laugh. I laughed back at my beautiful baby and she laughed harder. Her giggle was a manifestation of sheer and utter joy, an arrival into consciousness when baby first truly sees what is in front of her. She became a person on that day, and I knew I loved her more than air.

I pulled her to my chest, bursting into tears, knowing at that moment that some seismic shift had torn the fabric of my life forever. I didn't want to love this profoundly ever again; it hurts too much to love another with such utter abandon.

"Don't you break my heart," I had whispered into her uncomprehending ear.

From six weeks old, she has held my backpack. And she has never relinquished it. For 20 years, she has carried it without comment. I look at the beautiful woman sitting beside me and know: Inside her own backpack of happiness rests my little pathetic and torn bag; she has always left room for the weight of my longing. I may never be understood fully by anyone, but she carries the burden unconditionally. She, too, is different from the rest.

"I wish I were like you: a square peg trying to get into a round hole. In reality, I fear I'm a triangular peg trying to pass for half-a-square peg," I burst a cliché, seeking some kind of introspection. Better to look within for the answers.

"I think, maybe—just maybe—you're better now with Frank," she says at last.

I'm shocked to hear her say this. Does it pain her to admit she's wrong? Or is her statement even an admission of that? Perhaps she's just allowing me this small reprieve from self-sufficiency. Perhaps she is letting go the idea that I can be better than I am. If that's the case, I fear I've lost my best cheerleader. If Hélène has given up schooling me in how to behave, I may drift without the anchor she has been these past few years. She may finally be free of me, but I will be lost without her.

Letting go is so very very hard to do.

The Truth

It wasn't long before school backpacks, glue sticks and plastic organizers on the store shelves were morphing into orange plastic pumpkins, chunky faux corn cobs, and giddily smiling cardboard skeletons. Hallee was not looking forward to the holidays. From the impending deadline on the Pritzker to Janine's impossible shopping tasks to the prohibitive cost of shopping in New York City, Hallee felt more Scroogish than she had ever been in her 40 years on the planet.

Now that the boys were back in school, she should have been able to negotiate more time with Xavier, but she was still processing his level of commitment to her, and for the time being, work was her main focus. To some extent, she felt like she was hedging her bets with him when she snuck out every Thursday to have sex over her lunch break. The thrill of her time with X was always tempered when she got back to work, as she invariably was greeted with an oppressive "to do" list.

On this particular afternoon, Hallee returned to the office to Lauren's "Janine Report." The grande dame was awaiting a hired car to take her to her doctor's office; the car was not to be driven by a Latino or Eastern European; the driver was to use West Street and not the FDR to take her uptown; blah blah blah. Hallee had heard it so many times before, she truly couldn't understand why Lauren was explaining the instructions yet again.

Hallee's intercom buzzed. David's voice was beckoning her to come to his office. She turned the corner as the glass flashed brightness reflecting from the skyscrapers across the way. The air conditioning blew back Hallee's hair (or so she imagined) as she walked through a tunnel of uncertainty to the glass cave; the one good thing about being sexed up and high (thank you, Xavier!) was that Hallee no longer felt any trepidation in facing David. She sat across from him, waiting for him to look up from his computer screen. After a few minutes of tapping the keyboard, he slammed closed the laptop.

Hallee didn't even flinch. Whether David was expecting her to or not, he smiled at her knowingly.

"Hallee," he began, "when Lauren brought you to usss, I knew you would be an asssset to the company." Was his lisp more pronounced or was it marijuana fog? Hallee struggled not to grin stupidly at her employer. He was droning on about the future of the company before saying, "I'd like to know how you see yourself here. I'm extremely pleased with your efforts this summer. In fact, this is the best Pritzker package I've seen. Perhaps four's the charm?"

Hallee nodded, unsure of what she was supposed to do next. David was waiting. What had he asked her? Oh, yes. Her future at the company.

"To be honest," she said, "as much as I like working in admin..." a lie, "I would really like to be considered for the project manager position that has just opened." Hallee had been filling in, taking on many of the duties of the junior associate who had left to go to graduate school.

"But you're not an architect."

"I know," Hallee was careful in her choice of words. "The work I've been doing on the Pritzker is interesting and challenging..."

"You don't find being Arnie's assistant interesting and challenging?" David was peering over his stupid reading glasses. Why on earth didn't he just remove them when he wasn't reading?

"I am challenged, but not in the same way," she backpedaled. "I'm already performing most of the tasks of the project manager position, and it will probably be easier for you to find another administrator than someone who can hit the ground running in this position."

David's snaky eyes bore into her. Again, no flinching. "I'll consider it," he said. "I'd like you here for the long haul." Thinking that was her cue to leave, Hallee tried to stand. Her shifting weight sent a tingle up her spine. *Don't think of X now!* she chastised herself silently.

"In the meantime," David continued, and Hallee tried to sit back in the chair without further unwanted stimulation. "Alison has to go in for some medical tests, and she will be working from home for the next little while. I need someone here in the office to fill in for her, looping her in on everything, of course."

Hallee felt flush. Was David actually proposing that she become his executive assistant? It wasn't a project manager post, but it was as high as she would ever go in the admin pool. "Well, wouldn't you want Lauren for that? She usually backs up Alison."

David barely let Hallee finish her sentence before cutting her off with, "I think you're better suited for the job." He opened his laptop and began banging the keys again. He used his middle finger to push his John Lennon glasses up the bridge of his nose. "That's all," he added without looking at her. She supposed that meant she had accepted the position.

She hadn't even returned to her desk before the e-mail was sent out. David obviously had composed it before inviting Hallee in to discuss it. The notice was succinct, and as Hallee read it, she was almost positive David hadn't written it at all. Alison had composed it on his behalf; a similarly worded e-mail from her account went out time stamped seconds later with similar language. In short, Alison was taking a leave but not an absence. She would be working from home and should be cc'd on any correspondence with Hallee; she would be working with Hallee through the transition; depending on the outcome of her tests, she hoped to return to the office after the first of the year. Hallee felt a trickle of sweat down her spine. How was she to handle Arnie's schedule, the final Pritzker submission and inevitable follow-up, general admin, *Janine—never forget Janine*, and now David's needs, as well? The only small thing she had carved out for herself was Xavier. She had a few hours of "fun" with the boys on the weekend. That was *everything* she had for herself. David would expect Hallee to work weekends and to check her e-mail up until midnight (the man seemingly never slept more than three or four hours a day). Now she'd have zero down time. She felt as though she might burst into tears.

What stopped her was Lauren. Her co-worker was putting on her jacket. She was pale and had already started crying. A few of the junior architects were stopping by to offer Hallee congratulations; obviously they thought she was moving on up in the company.

Lauren gave a perfunctory congratulations, as well. "I'm sorry to leave," she said as she slid a stack of papers into a filing cabinet for later retrieval. "I have another migraine." Hallee doubted the migraine story but understood her friend's desire to be rid of both her and David Ormston-Meighton Architects Company, Incorporated. Her friend. Were they even friends anymore? Hallee doubted it. She didn't understand the office politics or why Lauren's years of indentured servitude weren't paying off. Hallee didn't understand why her efficiency and ability to multitask were being rewarded by backhanded promotions she neither sought nor particularly wanted. David's executive assistant? She hadn't asked for the job.

Lauren was barely out the door when the phone rang.

"Call 911!" the familiar voice screamed.

"Hello, Janine," Hallee said in monotone.

"Are you listening, you idiot? Call 911! I'm being kidnapped!"

"What?" Hallee wasn't sure if she should be genuinely concerned for Janine's welfare. It was New York, after all. Stranger things could happen than being kidnapped. "Where are you?"

"I'm in a cab!" Janine sounded apoplectic. "He's kidnapping me!"

"Janine, wait!" Hallee was scrambling to make sense of what was happening. "Tell him to stop and let you out."

"I don't want to stop, I want to go home!" Janine was screaming so loudly that Hallee had to hold the receiver several inches from her ear.

"Janine," she tried to speak over the woman's sobs and screams. Janine was cursing the cabby, calling him "a cock-sucking, mother-fucking Jihadist!" Oh, yes, that would go over well. If she were, in fact, being kidnapped, Janine was a poor negotiator for her own release.

"Let me talk to the driver," Hallee shouted.

"No, I'm not giving that terrorist my phone! I'll be dead if I do."

"Janine, just get out of the cab!" Hallee was screaming, and much of the office had taken notice. Sadly, no one felt this was anything out of the ordinary, having heard or seen it happen time and time again. "Just. Get.

Out. Of. The. Cab."

Hallee heard more shouting, screeching, and screaming. Then the line went dead. *Oh. My. God.* What on earth had just happened? A tiny evil idea popped into Hallee's mind that Janine was dead; the evil part was that the idea gave her pleasure. She called Janine back. No answer. She called her again. Still no answer. Finally, she called the car service.

The operator put her on hold, and the other line rang. It could be Janine, so Hallee put the hold on hold and took the call. A man's voice with a slight Persian accent was screaming back at her, probably having clicked redial on Janine's phone. "Who this is? Who this is? I already call police. They come get crazy lady who jumps from car!"

"Sir, sir, sir!" Hallee implored. Her heart was racing and her head ached. The pot had completely worn off, and now she was just exhausted by everything. Where on earth was Janine? "Where are you?" she asked the cabbie.

"Corner of Lexington and 29th!" The line went dead. Hallee clicked to the car service operator who, thankfully, had not yet returned to the line.

"Yes, the driver is still in front of the address," the operator said, repeating the address to make sure it was correct.

"What do you mean, the driver's still there?" Hallee asked, trying to make sense of a puzzle that was slowly coming together to create a picture only a student of Dali would understand. "She's in the car!"

"No, ma'am," the operator repeated. Janine had never gotten into the car. What car *had* she gotten into? Hallee thanked the woman and told her to send the driver to Lexington and 29th. Hallee grabbed her cell phone and headed out the door. She kept repeat dialing Janine, but there was no answer. On the street, she hailed a taxi and took it the few blocks to where Janine might have been. As the cab approached, she saw two police cruisers, a tall, dark-skinned man flailing his arms, and Janine walking around in circles, screaming what Hallee was sure were flamboyant epithets. Hallee threw a $20-bill in the front seat and ran from the vehicle, getting neither her change nor a receipt for reimbursement.

When she approached the melee, the police officer (a man, thank God; Hallee guessed it would be easier to appeal to a male cop than a female, "Look at this poor woman, officer, if she were your mother, you'd want her to be taken care of, right?") let her pass. After 20 minutes of Hallee's pleas and the irate cabbie explaining what had happened (he had been passing by the apartment when Janine waved at him, so he picked her up, how was he to blame, blah blah blah), Hallee paid the cab driver twice the fare, promising him and the police officers that Janine would cause no more problems. Reluctantly, the cops let Janine go with a warning.

Hallee attempted to get Janine into the correct car, which had now arrived at the scene of the "crime." Janine refused. "I never want to ride in a car again so long as I live!"

"Janine," Hallee began, "it's too far to walk you home. We're nowhere near the doctor's either. You won't make it on foot."

"I can walk to the office," Janine said. Oh, great. Now she would end up back at the domicile, and Hallee's day would go even further downhill. However, Janine was determined to walk, and at least the office wasn't far from their current location.

Hallee expected the walk to be torturous, but other than Janine's aversion to brushing up against other pedestrians, the return trip was blissfully uneventful. When David saw his frantic wife, he shot a sideways glance at Hallee before leaving for the day. *As if it were my fault!* Hallee thought.

Hallee spent the last few hours at work on the Pritzker. David didn't return, although he did call in to check his voice mail three times (leaving Hallee extended messages through the system every time he called in). He had also sent her a dozen or so e-mails. None of which had to do with the Prizker. It was all additional work. Apparently Lauren had called in sick, so tomorrow Hallee would be running the store. Thank God it would be Friday. Hallee considered calling Janine to see if she had recovered, but she knew no good would come of it and quite a lot of bad might.

Fortunately, Friday afforded her the opportunity to complete the majority of her work so that she could devote the entire weekend to the Pritzker application. Well, almost the entire weekend. Hallee really wanted to see X again before diving into non-stop-work-from-home, so she took a cash advance on a credit card (how was it she was working all these extra hours but only making an additional five grand? lots of takeout probably didn't help her budget) and got a sitter for the night, not wanting to encroach upon Mary and Ty yet again.

Being with Xavier those few hours was definitely worth the 18.99 percent she'd pay on the advance. He was generous and gentle, for which Hallee was grateful.

She was still sore from the previous day's lunch.

"I have something to show you," Xavier smiled knowingly. "It's a surprise." He jumped out of bed with enthusiasm, undeterred by his nudity. Hallee still was not entirely comfortable being naked around him, particularly when coitus had ended and they were chatting and lounging. She clutched the sheet around her midsection. He was rounding the L-shaped corner of the winding bedroom towards his magnificent bathroom. He paused to look back at her. "Well, are you coming?"

Hallee grabbed the most convenient covering she could find, which turned out to be X's undershirt. It barely covered her mons. She fidgeted between standing up straight, shoulders back so her boobs didn't droop or slouching to cover her graying pubes. The one thing she didn't want to do was stretch out his shirt; that would just be rude. Oh, why on earth hadn't she just pulled the damn sheet off the bed?

"Hallee?" X had hidden himself away in the walk-in closet just beyond the bathroom entrance. She couldn't imagine what he had in store for her if it involved his closet. She had barely stepped through the entrance when she stopped short. He was standing before two bare rods and was in the process of opening up several bureau drawers that also were vacant. He was beaming like a child—one of the Whoville children that sang before a missing Christmas Tree, not bowing to grinchiness—and seemed completely oblivious to her mood shift.

At first Hallee had felt a cold sweat coming over her, then gradually she began to feel irritation. This quickly morphed into a burgeoning rage. "What is this, Xavier?" she asked, and he could not have mistaken her tone as being affectionate.

"I made room for your clothes," he said matter-of-factly. He crossed to her, the joy gone from his face. "What's wrong?

"What is this?" she asked again, only this time she meant something very different. "What do you think," she motioned between them, her hand slapping into his chest with a bit more force than was appropriate, "is happening between us?"

X backed away from her. He didn't like being smacked, even if she hadn't consciously meant to hit him. He wasn't retreating. His demeanor was that of a man who had faced death and far worse. Her moodiness was not something that would cause him nightmares. Perhaps that was part of the problem; he never seemed affected by her. Sure, he enjoyed her company, her body. Why would he now intimate that their relationship was at a level that would require her to move some (all?) of her belongings into his apartment? Had he even considered her kids? Did he appreciate all she was juggling between work and motherhood and paying the bills and, now, him? When had they progressed from a summer fling into something more serious? Was this his way of asking her to move in or what? She was nearly furious at this point and would have screamed had she thought she could get away with it. Something checked her rage, however. She didn't want to lose him over this, but she felt utterly conflicted about being ambushed.

X was opening one of the other drawers. He pulled out a pair of boxer-briefs and slipped them on. They were dark blue and held his toned body perfectly. This certainly wasn't helping, as Hallee had always thought this kind of underwear—particularly on well-toned men—was far sexier than nudity or traditional briefs or boxers. More conflict rose within her.

"You know I have kids," she said simply.

"Are we really gonna do this again? Of course I know you have kids!" Now there was a hint of exasperation. He recognized that she was deflecting, but she had no interest in hypothesizing about their future together.

"So what about them? Are you clearing places in your closet for *their* things?"

"Are you saying you want to move in with me?" he asked with that penetrating stare that always disarmed her. Not this time.

"Are you asking me to move in with you?"

X leaned back against the dresser. He always seemed so calm, but she could tell he was weighing his words more carefully than usual. "What are you afraid of, Hallee?"

"I'm not afraid," she said, but she was pretty sure her stoic approach to their relationship was all about burying her fears.

"Alright, I guess I have to believe you." He wasn't going to start a fight, but he also wasn't ready to drop the matter. "I want you in my life, Hallee."

"And what does that mean?" Her voice was pitchy, and she could hear the grating quality but couldn't control it. "You never ask about my kids. You never ask me about my work..."

"Oh, you volunteer more than enough information about your work..." he interrupted, his voice rising.

"So, I'm not supposed to talk about my kids?"

"I didn't say..."

"I'm not supposed to talk about anything that bothers me? I'm not supposed to care about you because you say you don't believe in a committed relationship..."

"Now, that's not true. I never said..."

"You said the only honest relationship is an open relationship..."

"Yes!" Xavier was trying to control his voice before they escalated into a full-out fight. "That *is* the kind of relationship I believe in, and I want that kind of a relationship with *you*!" He was doing that pacing thing again, and this time Hallee was able to identify the animal resemblance as a tiger in a cage, but rather than pounce at her, he brushed past her and back into the bedroom.

He started changing the linens on the bed, walking back and forth—his caged tiger stride—passing her as he went from the hall and returned to the bedroom with clean sheets. He had this half-annoying, half-endearing tendency to busy himself when he was irritated, as though he risked throwing a chair through a window if he weren't otherwise occupied. When he came closest to her, he paused to hiss, "I'm not playing this game with you."

"Well, then, I guess you shouldn't have shown me the closet!"

X threw the folded linens against the wall, causing Hallee to flinch. She had never seen him exert force that wasn't sexual in nature. She held her breath. He stood over her, his body pressing hers into the wall, but the stance was one of power, not sexuality. She half expected him to strike her.

Xavier's breathing regulated. Seconds went by, but they felt like hours. Finally, he managed, "What do you think is going to happen between us, Hallee? I mean, what's the worst that happens in your most dreadful fantasy?"

Hallee felt immeasurably sad when she said it. "You die."

"Oh, now, that's total fucking bullshit." The statement felt like a slap, despite the fact that he was now withdrawing from her. She was free to move. "You're not afraid of me dying. You're afraid one day I'll just wake up and not want you anymore! That I'll reject you. That's why you haven't invited me over to meet your kids. You haven't even asked me to go out with you to meet your friends, Mary and Tyler. That's their names, right? I'd know, if you'd bothered to introduce us, but you don't want me outside the bedroom at all!" X took several breaths that would best be described as "cleansing."

Suddenly, his demeanor shifted. His tongue was at her earlobe, his fingers in her cunt. He was whispering, calling her nasty words, telling her how much she deserved to be punished.

He was touching her in just the right way that would make her come in less than a minute. She rocked her pussy against his hand.

"But this is a different kind of hurt," she admitted, her mouth finding his.

"Yes," he said. "I know you need it." He kissed her deeply, stifling her moan as she squirted all over his hand. He scooped her up in his arms and returned to the bed. He was kissing her clit, her belly, her tits (the T-shirt bunched up under her arms and over her breasts). He continued fondling her. She grabbed his hand and coaxed it to stop petting her. Somewhere from her subconscious, her head began to shake slowly.

"What do you mean," she asked, "that I need it?"

X cocked his head to the side. Hallee had never really minded before, but his knowing smirk reeked of condescension. It was irritating her now, like a blister forming on the back of her heel. "You need it. You need to be abused."

"What are you talking about?" Hallee sat up and moved away from him.

"Don't be defensive about it, Hal," he seemed to be forming a blister of his own. "Look at me." He grabbed her arm but she pulled it right back. This time, however, he didn't use his physical superiority to control her.

Despite the hour, he began pulling on his jeans and the dress shirt that he had been wearing when Hallee arrived (no T-shirt to go under, as she was wearing it). It felt incongruous, after initiating more sex, for him to suddenly be dressing himself. She felt dismissed somehow. After he finished dressing, he sat on the bed and motioned for her to sit beside him.

Hallee briefly considered joining him but instead shook her head and remained crouched at the head of his bed, the sheet gathered around her. Her mind was spinning. Was she in another abusive relationship? Had she really been the one keeping him at arm's length? Maybe he was right. Maybe rejection would be worse than death; knowing Jeremy left her for someone else probably caused her more pain (certainly more anger) than the inevitability of death. Hating God for taking someone dear away was much easier than despising a human being that was still living (possibly happily) without her. Was it possible that everything Hallee assumed about Xavier's indifference towards a relationship with her was actually her own distortion of his patience for her while she figured out what she wanted from him? As much control as he took in their sexual activities, had she simply assumed he would take the lead in their daily life? Or did he view her as a victim that just craved his spankings? She was utterly confused.

"Do I make you stronger?" he asked. His voice was all-business, but his face showed a hint of disgust. Hallee knew that look, and it made her recoil. *Not again*, she thought. *I won't do this again.* She stood and reached for her bra and panties, grabbing her clothes and heading towards the stairwell to the main floor. She finished dressing as he followed after her.

Once he caught up to her, X must have sensed that she was upset with how he was looking at her, because he softened his face along with his tone. "Is what I'm doing to you making you more resilient? Look at yourself, Hallee! You look younger, prettier, happier and, yes, angrier than I've ever seen you. I'm empowering you. I am providing a method of sexual expression that forces you to empower yourself."

"That is the most ridiculous thing I've ever heard!" Hallee was nearly fully dressed. "I don't need any of this, Xavier. If anyone needs this, it's you."

"I've had plenty of 'vanilla' relationships."

"Oh, really?" Hallee was mocking him now. "Any that fulfilled you?"

Hallee was in the living room, heading for the foyer door, but X followed, getting between her and the exit. "So, what? You're just going to leave? Run away?"

"I don't need you," Hallee turned to face him when she said this. She wasn't afraid of him. Maybe there was a hint of truth in what he said, but that was a disconcerting realization and not something Hallee wanted to consider at this particular moment. "You want to control and dominate and take pleasure from hurting other people."

"That is utterly unfair, Hallee," Xavier looked wounded. "We've always used safe words. We've had lots of sex that wouldn't be called extreme. I love that you are a woman who likes to do it all. I love that you're a slut."

"Don't be stupid," she was angry and felt tears welling up. But it wasn't slander; she felt like a slut. How did she end up here? *I will not cry*, she thought. "No one loves the slut," she managed at last.

"Is that what you truly believe?" The shock in Xavier's face was genuine.

THE TRUTH

"So you've bought into this whole notion that girls who like sex aren't worthy of love? Jesus, Hallee? What kind of human being do you think I am?"

"A man," she said simply and without any emotion. As she still struggled not to cry, she found her way back to the sofa, wanting to pull on her socks and shoes, but instead sunk into it feeling utterly defeated. She was no longer angry, just desperately sad.

"I know a lot of men are truly awful to women," he said in a measured tone. "And some women are just as awful to men." He came over and sat beside her. He picked up her hand gently and began to turn it over and back as though he were studying some unusual organism he had never before encountered. He didn't look up. "I'm not going to beg you to let me love you, Hallee. If you don't care about me, just say so, but don't blame me for your past experience with shitty men."

"Xavier, you've never even asked me out on a date," she managed meekly.

"That's actually not the case," he said. "I have broached the subject at least three times, and you always tell me you can't afford a sitter or that you have too much work. There's always an excuse. I'm tired of trying to knock down that wall you seem very attached to."

Hallee tried to process this, not wanting to speak defensively. She struggled with her words. "I have been trying... it's so much and it's so new... You're right, it scares me when I think about you going off and choosing someone else. I don't get the whole concept of not being monogamous. It's a lot to ask of me, Xavier." Her tone was measured, but there was still a level of anger simmering beneath her words. All her emotions seemed to be locked in an "on" position, and she wasn't sure what she felt about him anymore.

"I don't know how to explain this any clearer than I already have, Hallee," X tried nonetheless, his voice mellow and controlled once again. "You are the only woman in my life right now, and the only woman I'm looking to share my life with. But I cannot tell you that if I'm going back to Afghanistan or up to Hunts Point or anywhere in between that I won't want someone else. I spend half my life embedded in a world of death, destruction and chaos. All I have is today! That's it. Here and now. I choose you today. I choose you now. I don't want to promise you a future that is indefinite for both of us. I will be gone for months at a time, and I don't expect you to play Penelope to my Odysseus. I'm only asking for the same latitude."

If he was waiting for her to answer him, he showed no disappointment when she remained silent. She kept her eyes locked on his, but as much as she concentrated on the words he spoke, she was hopeless to respond. He probably only waited a second or two for her to offer a rebuttal, but it felt as though she had a bright light shining on her and there was nothing in the whole world that could protect her from the harsh glare. Nevertheless, he continued without her commentary.

"You know what I think?" he asked with no inflection. "You pretend to be indifferent to love. It's an act, self-preservation. I think you still have plenty of heart in you to break, but I will *never* intentionally hurt you. Never." He backed away slightly.

She didn't know what was true. Xavier had shown her more about herself than the prior 20 years had revealed. Perhaps everything he said was true. Maybe she did need to be abused. Maybe she did lump him in with her past relationships. Maybe she just didn't feel worthy of being loved. Maybe she couldn't feel love at all.

"I cannot make promises that I can't keep, Hallee, but I promise never to hurt you on purpose." He chuckled as a sly grin parted his lips. Hallee was strangely aroused by this unusual emotional display, and X seemed fully aware of this. He kissed her hard on her mouth. She winced.

"Unless you want me to hurt you on purpose," he taunted.

It was an invitation to return to bed, but Hallee was done. A single tear escaped down her cheek. She brushed it aside, but she knew X now understood that she wouldn't be accompanying him back to the bedroom. He shook his head. Was that pity she detected in his glance? It didn't matter.

"This isn't about me, Hallee," X sighed. "It's about you." He backed away from her, holding out his hands to suggest blamelessness or "choose your route."

"Goodbye, Xavier," she said and walked down the entry stairs and out the door into the cool Brooklyn night.

Had she not been completely overwhelmed with work, Hallee might have concerned herself with whether or not she and X had broken up. Instead, she spent the weekend getting all the final slides ready for the Pritzker. The only echo of her fight with Xavier was when she snapped at the boys for playing around the kitchen table and banished them to their room until dinner. At 2 a.m. Monday morning, she had the entire submission ready to go (saved on the company server and backed up on her home computer, her work computer and on an external drive, just to be safe). She double checked her e-mail to make sure no additional messages had come through from David (the last one had been at 12:10 a.m.) and fell into bed for four hours' sleep.

Monday was spent getting the mock-ups assembled for the final proof. The books were to go to the printer Tuesday to be shipped to the award committee on Wednesday, which would give them a whopping one-day grace period before the final deadline of October first. Hallee felt like she was nearing the final "point two" of a marathon. She could almost see the finish line.

She dropped the proofed book at the print house at 9 p.m. Tuesday night and headed home for the first full night's sleep she'd had in over a month. Apparently a full night's sleep was not the best of ideas, because she woke up late and had to rush the boys off to school tardy. Missing the bus meant taking the long walk to school, and by the time she finally made it in to the domicile, she was 90 minutes late to work.

On any other day, chances are she would not have been missed. However, on this particular Wednesday, the kind hand of fate reached back and said, "Enough," and bitch slapped Hallee so hard that she might have been concussed.

She was greeted in the hallway by Lauren, who ushered her into an elevator. "Where have you been?" she asked. "We have a major problem."

"My alarm didn't go off," Hallee stammered, not sure why they were leaving the building rather than going into the office.

"David is furious," Lauren explained. "You don't want to go in there."

"What happened?" Hallee said, fearing everything from Janine dying—and David blaming Hallee—to the CAD printer blowing up—and David blaming Hallee. No matter what had happened, the de facto result would be that somehow Hallee would take the blame.

Lauren was leading Hallee to Starbucks. David had ordered a double espresso, and Lauren had set out to get it. "Alison came in this morning."

"Okay, is she feeling better?" Hallee was wondering where the scarecrow and flying monkeys were, because she was pretty sure she wasn't in Kansas anymore.

"You don't understand, Hallee!" Lauren spoke to her as if she were some derelict homeless person. "The printer called and said the books were ready. Alison picked them up herself."

"And..." Hallee drew the word out. "Just get to the point, Lauren."

"She shipped them standard mail. They're gone and we have no way of tracking them."

Hallee was numb. "But there are back-ups. We can reprint them and still get them out in time."

"I'm working on that right now," Lauren said. Although to Hallee's mind all Lauren was working on was David's coffee order.

Hallee returned to the office with trepidation. David was screaming at everyone who came near him. It didn't matter if he had asked them to come or if they approached of their own free will; he screamed indiscriminately. Hallee braced herself to be next.

Instead of yelling, however, David simply gave her that stare. She wondered if he imagined little lasers beaming out of his pupils and cutting her in two.

"Of course," he said, "it's Laurel and Hardy to the rescue! What the fuck happened to you?" This was obviously directed at Hallee. She wasn't sure how to respond, so she did her best to explain.

"If Alison hadn't..."

"Alison had nothing to do with this!" David was turning purple. Legit purple. Hallee thought he might have a stroke, which probably would have been okay by her at this point. "Alison," he repeated, calming slightly, "has been my assistant since I founded this company. In all those years, she has *never* made a *sssingle* missstake!"

Hallee was befuddled. How on earth could she rationalize with an irrational person? Yes, she had been a bit late for work, but *she* hadn't taken it upon herself to mail the books off to the wrong address. Lauren cleared her throat.

"David," she said, "why don't we just have Hallee watch the front desk for today? I'm having new books assembled. I'm going to go back down to the printers and watch over them, maybe slip the guy a twenty to get him to rush the job. I really think that I'll have them out by four p.m., which means—if I ship them priority—they'll still be in Chicago by noon tomorrow. I'll track the package all night, if necessary."

And no doubt show up on time to work tomorrow morning, Hallee thought. What a bitch. She knew Alison—poor dear old deranged Alison, who never made a mistake in her life, of course—had created this problem. Lauren was going to step in and save the day, and throwing Hallee under a bus wouldn't be a problem at all. *Et tu, Lauren, et tu?*

Hallee marched off to "watch the front desk" for the day.

She was obviously persona non grata at this point, although some of the associates did muster weak smiles of sympathy. The junior architect that was building the new powder room even offered to buy her lunch when he went out to grab a sandwich. Everyone knew she wasn't to blame, but no one was going to stand up against David.

At 4:10 p.m., Lauren shipped off the books via priority overnight mail. David hailed her the hero for saving the day. He invited her over for dinner that evening with him and Janine, but Lauren declined, saying she wanted to "track that package," a concern she voiced as if she were head cheerleader at the FedEx Bowl!

David was more subdued, but as he was getting ready to leave for the evening, he stopped by Hallee's desk for one last dig.

"I have to sssay, Hallee," he coughed slightly, as though he were holding back an outpouring of emotion over his favorite child who had disappointed him completely and forever, "I had sssooo hoped for more from you. Do you even have half a brain?"

What Hallee wanted to say: "No, sir. In fact, I have an entire brain."

What she said: "I'm sorry for the *snafu*."

Something seemed to click in David's own brain, and he exited without bidding her goodnight.

VIII

What do you want?

**A life that has less pain than more... Medical tests that are conclusive...
Someone to take care of me...**

I hate doctors.

Many people claim to hate doctors whereas in fact they fear them. I do not
fear the doctor, my situational hypertension in the exam room notwithstanding.
I hate doctors because the first question they ask is not, "What is bothering
you?" The first question they ask is, "What's your insurance carrier?"

So much for the Hippocratic oath.

Doctors care first about money, next about getting sued (which is, let's face
it, really about money). I never go to the doctor until I must. I have been near
death several times. You may argue that if I had not delayed treatment, I might
not have been so close to death. I will retort that unless you have been sick
with a high fever for at least 10 days, the doctor will not treat you although
he will charge you to be seen. Thus, if the purpose of going to the doctor
within the first 10 days of illness is merely for him or her to bilk the insurance
company (or patient), then what is the point of going to the doctor before you
are at death's door?

I once had a conversation with several doctors about universal health care.
They were Canadian, and they felt it was the worst thing in the world. When I
pressed them for a rationale, they admitted that they worked long hours and
weren't paid very much. Oh, yes, like every other worker on the planet, you

mean? It was all about the money.

Don't get me wrong. I have nothing against Capitalists, in principle. I have seen the world and—for better or worse—capitalism is the best there is out there. The problem I have with Capitalists is that they aren't. Neither are doctors. They all want to capitalize profits and socialize losses. That's not true capitalism. That's called playing both ends. You want to take what you can get from a system that insulates you, bolsters you, benefits you on the backs of ordinary people, but if you fuck up, that same system gets to clean up your mess.

Plus, when it comes to so-called health care, now life is on the line.

I remember another conversation I had with a rabid Republican. He argued the problem with the medical industry was a lack of free-market competition. He insisted that if doctors were forced to compete for business, we would all be better off. I stared at him in disbelief (this man was not stupid by any stretch of the imagination). Finally, I said to him, "So, your son is bleeding copiously from the side of his head, and you plan to, what? Take him around to three doctors to get an estimate before seeking treatment? No, hon. If it costs you your house, your car, and everything you own, you'll pay the first doctor you see to staunch the bleeding before your son dies." At that, he turned and left me without a clever comeback.

And, if I am to be fair, I understand that the average wanna-be physician is no more corrupt than the average wanna-be politician. I think both get into the game with the best of intentions. Paving the path to hell with each cell of humanity they shed along the way. No doubt many of them look back upon the murky and fogged-in route they traveled and ponder, "How did I get here?"

My opinion of doctors aside, I know when I must buck up and consult one. Thus, it is with great reluctance that I go to the specialist to which my primary care physician has referred me. Even that sentence is too convoluted to be followed. If I had any sense, I would bail. I already know what she will say. I am only here to cross my "t's" and dot my "i's."

She signs on the dotted line of my file. I am to come back in two weeks.

Φ

THE TRUTH

Time has flown by, and Frank continues to visit for several "last times." In fact, the "last time" is our personal joke, a euphemism for "wanna fuck?" For a man not interested in a relationship, Frank sure does darken my door. Often.

"It's not fair."

"What?"

"It's not fair," I say louder.

"I heard you," Frank says. "I mean, what's not fair?"

"I want to have you in my bed." I admit.

"I'm in your bed," he says this as if he's reminding me. He has spent the afternoon with me, an increasingly rare pleasure now that Ryan-Claude has completely stopped filial visitations. My son is at a friend's apartment; I've started swapping with other parents to get a rare moment's peace. Or an afternoon of violent violations.

"I want more from you, Frank. I want you here, with me. Why is that impossible?"

It's a relief to tell him that I want him in my life. I've been struggling with this, knowing that he may rebuff me or—worse—misunderstand me, and then I will have no one left to whom I can turn. I am optimistic that his presence will give me the will to keep fighting the good fight, so to speak. I hate to need a reason to want to survive, but life feels long and tedious and overwhelming to me. Oddly, when Frank overwhelms me, I forego this feeling. Perhaps I truly do have a masochistic side silently seeking her own maelstrom; I feel calm in the storm. It's unnatural but also my truth.

"I can't," he says at last.

"Why? Why can't you? And don't give me your bullshit about not wanting a relationship. I don't buy it." Apparently Frank and I are about to have our first fight.

"There are things you don't know about me and you will never know," Frank shouts. Well, it's a "shout" for Frank. A man of quiet subtlety whom I often struggle to hear; this is the first time he has ever raised his voice to me.

"What the fuck does that mean?"

"It means you've got your head up your ass. You should just take what I have to offer you."

This is more than I can handle. Maybe Elise is right: She warned me that basing a relationship on sex alone would preclude me from having Frank as a more traditional boyfriend. Yet I have never felt that my understanding with Frank was only about sex. If it were, he wouldn't linger as though he dreads leaving me. He wouldn't keep coming back for one more "last time."

Yet now that I'm simply suggesting he be more involved in my life, he bristles. This goes beyond his hectic, highly disciplined life.

"People are hell," I state.

Frank sighs. He looks older, somehow. World weary, perhaps. "Please don't quote Sartre to me. He was a nymphomaniac that claimed he created his philosophy to sleep with women. It was what they wanted to hear, not what he really meant."

"Well, then," I am impressed he caught the allusion, although not surprised. "I guess he liked a very particular kind of woman, a kind of woman I've never been.

"You're good enough," he says as though it's a compliment.

"Well, I'm capable of fitting my head in my ass, so I guess that's something," I retort. I'm not warming to his calmer tones. I don't want to continue our fight, but I feel wronged in a way I cannot quite iterate.

"I am not capable of having a normal relationship with a woman like you."

"A woman like me?" I am flabbergasted. What does that even mean? I'm just a typical female of the species, albeit one that has made some progress in figuring out what I want from what little life I have left on this rock.

"You need to be used," he proclaims. Now I'm literally speechless. "I cannot mix nice with nasty. It's not how I work."

I struggle to choose the right words. Frank has been pushing boundaries every time we meet. He has certainly broadened my thinking about what I can or will do, but I have never taken the lead on any of this.

"You know, Frank," I try to speak without emotion. I'm afraid I'll either shout or break down in tears. "This is about you. It has always been about what you want. Not about what I need."

THE TRUTH

"Of course," he parrots. I wish he were being sardonic now, but in fact he is this self-absorbed. I've been a fool to think that my pleasing him would result in him loving me. Ryan-Claude was never pleased. Why should Frank be any different simply because he was more creative in the bedroom department?

"You lied to me," I say. "You told me you couldn't have a relationship with me because you had no time for a relationship in your life."

"That wasn't a lie. In fact, my company is transferring me to South America. It's just a matter of time."

I feel as though he has just slapped me across the face (not for the first time, but this time with such strength that I am knocked senseless). He's leaving? For South America? It's so ludicrous that I cannot help laughing aloud. There are tears in my eyes, not from the pain of losing him, but from the irony of our secrets. Despite unleashing everything physically possible between two people in a sexual scenario, we have kept our most pressing circumstances from one another. We belong to each other utterly and completely in one arena alone.

Frank will leave me. And I will never see him again. It's just a matter of time.

Φ

Perhaps the French have the paradigm figured out; if only I had arrived at this revelation a few years ago. If Ryan-Claude had found Monique and kept her on the sly (while tacitly approving my need to be used outside our marriage, a need I never fulfilled while married and over which I became embittered towards him), perhaps we would still be together, and my entire world would not be torn asunder. Maybe the only honest—truthful—relationship is an open relationship.

Ryan-Claude has his nanny, and I am doing my laundry.

There is a strange reality that is communal living: In a city like New York, we are all variously voyeurs and exhibitionists. And I'm not just talking about looking out my window and at any given hour of the day or night viewing someone *in flagrante delicto* from the hundreds of windows that are looking right back at me. I remember the shock of looking up from my toilet perch one day and noting that several rooms away a window looked out on my neighbor (meaning, therefore, that my neighbor could be looking right at me doing my personal business); from that point on, I remembered to close my bathroom door, even when I was alone in the apartment.

These are egregious forms of voyeurism and exhibition. There are far more subtle ways that we spy on—and reveal ourselves to—our neighbors. For example, the laundry room. My building has over 300 apartment units and a single laundry that houses roughly 20 washing machines with matching dryers. At this ratio, there is nearly always a queue to use the machines. Whenever I do my laundry, I set the kitchen timer so that no one is manhandling my panties (and other sundries besides my undies) before I have the opportunity to move them from washer to dryer to folding table to laundry basket.

I admit to taking a certain fascination in watching other people doing their wash. I stand now next to a 30-something Asian man. He's not bad looking; I see no wedding ring and wonder if he's single. It's early on Sunday morning, and he is meticulously folding his clothes. I pretend to have on my blinders, but we are standing literally inches from each other. I take my panties and create origami-like triangles that I pile up gently next to my son's boy briefs.

The man next to me must have a late summer cold or possibly an allergy; he is constantly clearing his throat. It pulls my attention into his weird little world, for what is our laundry if not a direct reflection on the world we inhabit? In fact, I am suddenly embarrassed, not by my undies which are remarkably clean and tidy—I remember folding my mother's panties as a part of childhood "chores" and being somewhat mortified that all the tidy whities had tell-tale period stains in the crotch that would never come completely clean, even with bleach—thank God for the invention of panty liners. But I digress...

My embarrassment stems from the realization that nearly every article of clothing I am folding is worn: Small tears and snags or full holes in the case of my son's jeans are found on each and every item. Some of these clothes are relatively new, but then there's the pajama top I got as a present two years before I met Ryan-Claude. Why have I held on to this shirt? If it had sentimental value, I've forgotten what it is. The cotton is soft, but the collar is tattered and there is a small hole just above the left breast where a pocket was sewn into the fabric but subsequently fell off; where the stitches had cut into the pajama front the hole now lives, announcing: this is an old shirt.

Throat clearing.

I take a stealthy, sideways glance at the laundry of the man beside me. Not only are his clothes immaculate, free of stains and snags, but he has folded them with military precision. The shirts look as though they could go on display at Brooks Brothers. The slacks are already creased, as though he had just pressed them with an invisible iron; my wash and wear never come out that crisp. No women's clothes in his many piles. He's single.

Then I note something odd: Either this man has not done his laundry for a month, or else he is folding clothes that belong to him and at least one other male. Boxers with military corners lie stacked next to briefs of various hues (gone are the days when my mother could only find white panties; even men have colorful drawers in the 21st Century). I don't know any man who keeps ten-days' worth of briefs alongside an equal quantity of boxers. Ryan-Claude almost exclusively wore briefs (he had one pair of silk boxers that he would flaunt upon occasion with a matching silk robe). Even my son wears briefs.

The man beside me is folding his lover's underwear. He's not old enough to be a single dad of a full-grown son. The competing undergarments have my mind reeling. Where is his "husband"? Still asleep? Upstairs sipping coffee while luxuriating in the Sunday *New York Times*? Since the throat-clearer is doing the laundry, does that make him a "bottom"? Is he submissive like me? Or is he just fastidious? Perhaps a victim of "Don't ask, don't tell," who never relinquished his orderly Laundry Queen training? *Semper Fi.*

Or am I wrong and he's just a business man who travels a lot and thus has a mountain of wash to do upon his return? I look at the other clothing piles. There aren't any that hold business attire. Of course, that would be at the dry cleaners I remind myself. The clothes are all darker in hue, which is strange considering that the summer has been brutally hot. Even if he works in air conditioning all day, he wouldn't be walking to the subway in dark clothes unless he enjoys being soaked in sweat on the 1 train.

Throat clearing.

Despite having a pile of clothes for myself and my son—an entire week's worth—I have finished folding my laundry. I hesitate. I feel that I have shared this bizarrely intimate moment with a man I can only pretend to know. I've been fantasizing about him for a full 20 minutes, creating a personality and providing him a lover based only on my assumptions about his basket's contents spilled (okay, stacked) on the table beside mine. My panties brushed his boxers (or is he the brief man?). My fingers glanced against his undershirts (or those of his lover). Yet I know not his name, his apartment number or his true orientation (he could be the Chinese laundry guy for all I know, taking in someone else's clothes for a little side cash). Chances are I will never see this man again; the apartment building is too big, the laundry room open 24 hours.

I want to wish him a happy Sunday. I want to acknowledge that we possibly know more about each other simply from viewing one another's folding habits than we consciously reveal to people in our lives. I am closer to this man, physically, than to any of my many "friends" that I chat up regularly on the Internet. I should tell him I like how he folds his clothes. I should ask him if he will be here next Sunday. I should say, "Have a nice day."

Instead, I pick up my fully loaded basket and return to my apartment, feigning obliviousness to his presence in my world.

Φ

Am I an idiot? Frank wants me. Work was hell but I could still make it there. Yet, somehow, a warm bath, a glass of wine and my cats seem sufficient. Have I devolved into my own cliché? Or do I just want, well, more? Frank wants me because I fuck among the best he's ever had. But I'm somewhat plain. Somewhat overweight. I'm somewhat. Nothing extravagant on the outside. Men are all wrapped up in wrappers. They judge themselves by the company they keep. More married to their jobs than their wives. It's no wonder I'm the afterthought.

I don't mean to lump Frank in with the rest of the pathetic lot, but I must admit to being baffled. I am exhausted of his "last" last time(s). It's the ambivalence that hangs over me and suffocates what remaining hope that is dying eternal. I am mired in existential Purgatory. How do people end up with the partners that they do? How did I end up alone? Why is the superficial held higher in regard than substance? Why does lying beget pleasure and the simple truth leaves you ostracized?

I have always struggled with lying. I suppose it is a sad statement on humanity that one struggles when one is honest. I remember being sought out as a youth when girls who loathed me for telling them the truth desperately needed to hear it and were forced to return to me (what an epiphany it must have been to the popular girl who realized that none of her entourage could be relied upon to tell her the truth!). When I was younger, I burned many bridges through honesty, and I myself was burned far more severely by not recognizing a lie for all its maliciousness.

Oddly enough, to my knowledge (and to that of Roget), there is no English language antonym to liar. Sure, you can create a hyphenate that all will comprehend (e.g. truth-teller, straight-shooter), but you cannot easily juxtapose a liar with his opposite. Perhaps that is what makes being a liar so easy. There isn't even a word for "he who does not lie," so why should I be shocked that no one wants to believe the truth.

The darkest truth that is the bedrock upon which all people—swindler and saint (ha!) alike—stand is that humans have a duality that can be repressed but not eradicated. Call it our animal natures. The religious will say it is a battle between good and evil for your very soul. Yet that is a simplistic excuse. To accept that every man or woman has a side that is nasty to mirror the one that is nice would be to blow open the paradigm upon which most civilized societies—and American society in particular—are dependent.

This is the dichotomy of 21st Century love: Man cannot rectify his animalistic urges with his need to perform lovingly, nor can woman exorcise her desire to be both a whore and a wife. Sadly, it is Frank who sums this up succinctly. He tells me I will never be the only woman in his life because he cannot mix the nasty sex with the loving sex. Elise says the same: She doesn't want her husband to ejaculate on her face, but whenever she finds an unfamiliar man attractive, she fantasizes climbing behind a dumpster and sucking him off until he comes in her face. I fear we will never lose the sexist paradigm simply because it's endogenous and evolutionary.

As noted previously, I have become a purveyor of Eleanor Rigbyism: looking at all the lonely people, and trying to figure out how they (i.e. I) ended up on the path where they (I) die alone. Yes, yes, of course, we come into this world alone and we exit it alone. That's not what I'm talking about, and you, dear reader, know this. There's alone and there's *alone*. I don't want to face death *alone*, but I know I shall be alone, simply because the handful of people who I want to be at my side when I die are the same people whose hearts will shatter at witnessing my death. Therein lies the rub. If they truly love you, you don't want them to watch your demise.

We are all destined to a life of solitude: In the West, relationships end with divorce and recrimination; in the East, men strap bombs to their torsos and crash planes into buildings while women self-mutilate and cast themselves onto funeral pyres. There is no Cinderella moment at midnight. "Life is suffering," is a platitude. Life doesn't cause us to suffer. Our own personal duality—what we long to be versus what we truly are—relegates us all to submissiveness. No matter the fairy tale we tell, in truth we are all victims and none of us rises above the degradation, even the celibate.

You are either overwhelmed or suppressed by your sexuality (and/or you overwhelm or suppress others and their sexuality). The best of us compartmentalize our basal urges. The worst rape, dismember and devour. The tragedy of man (or woman) is that we think therefore we disapprobate. No one is dominant. We all suffer in the end. And none of us enjoys it all that much.

Before Ryan-Claude, I had a lover. He was my first. He was married. Of course, I didn't know this small, insignificant detail (yes, that was sarcasm) when I met him. As a novice to love, I had no idea that married men cheated on their wives or the wreckage that would cause. He had two children, and I hesitate to write this because his carnage was caused by a dirty bomb long before that term became part of the terrorism vernacular. I have no wish to hurt anyone. I write this only because it is my last opportunity to leave my mark on a defiled planet. To come clean, in a sense. To tell the truth.

But I digress...

I met Dale (as you will eventually discover, my life experience has shown me this is a particularly cursed name, and if you speak in your head while you read, kindly get all Shakespearean on me and say "cursed" with two syllables: cursHEAD) when I was 18. I was lost. I was inexperienced. I was naïve. I was boarding a train heading for a wreck, and I was fucking clueless. I write this *mea culpa* on the infinitesimal chance that I complete this tome before I die and someone reads it and sees their father in it. You are barely past the age now that I was then. Please, forgive me.

It's funny how one chance encounter (or lack thereof) changes everything. I came home for my cousin's first wedding (she's had subsequent). I was maid of honor (in the truest sense) and thought the best man a good match. He thought otherwise, and hooked up with the third bridesmaid twice removed. In such a state (i.e. horny and dismissed—have I mentioned I've struggled with my sexuality?), I returned home on an ominous date (people fear the number 13, I say watch out for redundancy, as in 7/7/77 or 9/9/99; best to hide under the covers and not come out) to find Dale outside my door.

I was happy finally to be wanted by someone, *anyone*. And I felt love for the first time. It was like drowning in blood. Sticky, but warm. Leaving a metallic stench in your nostrils that is both nasty and life affirming, harkening birth. He chased me down as I traveled cross country (trying to find myself, I suppose, before heading off to college). By the time I found out he was married, his wife had found out about me. He decided he couldn't decide; thus making the worst decision of all.

I wonder what she thought, when she found him hanging from the basement ceiling like a side of beef. I wonder how the support beams held his weight, which was considerable. I wonder if his family's pain ever dulled to the point of being bearable. When I think about what his children faced growing up fatherless as opposed to what my "fatherless" children face, well, there's really no comparison now, is there?

This is not a diatribe against the opposite sex (I doth not protest too much, either, my friend, lonely in the night, reading this and hoping your kid—or your mom—doesn't look over your shoulder and go blind from truth so vulgarly writ). This is, in fact, a maxim to be accepted. If, as a woman, you can accept that you are attracted to a beast, thank God above that he does not behave beastly toward you. If, on the other hand, you are the rare male to read thus far in my tale, take some hard won advice: Accept the beast you are and tell your woman that it must have an outlet. Explain that porn is not a degradation of her but a way to quiet the animal that flares its nostrils at all that smells nasty. Tell her, that you feed the beast and save the best part of you as an affirmation of how precious she is to you. If you did not worship her, you would let the beast out and then never be able to possess her sublimely. She would end up nothing but a cum bucket, and your love would dissipate like issue discharged in a morning masturbatory shower.

In turn, on those occasions when your woman arrives home flushed and tussled, turn away and think no further upon it. You do not want a cum bucket as a life partner, but you must accept that she may crave being used as a slut by a man she will never love. Accept this duality, embrace it, and a floss of happiness will be extended for you to hold on to.

Or take a different kind of rope, and lash yourself to your ceiling. It's the only easy out.

Φ

Elise has given up coffee. She prides herself on being attached to nothing, having no real addictions or strong needs, be it shopping or sex or substance abuse. However, she found herself unable to get up and get going every morning without a cup or two of coffee. Thus, after a horrible week of cravings, crankiness and cranial cramping, she finally junked the java.

Her husband is back from Afghanistan, so we rarely see each other anymore. This is a treat for me, her presence here. She brought loose-leaf Mauritius tea from Alice's Tea Cup, along with two of the most amazing scones I've ever eaten: The first is raspberry and goat cheese; the second is pumpkin dripping in some kind of caramel sauce. Clotted cream with jam is held in plastic ramekins. We dip our scones in the cream and jam until there is no more, at which time we dip the remaining scone into the tea.

We sit quietly as choral refrains waft through my floorboards. How odd that a church is situated in the basement of a skyscraper. I know real estate is at a premium, but shouldn't services be held in the penthouse, bring the congregation closer to God? I know they're Catholic (I remember the hymns), but even they cannot possibly see the glory of the derelict homeless person who sleeps in the church entryway until around six, when he's gently shooed off with a croissant and cup of coffee handed to him by the keeper of the church keys. I try to be respectful, more from common New York neighborliness than any devotion I may once have felt. I sip my tea, and Elise and I chat with enthusiasm but in sacred tones that mirror the music. I note that these Halleluiahs are being sung far from Heaven.

We both have news, although I am unaware of it at the moment.

"I've met a writing partner," I tell her. "We are getting together on Tuesday evenings at the Union Square Barnes and Noble."

"That's great," Elise says. "Maybe you'll finally finish your novel."

"Well, it can't hurt," I admit. Having a weekly deadline means I will force myself to sit at a computer and type up something. "Actually, I went back and reread some of my pages for him. I was shocked."

"Shocked? By your own writing?"

"Yes," I admit, choking down a clump of soggy scone that has drifted into my tea. "What I wrote is truly brilliant. It's amazing." I'm surprised by the neutral tone of my voice that belies the arrogance of the statement. I'm not feeling boastful. Just truthful.

"Wow. That's great," she says in a tone that belies the words of praise. Elise is generally more effusive in her commentary, but this morning, she is subdued.

"Yes," I start to laugh. "It's either totally brilliant prose or else the most pathetic turd ever put on paper." She joins me in laughing. It's the first genuine interaction we've had this morning.

I've known Elise for two years, the entire time her husband was stationed abroad. I've missed her terribly since he came home. I admit to being jealous, but in the best way. I've given her some space to enjoy him these past couple of months. Despite my own difficulties, I haven't burdened her with any guilt trips or tried to impress upon her that her absence has affected me in ways she cannot comprehend, not being in possession of all the facts.

I resolve to tell her what has been going on with me. Beyond Frank, beyond the new writing partner, beyond this long hot summer.

"There's something I should have told you by now," I begin.

"I need to tell you something, too," she answers. The benign distraction in her face changes to worry.

"You go first," I offer. Now I am more worried about her than for myself. It turns out my intuition is not at its best.

"Todd and I are moving back to Texas," she blurts out with no preface. "We leave the end of the month."

I want to parrot Elise: *Wow. That's great.* Only it's not great. I should have known Todd wouldn't want to stay in New York City. Elise had said he was finally getting out of the Marines, so no more tours of duty. After three tours in Iraq and a final one in Afghanistan, her husband was home safe. Probably longing for some peace and quiet that would never be found here in NYC.

"The end of the month is next week," I manage weakly, my voice almost monotone. Suddenly, the scones don't taste all that good.

"I know," she answers apologetically. "I didn't want to tell you until I knew for certain. We weren't entirely sure what he'd be doing next, but he got a teaching job in Austin. Lots of libraries in Austin." I know she wants me to be happy for her, that she has Todd back. I lean in to hug her.

"I'll miss you," I choke.

"We'll see each other again," she offers. "Maybe you can come visit at Christmas. You hate Christmas in New York." That is true. I probably won't be in New York at Christmas regardless.

"You're right," is all I have to say.

"What were you going to tell me?" Elise asks.

I have no idea what to say. Her news has deflated me. I'm woefully tired. I want to crawl back into bed and go to sleep.

THE TRUTH

I say the first thing that comes to my mind.

"I met Eric, that's the writing dude, on Craigslist."

"You and your Craigslist."

"I swear by it."

"Okay," she says, back to an easy banter, not sensing the change in my mood. "So you met Richie on Craigslist?"

"Yes, when I wanted a drinking buddy."

"And Frank?"

"Yes, when I wanted a fuck buddy."

"And, now, Eric?"

"Yes, my new writing buddy."

"You know," Elise says, "I once bought a teapot on Craigslist. It was an antique." She laughs and it is infectious enough to spread to me.

"How is Frank?" she asks tentatively, after a slightly awkward pause during which we finish off our tea.

"He's leaving me, too."

"Oh, I'm sorry," Elise says, and I know she means it.

"His firm is sending him to South America," I explain.

"You'll find someone else," she says. I nod, but I know she is wrong. I will not find a new "Frank" any more than I will find a new "Elise." My days of finding anything new are waning.

"I guess all these changes really screw with your inner Zen," Elise tells me. The juxtaposition of Frank, screwing, and Zen hits us both as we burst into laughter together one last time.

Φ

Today something extraordinary happens. I find a confidante. I didn't even have to resort to Craigslist to do it. I see her reading beneath a tree at the park, and I notice her because my son could play triplet to her twins. Toe heads all, with a sunny disposition and a distinct lack of awareness that dissipates all too quickly along a little boy's path to adolescence. The three boys hold hands and entertain one another in that way boys still do. Her older son is already too self-conscious to hold hands in fellowship. (I'm guessing he'd hold a brother's hand to cross the street—already the "man" of the house.) I am completely exhausted, sipping wine surreptitiously to tamp down bouts of pain and nausea. The four boys are hungry to play at full force, enjoying a perfect fall day on the Hudson. While the boys tumble and dig in the sand pit, I hunker down with her (okay, I've invited myself to invade her space) and share a Chardonnay that's as oaky as the early Autumn day.

I tell her the truth. I tell her everything. She is the first to know. She is the only one I've told.

I have no more secrets.

The Encounter

It was one of those intensely amazing New York autumn afternoons that for the first time since the move east made Hallee feel at home. The entire city had turned golden. The near end to daylight savings had cast a low level yellow haze of a sunset over the park. White caps on the Hudson; yellow leaves of cherry, birch and oak blowing past her golden-haired boys. They were kicking a yellow soccer ball. She was reading *The Girl with the Dragon Tattoo* (with a yellow cover). It was one of those moments that come and go so quickly, Hallee would later wonder if it ever happened at all.

When Hallee had returned to the office on Thursday, David was still proclaiming Lauren's praises (the package had arrived to the correct address before the deadline). Everyone was in generally good spirits (whither go David, there go all), so when Arnie called her in to his office, she assumed it was to review his upcoming travel schedule. He had three trips to make the following week, trying to get more jobs inspected before winter weather made it more treacherous.

"Hey, Hallee," Arnie began, his soft demeanor a balm for the week's woes. "I need to talk to you about your position here."

Hallee's heart sunk. He wasn't going to talk to her about travel. He was going to fire her.

"David has decided that you're best suited to the front desk," he sighed. Audibly. "He has asked that Lauren take over as my executive assistant and Alison's backup."

"I see," Hallee said coldly. Everyone was turning on her.

"It's not personal, and your job is still secure," Arnie was trying to be reassuring, but Hallee wasn't buying it. "We aren't even going to put you back at your old pay, so you'll be making more for doing less."

What Hallee wanted to say: "What you mean to say is, 'Enjoy that raise, because it's the last you'll ever get.'"

What she said: "Do you really think I'm a fuck-up, Arnie?"

"God no, Hallee," and she could tell he was sincere. "Look, I tried to reason with David, but to be honest, it didn't help that whole thing with Janine and the taxi. She blamed you for it, so you were already in the doghouse. So to speak."

Of course Janine's little machinations were involved. Hallee exhaled. As she took it all in, Hallee mourned the fact that she couldn't just up and quit: Without a job, she couldn't afford to live here. She had no idea where she would go. Back to the front desk, she supposed.

Hallee was determined the demotion would be a blessing in some ways. She would no longer care about her work. She would do only the bare minimum, forcing herself to work less efficiently. If Lauren noticed, Hallee would guilt her into feeling bad about the back stabbing. Or simply remind her that without Hallee, David and Janine would only have Lauren to blame when things went sour. Hallee would leave work at 5 p.m. and never arrive before 8:30. Since she was being paid for a 40-hour workweek, that was all she was planning on working moving forward. Thus, she wasn't happy with her new reality, but she wasn't miserable. Especially on a day like today: the cool autumn, reading her book, relaxing, playing with the boys.

When the woman sat beside her on her blanket, therefore, she was a bit startled. The stranger had red hair—not the carroty-kind, but rather that auburn color that Hallee always meant to try out but never had—and delicate pale skin. Too pale. And her hair was freshly washed but very thin, as though she was experiencing hair loss. The woman wasn't well, but she was well dressed. In other words, not some derelict homeless person. She seemed incredibly tired. Or sad. Or sullen.

She had snuck a bottle of chardonnay into the park and poured some into a thermos-type coffee cup for Hallee. Rather than be afraid of the familiarity, Hallee embraced it. She sipped her wine, introducing herself to the woman. It had poured several inches of rain for the better part of two days, (given Hallee's mood upon being demoted, it seemed apropos to what she was feeling; at one point she hoped all of New York City would wash away in the downpour). Today was dry and the park's lawn still open for play.

The woman had told Hallee her name, and Hallee had promptly forgotten it. Now she was too embarrassed to ask for it a second time. Even though she knew there was no harm in needing a reminder, she felt awkward and irritated by the thought she had forgotten the name of this woman as though she were already an afterthought. How easy it was to dismiss information that held no direct importance to her.

The woman had brought her son to the park, and he appeared to be the same age as the twins. He joined them in soccer and seemed so very happy that it made Hallee's heart clutch. Were her boys happy? She was struggling so hard to make a better life for them all, but were any of them happy?

Hallee had started up a conversation with the woman. At first, they spoke about only the weather, then it turned more serious. Hallee said, "I used to be proud of my work. I was a project manager for this huge import-export company. Some of it was really technical, but I just felt like I was doing something important. Now, when people ask me what I do, I say, 'I work for an architect.' I usually tell them quickly about the buildings he's designed, especially that one on the Lower East Side that everyone knows. That way, they get distracted thinking about David's buildings and don't ask me if I'm an architect myself. I feel degraded when I say, 'I work in admin'."

"Well, a lot of people make a good living doing admin," she replied. She wasn't judging Hallee, but she definitely seemed put off by the notion that Hallee was being elitist.

"I'm sorry," Hallee continued. "I know administrators are the ones who keep the office going, but the very best they can do is make their boss look good. And in truth, with my boss, I don't think I want to make him look good." The woman laughed. She was coughing, too. She had a small hand towel, which she used to cover her mouth. She was not small boned, but her skin was hanging off her skeleton as though she had recently been ill and lost a great deal of weight.

Hallee continued, "Here's what my job is: I spend my days searching for a particular coffee bean brewed on a particular date, and then the next day my boss sends out an e-mail cc-ing everyone, telling them how stupid I am because I got him the wrong kind of coffee. That's my life, and I accept it. But I have to believe that I have more to offer than this. Yes, my work facilitates these great buildings being designed, the construction of architectural wonders. I can look at that building a few blocks from here and say, 'I took part in that,' and feel a glimmer of pride." Gavin ran over to snuggle up against his mom. The twins were still playing in the sandpit with her new acquaintance's son.

Hallee sighed. Other than Xavier, she had probably shared more of the intimacies of her life with this odd woman than she had with anyone else in the past year. "Then, after I stop thinking about the buildings, I go and check my e-mail where I have a list of groceries to collect and haul to work for two people that can never be pleased, no matter how fresh the Swiss chard or how delicate the cornichons."

"Why do you try so hard to please them? Are you hoping for a raise?" Hallee shook her head. The red haired woman continued. "A promotion, then?"

"No. I've had some difficulties in that department, and a promotion is unlikely," Hallee admitted. "I think it's just my nature."

"So you're submissive? Or a masochist, maybe?"

The blunt question took Hallee aback. Who was this woman and how dare she assume anything about Hallee? The fact that she had summed her up so easily made her feel ashamed.

Despite the cool breeze, Hallee flushed, and the woman across from her either saw or guessed at her embarrassment. She turned her glance away, as Hallee whispered for Gavin to go back and play with the others.

"You obviously aren't 'out'," the woman commented, watching Hallee's son venture off.

"I'm not gay," Hallee sputtered.

"No," her new comrade sipped wine, "but you sure are defensive."

Of course, Hallee's immediate reaction was to say, *I'm not defensive!*, which would have been quite defensive. She reached for the paper-clad wine bottle and poured what was left into her own cup.

"I believe that most of the planet lives in the closet when it comes to sexuality," the woman attempted to explain. "Look at the gay rights' movement, for example. They want what everyone else has: this normal, pathetic, pair-bonding blah-ness. It's sad, really."

"I don't think it's sad," Hallee admitted. "Why shouldn't they want what everyone else has?"

"And what do you have, exactly?" the woman questioned, knowingly. "You hate your job, you are here alone with the kids... is that by choice?"

"It's my choice for today!" Hallee continued, *not being defensive*.

The auburn head bobbed in acknowledgement. "I just think most people haven't 'come out' sexually. Think about all the taboos. We can't even determine where 'normal' ends and 'perverted' begins; the lines keep shifting."

"Well, certain things are completely wrong! You must know that!" Hallee was thinking of people who abused children or animals.

The woman seemed infinitely patient, as though all the "fight" had drained from her being. She probably would sit here for hours, lecturing Hallee on bizarre topics if Hallee let her.

"I think there is something to be said for consenting adults, if that's what you mean," the woman paused again. Hallee couldn't decide if hers was the air of someone who had not a care in the world or if she was indifferent to life or just some odd philosopher time traveling in the hopes of finding a sympathetic audience. Regardless, Hallee felt profoundly discomfited by this discourse. While parts certainly seemed rooted in common sense, the rest simply felt "out there."

"I don't mean to make this about me," the woman said, "but 'me' is all I truly know, and I came about self-understanding relatively late in life."

What Hallee wanted to say: "If you want to blabber on about yourself, I won't stop you."

What she said: "Go ahead."

"For almost my entire life," the woman continued, "I felt that I was a bad person. Never mind the reasons why, whatever messages I received along the way... I internalized this self-loathing because everything society, religion, my family taught me was that girls were to behave in a certain way. I began to wonder if we weren't all walking a proscribed path in that instead of choosing where we would go, we simply went where we weren't forbidden to go. Like all of life is one great big, 'Keep off the grass' sign."

Hallee could relate to some of this, even if it was literal: How many times had she seen a luscious green completely devoid of activity? Which was, probably, why the green was so luscious. All it took was a few human footprints and the grass would be worn down to the dirt. Yes, stick to the sidewalk, don't touch the beauty.

"Anyhow," the woman was trying to pour remaining drops from the wine bottle, shaking it into her cup. Hallee felt bad, so she poured half of what she had into Chatty Cathy's plastic mug (no, her name wasn't Cathy either). "Oh, no," the woman mocked, "You aren't a submissive. Why did you give up half your wine?"

"To be nice!"

"You mean you wanted to be pleasant?" Hallee nodded in response. "To please?" the woman asked with emphasis. Hallee would have left by now if she wasn't intoxicated. When had she last eaten? She was pretty sure it had been breakfast. She was better off sharing what was left of the wine if she was going to get the boys home without dozing off on the subway.

"Anyhow..." the woman was beginning her train of thought again. "I was only invited to be my true self late in life, fairly recently in fact, and by total dumb luck. I met a man who would best be described as quite *artistic*. His artistry is in delivering sexual pain. Do you understand what I mean?"

Hallee didn't answer. Her red cheeks told all.

"Okay, then," the woman continued, "so you do understand. Anyhow, he showed me a world I never before knew. I mean, perhaps I was intrigued by the potentiality, but he did things to me I never could have imagined, and I endured them."

"Did it make you stronger?" Hallee desperately needed to know.

THE TRUTH

"Maybe," she admitted. "Maybe he just peeled back all the callouses that had metaphorically manifested throughout my lifetime. Gave me back my raw and unadulterated self. I just know who I am now, and I don't try to be someone else. I still want—like you do, obviously—to please," and with this she toasted Hallee with the last of her wine. "But I won't do it by pretending to be something I'm not. You shouldn't either."

"I don't," Hallee protested.

"Tell that to your boss."

Hallee wasn't sure if she was affronted or not by this woman's familiarity. After all, it was Hallee who had revealed so much about her unhappy professional life. Maybe the advice—ill-advised or not—was to be expected.

"I'm sorry to be so direct," she began. "Actually, I'm not sorry. I'm sorry for nothing these days. You see, I have only a few days left."

Once again, Hallee found herself thrown off guard. She stammered, "What do you mean?"

"I have stage-four cancer," the woman said completely nonchalantly; she could have been talking about what she had for lunch. "By the time I felt sick enough to see a doctor, it was in my lymph nodes. They told me six months at that point. *With* full chemo and radiation. I said 'no thanks.'"

"What?" Hallee was beginning to wonder if the woman across from her was psychotic. Considering what she had seen over the year with Janine, Hallee felt certain the woman sitting beneath the tree—squeezing intimately close to share the bottle of illicit wine—was "normal" in so far as anyone facing death could be. "Why didn't you fight it? Why don't you fight it?"

"I've never liked life that much," the woman said bluntly. There was a tremor in the woman's voice, however, and Hallee suspected she was lying, but maybe lying that life isn't worth living is all there is to be done when facing imminent death.

"What about your son?" Hallee was pleading, and she couldn't understand why. This woman was nothing to her. Just a sister mother with a son the same age and physical type as the twins. If this woman fell off the planet tomorrow, Hallee would not think twice about her.

"We all die," the woman was elongating the vowels, as if she were fomenting an idea. Or maybe she had a head start on the wine before she met up with Hallee. "You know, the notion that you will be here tomorrow, that you will have your job, your home, your family, it's all illusion."

Hallee thought this to be far too metaphysical a discussion for an early fall afternoon. Perhaps the cancer had already made its way to this woman's brain?

"If you're saying we can't predict the future," Hallee said, "Then I agree with you. But that doesn't mean we give up living."

"Exactly!" The woman's hair was flitting in the breeze. The air was salty, stirred by the wind coming off the Hudson. Looking at her, Hallee realized the appearance she had taken for sullenness was, in fact, death. The woman across from her couldn't be much older than Hallee; she may have been younger. With her sunken cheeks and wispy hair, however, she was almost as frail as Alison. More frail than Alison, because this woman still had all her mental acuity—so much for brain cancer—with a waning shell in which to contain her intelligence. At least Alison was blissfully unaware of her misfortunes.

Hallee took another sip of wine. "That person you were talking about? Your dominant lover?" She felt a slight shudder that had nothing to do with the autumn breeze. "His name wasn't Xavier, by any chance?" she asked.

"No. Francis."

"I thought you said your dom was a man?"

The red haired woman laughed. "Oh, he's definitely a man. Frank. Christian name, Francis."

"Oh," Hallee flushed again. She wasn't sure why the topic was so disconcerting to her, but she was ready to get away from this encounter. She looked to the sad, dying creature beside her. The strange woman probably had been very pretty before she got sick. She still had deep blue eyes, the kind people would call "violet" even though it was really just a shade of blue. Hallee wondered what all this woman had seen in life. The thought that Hallee might only gain such clarity and sense of purpose on her deathbed made her break out in a cold sweat. Certainly life was more than what this woman with the knowing violet eyes had seen. Living a life less meaningful only to sum it all up at the end? Hallee hadn't moved all the way from San Francisco just to give up and die. So what on earth was she doing with her life? Was she—like the dying stranger—just marking time, waiting for some revelation into the deeper meaning of her presence here on Earth? Was Hallee just biding time until her time was no more?

All the questions mulling around in her head were making her nauseous, as if someone had stirred up a big smelly pile of crap. "I probably should be going."

"Yes," the woman said, gingerly raising herself up off the ground. "Me, too. I have to put my son on a plane to his grandmother's."

"Really? By himself?" Hallee thought the boy was too young to fly alone.

"What part of 'I'm dying' did you miss?" The woman's smile was gentle. Hallee so wished to remember her name. "It was nice meeting you." She held out her hand to Hallee. Despite her frailty, the handshake was firm.

"I'll let you in on another secret," she said, still holding onto Hallee's hand. "It takes tremendous strength to be a submissive. You're far stronger than you know." She released Hallee's hand.

"Thanks for the drink," Hallee said.

"I'd say 'anytime'," the woman shouted over her shoulder at Hallee, walking away and towards her son, "but I'd be lying."

As the woman disappeared down the Esplanade, Hallee gathered her boys close to her, kissing each of them repeatedly until Gavin said, "Mom, stop! You're embarrassing us!"

IX

"You won't disappoint me; I can do that
myself... Now, if you don't mind, leave.
Leave, and please yourself at the same time."
Leave, Glen Hansard

What do you want?

To grow old with someone by my side... To feel loved... To know I made a difference somehow...

It has taken me awhile to sort this out. I guess I've muddled through to this latest epiphany since these days I have time on my hands, as they say. I am unraveling what it truly feels like to love and be loved. When I was with Ryan-Claude, I don't remember a day that went by when we didn't tell one another, "I love you." However, I now accept that whatever my intentions, he didn't feel my love. I know what I felt for him, but it didn't get through. Conversely, I now know that Ryan-Claude didn't love me (or at least he didn't those last ten years we were together) despite my belief that he did. I thought I felt his love, but it was just another one of my fantasies I've created to get through a life less lived. I don't know why. I guess there's plenty of fault to go around, but no one to blame.

Now I try to understand Frank's intentions. Why he goes to extremes to keep himself insulated when it comes to any meaningful relationship. Yet what we have *is* meaningful. Perhaps this has been the most meaningful relationship of my entire adult life. And although he has never once told me he loves me—in fact to an outside observer his behavior to me would indicate the opposite—for some twisted reason when I am with him I do feel loved. It's a kind of ethereal grace that confounds and distracts me. And this time it doesn't feel like a fantasy. There is no romantic twist to this particular tale.

When I am in his presence I wonder what he feels in return. I do hear him when he tells me he cannot love a woman to whom he is "nasty." Yet I think he is most alive at those times. Which brings me to the only truth: Love is not a term in his vocabulary but he is completely and utterly consumed with me (and I by him) when we are together; the external world ceases to be; it is as though with every lash, every violent thrust, every bite, he obliterates reality.

I know that Frank cannot be with me not because he doesn't love me but because to give in to his monster would be to destroy the meticulously ordered world he has created for himself. His strict diet, the meditation, the martial arts training, the high-pressured job would all implode and collapse upon him were he to devolve to his purest essence. Yet, with me, he is he. He allows himself to be himself. He "rewards" me with the punishment of his raw being. However, I cannot find the aberration. I know what I feel for him. He sees the love in my eyes every time I don't scream and beg him to stop. In that moment, his hubris is obliterated and he has lost control of his entire fabricated world. I doubt I am the nirvana he seeks, but I now understand that he cannot remain in this enlightened state indefinitely.

I have always been puzzled that for all the times Frank insists he will not see me again that he never rushes out the door. In fact, he seems not to want to leave at all. Now I appreciate why this is. No one wants to go back to the precariously controlled illusion that is life. Frank is more tightly wound than any person I've ever known. His regimen is intractable. Excepting those hours that he lets me invade his world order. He says he needs nasty; I think he needs chaos. If only to feel truly alive for a little while.

But it's not a place to build a home.

The edict is decreed late one night on Yahoo chat. Summer has ended. Life as I knew it is over.

> Frank.S: I got the news today.
>
> Ace: About a lucky man who made the grade?
>
> Frank.S: Funny.
>
> Ace: You home?
>
> Frank.S: Nope, why?
>
> Ace: Okay. Not home. But in front of a computer. lol
>
> Frank.S: No, actually I'm at the dojo.
>
> Ace: On a computer? wtf?

Frank.S: This is on my blackberry

Ace: Ah, cool. Technology.

Frank.S: Duh!

Frank.S: Yup, it's mobile too

Ace: I don't want my employer to track my sexting. I figure it's bad enough if YOUR employer tracks my sexting.

Frank.S: I thought you quit.

Ace: I did.

Frank.S: Wanna talk about it?

Ace: I thought my personal life was off limits.

Frank.S: That's not what I said.

Ace: I know what you meant.

Frank.S: My employer has me leaving for South America next week.

Ace: Next week? Wow. You're just full of surprises.

Frank.S: I didn't want to tell you until I was sure.

Ace: Yes, it's certainly better this way.

Frank.S: Like you share your shit with me? Every time I ask, you deflect.

Ace: It's a long story. Maybe I'll share it with you one of these days after you've fucked me. If I ever have the pleasure/pain again. ☺

Frank.S: I'd like to get together for, wait for it...

Ace: ONE LAST TIME!

Frank.S: One last time

Ace: sigh...

Frank.S: Then SP.

Ace: SP?

Frank.S: Sao Paulo.

Frank.S: 2 new bosses, both brilliant and wanting me to do a lot

Ace: One lover. Really brilliant. Wanting you to do a lot. :-P

Frank.S: Ha ha ha. They still aren't sure if I'm going to Buenos Aires or Sao Paulo. Prefer SP.

Ace: That's on the PATH, too, right? Couple stops down?

Frank.S: I believe so.

Ace: Why Brazil?

Frank.S: Cos I don't wanna be figged to learn Spanish

Ace: Do you speak Portuguese?

Frank.S: Eu estou fluente mais ou menos, e voce tambem? Fala?

Ace: Okay, then. Um, you do know that Spanish is WAY THE FUCK

EASIER than Portuguese, right?

Frank.S: Yes I know. I can read it

Ace: Well, the only thing I'm fluent in is enduring pain.

Frank.S: And apparently Portuguese

Ace: Yes I know. I can read it

Frank.S: Funny. Anyway - gotta go. Class soon.

Ace: When u wanna see me, you got my number.

Frank.S: I have it.

Ace: TTYL

Frank.S: Ttyl

Φ

When I first realized I was going to die, it was hardly a revelation. We're all going to die, it's just a matter of how and when. I've never feared death *per se*; I've often feared dying. I'm not good with the unknown, although Frank has been pushing my boundaries into exploring those fears. I always thought that if given the choice to know my fate, I would absolutely want to know how and when I would die. In that sense, I suppose my wish has been granted.

When I first learned about the "how" (i.e. Stage IV pancreatic carcinoma that has now spread to my liver, stomach and lymph nodes), I had to appreciate my bad luck: I am the first in the history of my family to die from cancer. When I was told the "when" (i.e. very soon), I found myself to be unfathomably sad. I wasn't sad that I would soon be dead. I wasn't even sad for my kids who would have to go on without me or my parents who would not predecease me. I was sad because my life never amounted to much of anything. I had intelligence and good fortune (maybe not on the Brooke Shields' Knee Sock

Scale, but certainly in the first-world problems' arena). I even had some talent (I think... Here's to posthumous publishing potential!). Yet I never did anything remarkable or even lasting. I procreated... which is hardly an achievement. I figured out far too late of what I was capable. And I chose distraction as my drug of choice; rather than swim against the current, I fantasized I was floating in a glorious pool of rejuvenating glacier-fed waters... as opposed to the sewage in which I swam for more than 40 years.

The most I can really hope for as epitaph is that somehow the love I made was equal to the love I took... but I know no one will write a song about that. My love was common and banal. In fact, this makes me saddest of all: I have—had—the capacity to love to the extreme, to give myself fully to another human being, to belong utterly and completely to the grace of another. And no one wanted me.

I suppose some of my regret stems from an overly romanticized imagination. I may have been able to see through the Princess/Rom-Com culture into which I was born, but I wanted the happy ending. I wanted the union of two souls. I wanted to be lost in the longing of one other human being who would lose himself equally to me. Yin and yang.

If I had been born lucky, I would have met at 18 not some man hell bent on self-destruction but someone who recognized me for what I was. Someone who would have taught me my full potential at a formative stage in my development. Not an abuser, but someone controlled and certain of the pain he would inflict. Or she. A nice dominatrix, if that's not an oxymoron. A "Frank" of my youth. Only when my mentor left me, I would have known my own strength and have been afforded the grace to live on and live fully. To tell the truth and love in the only way I ever was capable of truly making love.

Instead, the truth tarried. I found out all-too-late in life what could have been. I am sad, not because I didn't live long enough, but because I never lived to my potential. I was always waiting for things to change. For Ryan-Claude to change. For my job to get better. For someone to recognize my talents and encourage—or at least inspire—me. I found the truth at last. Is this the irony of life? Isn't the religious notion that when you die all will be revealed to you?

THE TRUTH

Nirvana at last. I understand everything, but it is too late to take the teachings of this lesson and apply them.

I worry that if these words reach you, dear reader, you will despise me for my pedantic ways. Forgive me, if you can. I wish I could rise up like a modern-day personal Jesus and tell all the young people what I've learned: that only by knowing oneself can you ever live life fully. That to pretend you are something you are not (and, sadly, this society seems hell bent on making its youth ever more stupid with regards to introspection as the years go by) will only lead to pain, self-inflicted and otherwise. Of course, the irony for me is that I lived a life without love because I tried to avoid pain at every step of the way, always trying to be the "good girl." Perhaps my teachings to the youth should be to embrace all the pain you can endure, the pain that motivates you to be stronger, the pain that forces you to get up off your ass and make your world—*the* world—better.

I've never subscribed to the theory that in order to create great art the artist must suffer. However, I can now see where pain can be liberating. When you run a marathon, for example, your feet bleed, your toenails fall off, your tendons rip. The grace comes from understanding that you endured. You did something remarkable, through which many others will be incapable of suffering. I suspect survivors of the gulag or concentration camp feel the same. The simple act of enduring pain makes us stronger, but to proceed from that point is to love your callouses, the abrasions, the scars that linger long after the pain has ended. It is, in fact, to *remember*. I wish I knew that facing pain would release me from the hallucination of living in fantasy. Pain truly makes you embrace the moment. There is something genuine to be learned from this. I wish I had more of such moments and fewer bogus dreams. I wish I had more time to live for now rather than plan for later. The pain of underachievement was never acute enough to make me face my reality. Banality and mediocrity is a dull, throbbing annoyance. A bone breaking with such violence it tears through the skin will definitely shake you from antipathy and indifference.

If only I had known this, I would have loved my pain, and probably myself by extension. I would have sought out "healthy" pain and left the abusers in my dust. The cliché "no pain, no gain" comes to mind, but it's rarely uttered by those who truly understand the power of pain. I've only heard it spoken by over-zealous gym rats. I still wish my children (and anyone else I've managed to love in spite of myself) a life free of hurt. I apologize for any hurt I've caused by "the love I took." There's a difference between hurt and pain. I know this now. If you can face life's pain, you will learn from it. And learn to live.

Φ

The final fuck is, in Frank's word, "quick." I think, "messy," but it seems indelicate to say so. I don't want him to leave but sometimes life, like sex, is messy. So, the last time isn't the best time, but it is better than the previous last time, or the last time last month. I tell him he doesn't have to run off, so he sits at the piano and plays for me. For himself, I should say. But I sit and take it in. This strong complicated man with his complications. He plays Grieg and Bizet and his own compositions. At one point he plays Howard Jones' *No One is to Blame*. Does he sense the irony of his choice? I think so, only because he is surprised when I know the tune. In fact, I consider it my anthem, and I tell him so.

I want to say, "Don't move to South America. Choose me." But that would be a promise I don't know if I'm ready to make. It's certainly not a promise I'm able to keep. He's probably close to perfect for me, but it is the wrong time and I'm in the wrong place. No one is to blame.

I like to think that he wants to say, "How about I don't move to South America? I choose you." But that would be a promise to involve himself in my life, out of the bedroom and into the living room, and not just to play the piano. I see the series of photographs on the top of the instrument he plays unselfconsciously. Could he ever be a picture on that mantle? He certainly has claimed he doesn't want to be. And if he stays a bit longer would he want to be there at the end, when the really messy stuff happens?

How many times has he told me he would leave me? How many times has he been unable to stay away? The kaleidoscopic projection of my heart sees the truth at last. The word "love" has never been uttered between us, but whenever we're together, love cradles us, two broken people who found each other against all odds. Two people who have said, "I love you" umpteen-million times and never felt it (even if we meant it), who have heard the iteration from others who never meant it (even if they felt it). Frank or I should say the words. Recognize that the real elephant in the room is our self-loathing, which has kept us from being able to allow others to love us. I know Frank loves me as surely as he knows I love him. Yet to put our feelings into a phrase tossed about as haphazardly as, "I'll take fries with that," would sully the one clean feeling we've ever managed. And we found it together.

Whatever we may want to say goes unsaid. We discuss music. We discuss politics. We discuss the inanity of the masses. Now he's putting on his shoes. He kisses me. It's a passionate kiss, but not the passion of lovers. He barely touches my lips, then leans into my cheek, then his full weight is at my neck, breathing in my hair. It's goodbye, but neither of us says anything. He just looks at me with that tired look he has (a man who does too much but doesn't know how to stop).

What do you want? I want to scream so loud that the world would shatter; not just mine, not just his, but the entire God-forsaken planet. I want for Frank to hold me and lie to me, just this once, to tell me I didn't waste my life. I want to begin again, make smarter choices, choose a better path that I eschewed not from deliberation but because I was lost and lived a life that was thrust upon me. I want him to tell me he loves me, to hear him say that I've made a difference to him in some significant way. I want immortality.

I want to say something profound: *We loved well enough.* Would that sum up what we have been to each other? It certainly will not sum up what he has been to me.

Neither of us says what he or she wants. Neither of us discloses his or her closely held secrets. In the end, all of it—the relationship, the sex, the conversation, the pangs—seems utterly diaphanous.

I hear his soft tones: "You are the good slut." It's possibly the kindest thing anyone ever said to me.

Then I look up, and he is gone.

End of chapter.

The Resignation

Ever since the combination "Pritzker press problem" and meeting the odd woman in the park, Hallee could not stop thinking about the many new ideas that the past two weeks' events had fomented. In fact, she had begun to think of the "stirred up shit" metaphor that was stinking up her life more as a fertilizer. Or a compost—something natural, organic, non-toxic—which stunk a ton but gave rise to life after death. Despite her Catholic belief, Hallee didn't really believe that something good would be out there after her life was over, but the seeds that had been planted these many months since moving to NYC were starting to germinate and flourish after the compost-park encounter with the woman whose name Hallee still couldn't recall. She had even combed the *Times*' obits instead of the marriage announcements these past few weeks on the off-chance the sickly woman's near death tale was true. If she had died, her obit hadn't warranted a photograph. Hallee had seen no trace of her in the news. She even had returned to the park intentionally to seek her out, but the woman was nowhere to be found.

It got to the point that Hallee wasn't even sure the woman had truly existed. She had asked the twins about the boy they were playing with, and all Josh managed was, "We played with a lot of boys." She had to break down and ask Gavin if he remembered the woman, and happily he had, thinking she was "scary looking." At least Hallee wasn't completely losing her mind. That aside, she really just wanted to find the woman to talk to her more, to seek additional counsel. Hallee felt utterly alone with no one to turn to. She had waited for Xavier to call, but he hadn't and she couldn't bring herself to call him. Lauren was distant and cold to her, perhaps out of guilt or perhaps because she regretted having brought Hallee on in the first place. Hallee couldn't even imagine breaking down and calling her mother, whose solution to the problem would vacillate between encouraging Hallee to move in with her and—worse yet—needling her that she should never have left Jeremy. No matter how lonely she was at this moment, no matter the mistakes she had made since moving east, she knew she had made the right decision to leave her past life. That was the only truth she could cling to at present.

With regards to work, Hallee felt a sea change in her efforts. She had been true to her word and left work every day at 5 p.m., leaving Lauren at the front desk to cover. Hallee hadn't requested a change in her schedule; she just packed up her things and left without fanfare, sometimes sensing they were glad to see her leave the premises. It was as though she were carried out the door on the wind of the staff's collective exhale.

Not everyone appeared to be avoiding her, as though she would taint them by association. Arnie had tried once or twice to engage her in banter, but the effort was forced and Hallee felt deeply disappointed in him. Arnie Jacobs could launch his own firm and probably take half the architects with him. Who knew? Maybe he had a non-compete clause. Maybe he was afraid if he stared Arnie Jacobs Architects Company, Incorporated, he'd become the infernal ass that David was. Hallee doubted it. In fact, she believed that Arnie just lacked the strength to strike out on his own. He was fulfilled in his work, which was more than most people could claim. Certainly more than Hallee. Plus he had his family to consider; his wife was expecting a third child.

On a more petty level, Hallee also couldn't forgive Arnie for having brought Xavier to the office and inadvertently introducing them, even though she was fully aware he had held no sway on Xavier's attraction to her or the subsequent affair. Every time she saw Arnie, he reminded her of X. Had the two of them discussed her? Was that something grown men did, even as former college frat mates? Was Arnie spending time with X? Had her boss known the depth of the affair, Hallee would have felt genuine shame.

As it was, Arnie barely took notice of her lackluster efforts, but Hallee knew it was only a matter of time before her flying under the radar was observed by David. She didn't know if it would result in her being fired; at this point, maybe that would be the best outcome. Let someone make the decision for her. Now why did that sound familiar?

It was nearing Halloween when David decided to play "trick or treat" with her. He approached her in the morning and pointed to his daily schedule. The line beside his bony middle finger—*Why on Earth did he use his middle digit to point at everything?*—read: **15:00-15:15 Meet with Hallee Thompson.** She supposed that was his way of an invitation. Not a moment of the day went by without her attention being diverted by the clock on her computer, the clock on the wall, the timestamp on her e-mails, the reference to her cell phone. She was on edge, feeling—she imagined—like the death row inmate contemplating a last meal before hearing the clarion call of, "Dead man walking."

It was in this mindset, therefore, that she startled when she rounded the corner into the kitchen to see Lauren syphoning a sad little soup as her quick lunch break. Such was the nature of their relations at this point that Hallee hadn't even known where in the building Lauren had ventured off to. The two colleagues stared awkwardly at one another. Hallee turned away to fill the electronic kettle with water for tea (herbal, Hallee had decided; no caffeine to make herself even more jittery than she already was).

Hallee was both surprised and elated that Lauren didn't bolt from the kitchen. She took her brewing cup and sat down not quite across from her co-secretary (how else to define their relationship at this point?) at the round Formica table. Perhaps it was a subconscious gesture on Hallee's part, that she sat 60 degrees away: not as the adversary directly across the table but also not sitting close enough to be construed as being on intimate or even, she supposed, friendly terms.

Hallee held the teabag by its tag, bobbing it in the hot water in an effort to brew the right level of flavor. "You seem to be doing well," Hallee finally managed, wanting to open the channel of communication without sounding snide or bitter. It was an effort.

"No thanks to you," Lauren snapped back. Okay, so this is how it was going to go.

"You cannot possibly believe that I had anything to do with that whole

THE TRUTH

Pritzker screw..."

"I'm not talking about the Pritzker mailing," she interrupted. At this she leaned in toward Hallee; from a distance it may have appeared conspiratorial, but up close it was sheer spite. "I vouched for you when I brought you in here. I told David you could handle the pressures of this office. I'm the one he looks at now and questions my aptitude and decision-making skills."

Hallee was stumped. On the one hand, she was disarmed by the thought that Lauren truly felt that Hallee had impacted her standing in the company. On the other, Hallee was disgusted by how Lauren had made Hallee's troubles into something all about her. How many other admins had she hired (and fired) over the years? Was her good standing wrecked by *those* decision-making skills?

"I'm just so disappointed in you."

Hallee choked back a gasp.

What Hallee wanted to say: "Are you fucking kidding me? I've bent over backwards for this job!"

What she said: Nothing. She had no words. Her only feeling was devastation. Had Lauren stepped out in front of a bus and been struck dead Hallee would not have felt worse. No, they hadn't been close these past few months, but once upon a time they had been the best of friends. And for years they kept up via letters, with frequent phone calls and—in recent technological times—by e-mail. They were the truest of friends, and whether or not Hallee had indeed let down Lauren, she knew without a doubt that they were friends no longer. Hallee didn't think it was possible, but she felt her already broken heart crack further.

"What happened to you?" she asked Lauren, no longer hiding an accusatory tone. "Why have you stayed in a job that has impacted your health, your intellect, even your morals? Do you honestly believe that how you are treated by Janine and David is appropriate?"

Lauren barely drew breath. "What you fail to understand is that David is a *genius*. We facilitate *genius* here. Long after you and I and even David are gone from this earth, his work will stand. We will be remembered long after our deaths for the great things we accomplished."

"Don't you mean the great things *he* accomplished?" Hallee replied with deliberate malice.

"See, that's what's wrong with you, Hallee! You just don't get it. We're a team here. Every architect in this office is here by choice. We support them. We make sure that David can be free to create, and you just think you're too good to be a supportive team member!"

Hallee tried to remain calm, but she felt her blood pressure skyrocket. She glanced down. Lauren's half-eaten soup looked like gruel. Her collar bones jutted out of her chest. Hallee's own chest was lurching in and out with the hyper beating of her heart. She tried to summon sympathy for Lauren; whether or not she truly believed what she was saying, Laruen certainly was ill. On many levels.

"I'm not going to have a fight with you, Lauren, but you're wrong when you say I'm not a supportive team member."

"Oh, come on!" Lauren's nostrils were flaring. "You spent more time fucking Arnie's best friend this summer than you did paying attention to your job!"

Wow. So there it was. Lauren had descended into cliché. The jealous best friend. As much as Hallee wanted to rub her nose in it, at this point she hadn't the energy.

"We broke up, actually," she said, and there was a flicker of humanity on Lauren's face.

Or maybe Lauren's surprise masked a nasty streak of glee, because the next thing she said was, "Well, it serves you right for ingratiating yourself like that with Arnie."

Hallee just smiled sadly. Whoever was now sitting—not quite directly— across from her was an absolute stranger. She no longer felt any ties to Lauren, and the grief weighed her down and made her sleepy. She wanted to get in a jibe, to be cruel to Lauren about how she was more interested in being on David's support team than on creating a life of her own. A life with love, children, a true home...

THE TRUTH

Hallee suddenly felt that she had everything that truly mattered to her, even if some of what she had had been fleeting. Looking at her old roommate, she didn't feel hate. She only felt pity for her.

"I'm really sorry you found me a disappointment," she said, taking her unsipped tea and tossing it in the sink. She rinsed the cup, trying not to show her shaking hands to her co-worker, turned her back on Lauren and went back to her desk.

Promptly at 3 p.m. Hallee went into David's office. She had been dreading the confrontation, mostly because after her lunchroom altercation with Lauren she was sure she would break down in an emotional confession in front of David. Her goal was not to show that to him, not to embarrass and demean herself before a man who didn't deserve to see her most vulnerable self. She stood, straight-backed, and walked towards the gallows.

"Close the door," he commanded. She shut the solid plate of glass behind her. He continued the ruse of typing on his keyboard as if she hadn't even entered his sphere. Nothing had changed in the domicile. Nothing, except for her.

At long last, he closed his laptop. He flexed his fingers outward, and she heard the crack of his knuckles.

David sighed. Audibly. A moment passed. Hallee thought he was waiting for her to say something, but she remained silent.

"I have been waiting for the air to clear to ssspeak with you again about your status here," David said with a weary attitude. Hallee said nothing. David seemed to study her with his snake eyes, but Halle was an expert at the staring contest. He blinked first.

"I still believe you have a future here, despite the misssstakes that were made," he said. Hallee wondered if he was trying to get a rise out of her or if he were truly deluded into believing the fiction he had created around her. "I would like to see you ssssucssseed here at David Ormston-Meighton Architects Company, Incorporated."

"Why?" was the only response she could manage. She wasn't sure which part of her brain—conscious? subconscious? manipulative?—wanted to know the answer, but her body betrayed no reaction that she didn't genuinely seek an answer. This might be the only chance in her life to ask someone so cruel why they wanted to see her remain a victim.

Hallee was in treacherous territory. No matter what he said, her response was bound to be wrong. There was no way to be the good girl in this situation. She thought of the strange woman in the park. The one who was by now, probably, released from life's suffering. She had scared Hallee. All the truths she had told that Hallee couldn't embrace at the time were reeling through her mind now. The dead woman was open: She knew who she was; she was, as she had noted, "out." Was Hallee going to wait until she was already dead to accept who she was?

Xavier had taught her something: There's a time to suffer and a time to be brave. No, not brave. Strong. This was Hallee's time.

What Hallee wanted to say: "I have another job in my field, and I'm moving on. I really thank you for taking me on and showing me how things are done in New York."

What she said: "I was not raised in a terrarium, you husband of a bitch!"

She thought of Xavier whipping her with a belt. She could endure anything David might throw her way.

David stammered. His green eyes shifted. He wiggled in his chair. He actually opened his laptop and closed it again.

Suddenly Hallee felt powerful.

"You know," she began, "I have a college education. I've worked for companies 50 times the size of this for bosses with one-fifth the superiority complex. Have you even bothered to look at my resume? I took this job because I needed out of a bad situation, and Lauren *begged* me to help her here. I never expected anything from you but professionalism, but I did *you* a favor. I don't know what your mommy and daddy did to you that made you marry that cunt and take her abuse and then diffuse it to your staff, but I'm not taking it anymore. I quit!"

Hallee smiled, feeling that she had finally completed a marathon or climbed Kilimanjaro. She had spoken clearly and with emphasis, in even tones. No screaming, no crying. Aside from the name-calling, she had handled herself well, she had to admit. *Oh, fuck it. The name-calling was justified, too.*

"I. Know. You." She leaned in as she said this, flaunting her considerable cleavage deliberately. She had no need to mention that he long had been emasculated; that was an obvious point not needing to be said. He recoiled, so Hallee took her retreat. But one step back only.

As she stood before him defiant, David was speechless. Hallee waited for him to say something. When he didn't, she returned to her desk and managed to finish out the day. She shook when he passed by her several times, but he didn't speak to her again.

Shortly before 5 p.m., Hallee felt her cell buzzing. She immediately recognized the number on the caller ID. It was Xavier. The fun just kept on getting funnier. She wasn't ready to face him, even by phone, but it had been four weeks since they last spoke. Maybe he was calling to apologize. Maybe he was calling because he had expected her to apologize, but when she hadn't, he felt obliged to get in touch. Either way, she couldn't avoid him forever. She snuck off to the server room, which was unbearably hot but usually the only place in the office that would guarantee privacy.

"Hi," she said, and without meaning to added, "I'm really sorry about our fight." Well, it wasn't quite an apology. At least she hadn't taken the blame.

Xavier's voice was low. He whispered, "Yes, I'm asking you to move in with me."

"What?" Xavier thought he had spoken too quietly for her to hear, so he stated his offer more loudly. Actually Hallee was shocked. The "what" was exclamatory, not a request for him to repeat what he had said. When he had showed her the closet a month prior, she really didn't think it was an invitation to live with him. In fact, she wasn't conscious of any rationale for him affording her a place to store her very few belongings. She never valued herself enough to consider that a man like the mythical "Xavier Sebastiani, world explorer" could actually fall in love with a woman like her.

What Hallee wanted to say: "Xavier, I love you, and of course I'll move in with you. I'll be your doting wife/girlfriend/cum-bucket. Whatever you need me to be!"

What she said: "I don't think so."

She sensed immediately that he had assumed she would accept. She didn't want for their relationship to end, but she needed to be honest. With him. With herself. "I think I understand what you mean about us, Xavier. Whether it's open or kink or whatever down the road... I just know that if I don't figure out how to stand on my own, take care of myself, I won't ever be the woman you see in me."

Hallee felt as though her voice had come from someone else, as if she were the wooden sidekick of a nearby ventriloquist. X was silent. Her mind was reeling. She had just quit a job that she hated; she would soon be desperate for money; she longed to be protected and loved and cared for; and her appetite for sexual exploration had grown exponentially of late. Here was a man that could have solved all these problems with one fell swoop, and she had rebuffed him.

"Okay, Hallee," he said simply. "Take good care of you."

Her conscious mind was screaming at her, begging her to tell X she had changed her mind. But some faint murmur—like a dying ember that flickers its last flame... and with it sets off a firestorm—was telling the loud conscious voice to sit down and shut up. Hallee was terrified of where she was heading, but she knew that she had finally set off on a new path. One that could lead to anywhere. Her way may be more treacherous than before or full of light and grace. All Hallee knew for certain was that she was walking a route she had never walked before.

As the end of the work day approached, Hallee packed up her few belongings and sent a "goodbye" e-mail to a handful of her colleagues. She bcc'd them out of consideration, but Lauren wasn't on the list. The only bridge she cared about was burned, but Hallee hadn't started the fire. The message read:

THE TRUTH

I do not believe in platitudes. If you are receiving this, it is because I value you and believe you deserve better than working for a megalomaniac. No amount of "genius" excuses the treatment we collectively suffer here on a daily basis. You do not have to live in this abusive situation. Believe in yourself and walk away. Know that you are strong. You are not a victim. Great things await you.

Thank you for being my co-worker.

Hallee.

When she left the office, there was no fanfare, for which she was truly grateful. She needed no send-off. In fact, she sighed with relief upon exiting the building. Whatever lay ahead, whatever the uncertainty, anything was better than what she had endured at David Ormston-Meighton Architects Company, Incorporated.

She left work on a Friday. The following Monday, the Pritzker Award was announced. David had won the highest achievement in architecture. Another framed picture to go on his wall. Another genius awarded accolades while Hallee just shook her head in disbelief and befuddlement.

X

What do you want?

To feel the presence of God.

I am an old soul. If I am to embrace that statement, I thus have been seeking the truth for millennia. Marilynn (30 hours my senior) drifts from religion to religion, throwing herself fully into whatever practice finds her. First, she is devout. Then, she is disappointed. Then devout again.

I became agnostic sometime in my teens. I used to say, the difference between an Atheist and an agnostic is that the Atheist believes there is no God; the agnostic doesn't believe there is a god. While the difference appears to be semantic, I was able to explain myself more fully decades later: Atheism *is* a religion. These people preach and proselytize as strongly as the evangelicals, trying oh so hard to convert the believers into their camp. I've heard the argument that if you don't believe in God, you are an atheist and to identify as otherwise is a bit of a cheat. However, I suspect most agnostics identify as such because we feel we are simply faithless, lost souls, aware of our essence but unable to embrace any meaningful continuation of it. The best of agnostics live for the moment and appreciate every day on earth. The worst of us simply feel abandoned. A life full of questions with no answers.

There have been a handful of times in my life when I thought I felt the hand of God in my life. A glimpse, as it were. One of the most profound experiences I had was when I was considering converting (back) to Christianity. I was preparing to join the Catholic Church at mid-life. I was having serious reservations: about my priest (these turned out to be justified), about the Trinity, about a virgin birth (Talmudic law would have precluded Mary being a virgin, and any scholar would know that), and about God in general (oddly enough, I've never doubted the existence of Jesus Christ, whom I hold as one of the greatest historic figures of all time). I just didn't know if conversion was the right thing to do or if I was doing it for the right reasons. Even my husband admitted that it was a religion he was born into and there was no reason for me to choose it.

I think the main reason why I wanted to convert—ironically enough—was because I wanted to be married in the Church, as if somehow, that would in the end make everything better in my marriage. That if God blessed it, my marriage would last and be eternal or—at the very least—last me to my end of days.

But a few days before my conversion, which was to take place on Lazarus Saturday, I was getting cold feet. I mentioned this to my priest and he showed what seemed to me to be less disappointment and more disgust. He told me "Don't do it then." And left me with no counsel.

I must digress...

I mentioned earlier that among the many problems in my marriage was the fact that I wanted babies. More babies. Many babies. I had one perfect child and I had accepted my lot in life. After years of begging my husband for another child, I gave up and moved on. Perhaps I had moved on in ways that doomed my marriage to failure, or perhaps I just stopped wishing for what I didn't have.

Yet at one point my husband saw his own mortality and suggested we stop using birth control. I laughed and thought, "Okay, whatever." What I failed to mention before was that we had had a great deal of difficulty conceiving our daughter. It took us months at a relatively young (read: fertile) age to produce that embryo. Ultimately, I learned a lesson in willful reproduction: When a woman wants a child, you try and try and try again, generally "making love" and after many attempts and failures, you end up pregnant with a girl.

When a man wants a child? He drinks a lot of beer, bends you over, enters from behind, and on a one-shot deal you get preggers with a son.

And thus it was, the Friday before Lazarus Saturday, I got the news that I was pregnant (I wouldn't find out about the boy for four months, of course). I considered it a sign from God: My prayers were answered and I was being given a child. (In fact, I was being given *back* a child, but that is a story for another day.)

So that was—perhaps—a glimpse of God.

For what follows, I am now prepared to burn in hell should mercy be denied me. Dear reader, if you've stayed with me thus far, I hope you will see both humor and irony of what I reveal to you now.

I finally witnessed God at the not-particularly-youthful age of 40. I submitted.

There isn't much more to say about that for those who understand. For those who don't, a 300-page tome probably will titillate but not suffice. I submitted to Frank on Palm Sunday, 2010. It was above that same Church. I note the circumstances because I don't want to forget that final fuck. And although it didn't actually turn out to be the final fuck, I don't want to forget the date of the most meaningful fuck of my life.

It sounds hyperbolic, but for those who aren't submissive, try to comprehend 30-plus years of being lost in your sexuality. Of not knowing who you are or what you need. Of wandering from one bad partner to another, thinking that suffering is okay because you will eventually please and all will be good. Of course, the difference between submission and abuse is the difference between discipline and torture. An athlete knows discipline; a prisoner of war knows torture.

I went to Frank with no expectations or agenda. I just wanted... to know. At some point, I not only realized that I was powerless, but I understood that some... one... had complete control over me. I was at the mercy, the grace, the amusement, the need... of something "other." I felt complete and utter faith in my master; I knew that I was going to be used and pleasured and that I would do everything my master wanted of me; and in the end he would be pleased with me and let me love myself. I was out of control and no longer trying to fight it. I let go and let "god." In the purest sense.

The first time he spit into my mouth, I honestly was lost. Not in the way you generally think of being lost, as in misdirected or even rudderless. I was literally lost: I had absolutely no frame of reference for what I was experiencing. On my knees, my head back with my mouth wedged open, I expected to be force fed a cock... not to receive a goober of saliva. Having no religious epiphany to draw upon, I later wondered if this wasn't exactly how the truly devout felt upon drinking the blood of Christ. You have God before you, and whatever bodily fluids he gives unto you, you accept with grace and gratitude. In that sense, it wouldn't matter if it were blood, sweat and tears, or semen, saliva and piss. It's the same DNA, after all. And when my consciousness finally took hold, I was forced to admit that among those options, piss was the most sterile. So much for sensibility.

I certainly could digress and discuss the inherent dom-sub, sexually charged atmosphere of receiving communion at Church. Kneeling and opening your mouth before an allegedly chaste man (invariably a man) to be fed that wafer. There is something rather twisted in this set-up, but who am I to judge? In fact, I now wonder if Jesus also was a true submissive. After all, he allowed himself to be beaten, mortified and nailed (no pun intended), all for some commandment by a Being he wanted to serve. To please my Lord.

It took me days to come to terms with Frank's "offering." He probably chuckled at my naïveté. He had his pick of submissives, but for some inexplicable reason, I was the one he could never shake. What he taught me was everything, but what he left me with was nothing. For we brought nothing into this world...

At the end I was rattled and unsure, but I knew that I was loved at a level no earthly love had ever achieved. In that moment of extreme stimulus, I knew what omnipotent love was. I felt in a state of grace as I took Him in and let Him have whatever He wanted. Had He told me I must die for His sins, I would have done so with extreme gratitude.

It is difficult to explain the irony of submission. How letting someone do "degrading" things to you actually empowers you. It's all these labels, perhaps, that make us feel insecure. The tropes and mores that lead us not into temptation but land us in the midst of evil nonetheless. Maybe the vocabulary is insufficient: to be used versus to serve. Maybe it is the eternal question of free will. Christ made only one choice: To show up and endure whatever was done unto him. He could've tucked tail and run. He chose to submit. For me, I understand this acquiescence. Ultimately, however, I feel power for the first time in my life. I was given a choice—free will. I chose consciously and deliberately and came out of my baptism reborn. And for the final months of my life, I am home at last.

Φ

My oncologist is angry. She begged me to remove my pancreas two months ago. She told me a pancreaticoduodenectomy along with intensive chemotherapy would prolong my life by at least three months, possibly six. I laughed at the time, thinking what quality of life those six months would afford. She sighs with exasperation. She's lucky I kept the appointment.

It turns out, I've lost almost eight pounds since my last visit. On top of the 13 I had already lost, that's 21 total. I smile. My goal for the year was 20. I have quantifiably met a resolution. My first.

"How much longer?" I ask, and she hears the sarcasm over my sorrow.

She sighs. "Days." She shakes her head. Under her veil of anger is a hint of shared grief. She doesn't want to pity me. She doesn't feel sorry for me. In fact, she knows that I know that she would have chosen the same route. "Is the pain bad?"

I smile. No point for lies now. "I scored some 420. Do you know what that is?"

She chuckles. "Yes. If this were California, I would have given you a script. Is it enough? I mean, I can get you morphine pills."

"Enough to end it?" I ask her. Am I serious? I don't know. The pain is quite intense, but I've felt worse at the end of Frank's belt. I smile. I now understand the need to endure controlled pain. I shake my head. "No, I'm good with the pot. But thank you. For everything."

Her eyes are moist. She clears her throat. It's the same sound the Asian laundry buddy made that Sunday morning months ago. I remember his neatly folded boxers, the military corners, the button flies. I have the urge to clear my throat as well, but my mouth is dry. There's no phlegm to hack.

The doctor's voice interrupts my reverie. "You need to make arrangements," she says.

"I have, actually," I answer. "In my way."

"What's your way?"

"Well," I hesitate. For a doctor, she wasn't horrid, had some humanity left, at least a sense of humor. How much do I tell her? How far to debase myself? Is there any shame or humiliation left in me? "I made arrangements for my son..."

"That's not what I mean," she speaks slowly, as if the cancer has spread to my ears. For all I know, it has. "You are alone, right? You shouldn't be. You need someone."

"I made arrangements for my son," I continue, my doctor being more patient than my insurance policy will probably allow. "I went to my husband—we never filed for divorce, so I guess he's still my husband—and asked him to look after our boy." I'm choking up, which I hate most about myself. I wish I could not care. I wish I had the ability to let go and forget. Not to feel so acutely. I inhale and begin again, "His girlfriend—and the emphasis is on girl—is pregnant. He says it's too much stress on her to have another child in the house. How can men do that? How can they move on so easily, forget their flesh and blood even? You're a doctor." I'm disgusted with myself. Why do I begrudge him happiness at this point? He's creating a life for himself, but all I see is my own anger, frustration and loss. I want to blame him. Still. I looked at my doctor and implore, "Why can men leave and women not?"

She sighs. "Some women leave."

"I'm going to leave," I whisper.

"That's different," she shuffles through my file, pen in hand. What is there left to write? "I don't know the answer to your question. I wish there were a medical reason for why some people—not all—do not value their human connections. I'm sorry."

I dry my eyes. Will God be there to answer my heartfelt quandary? I'll know soon enough. No one is saved, I suppose. Father McKenzie wipes the dirt from his hands.

"Where is your son now?" she interrupts my reverie.

"I sent him to my mother's."

"Your mother should be here," my doctor continues. I shake my head. "Your daughter? Someone?"

"There's no one," I say, honestly. My daughter is safely abroad, and I won't witness her heartbreak (hers being the only heart I am capable of breaking at this point). I could ask Richie, I suppose, but I don't want to receive solicitation in death. Why should my exit be any different than my entrance and the tedious walk across the interim that was my life? Why should anyone care for me now that it's too late to mean *anything*? I feel myself descending into melancholy and self-pity. Wasn't I supposed to be more sympathetic? Didn't I touch people along the way? What had the doctor said? *Some people do not value their human connections.* Guilty as charged.

She scribbles something on her pad, tears a sheet, then writes on the next page. She hands both to me.

"The first is morphine," she says with emphasis. Back to business. Her eyes are limpid blue. "The second is the number of our Hospice Unit."

"Hospice?" I ask, barely hearing her, the tumors echoing in my ears, figuratively if not literally.

"They will sit with you, care for you," she explains. "Until the end."

"I don't..."

"Call them," she commands. "Otherwise, I'll have you admitted."

She should be glad I'm very good at doing as commanded. I dress, leave the office, and am punching in the numbers of the Hospice Unit before I hit the R train.

Φ

He's perfect.

I'm bleary from pot and morphine, but I see my hospice nurse and he's lovely to behold. Reminds me of Lafayette from *True Blood.* Or Robert.

THE TRUTH

Robert was a beautiful black bull queer who worked at Goatfeathers in Columbia, SC. He once squeezed my tits in that pseudo-judgmental way gay fashionistas have and told me I would be perfect if I had implants. He wore eye liner and had the most incredible body I had ever seen. He was both fey and ripped. He swished wherever he went, and he wore the stereotype before it was fashionable (or accepted). He was a *black gay man in the south*! I didn't know it at the time, but he was the bravest person I ever knew.

One of the bar's policies was that no cocktail waitress could walk to her car alone. Columbia had the highest per capita rape rate in the nation. Dail Dinwiddie disappeared there after a U2 concert I attended with my then husband. Public Enemy opened. Dail was gone. I later sold a puppy that appeared to have gone to her parents (it was on the news). It was a poor substitute, and had I known who they were, I would have given them the puppy for free.

Columbia was particularly hard on the "Dails" of the world. My good friend, Dale (this one a woman à la Dale Evans), died of a brain tumor (trust me, the irony is not lost on me... how many Goatfeathers' employees have succumbed to cancer? At least one more than starred in *Sex in the City*.). Another Dale disappeared into Tibet, never to be heard from again.

But I digress...

The policy at the bar required a male escort for each female. Then one day, one of the busboys was mugged. He talked about it in equal measures of pride and shell-shock.

He was relieved to lose nothing more than his wallet. A week after his near-death experience, Robert was whiling away the afterhours at The Elbow Room. He danced, he flirted, he rubbed against, well, everything. He sashayed out the exit, vaguely aware of being followed. One big red neck nodded to a buddy. That buddy nodded to another buddy. Soon, the party of three was trailing him.

Robert sensed them before he saw them. He regulated his breathing. His hips shook gently, from left to right, and back again. His tight satin black pants framed his sculpted ass perfectly. His biceps rippled in the streetlight on the corner of Harden and Devine. His car was 200 feet from him. That's when he heard the first whistle, followed by a catcall.

"Hey, faggot!" the desultory voice rang out in the near deserted street.

"Not just a faggot," his drunken buddy slurred. "A nigger faggot."

They laughed. Robert's hips swung as he grasped his keys in his dominant hand (and not being in the majority population in any fashion, that hand happened to be of the left persuasion). He fumbled slightly with the keys, making sure the pointiest one was jutting out between his thumb and forefinger. His car was just in front of him, and his predators within feet of him. He felt a single bead of sweat drip from the spot where his hair should have begun, if he didn't shave his head. He wasn't puzzled by the fact that he could sweat from his non-hairline. He lightly brushed his brow with his right hand and the bead was gone. A thing of the past.

His pursuers upon him, Robert could smell the alcohol and nicotine residue on them, and he was repulsed. His hand trembled slightly with the key still sharp and pointed out.

"Whacha gonna do, fag?" the third musketeer hissed.

But it was too late.

Robert's key was in the trunk lock. The trunk opened almost instantaneously with the keys launched moon-ward. In thrust Robert's good left hand and out thrust a crowbar.

The pursuers were bloodied and on the ground in no time. Some claim Robert said, "You want a piece of me, bitches?" and that he was more masculine looking in that moment than he had been since the age of 12. No charges were filed. Less than a moth later, Robert was living in San Francisco.

So, what is he doing here, now, at my bedside? He rolls my joint, injects me with morphine. He smiles. His slurred words (my slurred hearing) ask do I want a massage. I laugh. I think I laughed. In my mind, I laughed. I say, "No thanks. Do you want a hit?" and I offer Nurse Lafayette-Robert my joint. He politely declines.

"What day is it?" I ask him.

"Sunday," is his answer.

"No, I mean the date."

He hesitates, and then he remembers, "It's October tenth."

In my fogged state, it takes a moment to put together two and two. Or 10 and 10 and 10. It's perfect. Triple witching. Beware the alliterative dates. Maybe there *is* a heaven and God is either laughing or smiling at me. I will die on 10/10/10. It suits me.

"I was reading a book," I mumble.

"What book, honey? I can read it to you."

I gesture with the back of my hand in the general direction of the desk. He goes and looks through the notebooks, post-it pads, the desk calendar, occasionally holding up something for me to reject. "I don't see any book here," he says.

"The manuscript. It's not finished. I tried, but I failed."

He finds the loose leaf in the manila folder and brings it over. "We all try and fail, honey," he drawls. "That's called life."

"Or death," I mock.

"Oh, no, hon," he sasses right back. "We all succeed at death. Eventually." He's looking at the manuscript. "So what is this?"

"A book I was writing."

"Fascinating," he says genuinely. Reading the title page, he questions, "*Love, Lies and a Life Less Lived?* What kind of title is that?"

I try to explain about my passion for alliteration. I also want to draw him the cover art I had imagined for this book, my in vain attempt at writing and being published one day. Another dream thwarted, but he hands me a pen.

"I thought it could be shortened: 'L' to the fifth power," and I draw on the folder:

$$L^5$$

"Do you mind if I read it?"

I nod, which could mean either I mind or I don't, but he assumes it's okay to read on. And read he does, stopping only sporadically to tend to me, which in some ways his neglect is the highest praise I could receive. He occasionally laughs, sometimes he frowns, once he says, "Awe, honey, this is *nasty*."

"Well, that's kinda the point," I admit. No apologies.

I don't know why he continues to read. His comments are thoughtful and would be helpful if I had any rewrites left in me. At last he glares at me; it's not an angry accusation but more along the lines of ocular penetration, as if he's trying to figure out what I meant when I wrote what I did.

"How much of this is true?" He holds me with his black eyes; I cannot differentiate between pupil and iris. I smile.

"It's a work of fiction," I reply.

He whistles. "Honey, you are a piece of work. You gotta change the title."

"All I have to do today is die."

"The title is long and tedious."

"Kinda like life?" I ask, stating the obvious. "That's the point. I wasted my life."

"No one wastes a life," he consoles me. "What's the saying? 'A lot of failures are happy because they don't know they failed'? Something like that." His smile is pure benevolence. "I know! You should title it, 'The Truth.'"

"It's a work of fiction," I reiterate.

"Well, it's more truthful than any book I've ever read. You say a lot of important things about sex, but there needs to be more *sex* in this story. A *lot* more sex. That's what sells."

"Maybe I should call it, 'All About Sex,' then."

He waves the loose leaf pile of prose. "It's a bit thin. It feels unfinished."

I bark a guffaw. "That's what the agent said."

He finds a pen from the mess of my side table and positions himself as a secretary ready for dictation. "Tell me," he commands. "Tell me and I will write your ending."

"My ending has been written," I state. There is no more to tell that isn't inevitable. *The book needs more sex.* More sex.

"I could tell you a story from the middle," I attempt to sit up but it's pointless. He adjusts a pillow beneath me so that I'm not completely supine.

"Tell me the middle, then." He resumes his secretarial stance, and I tell him a story. I reminisce about a trip I took to the edge of the earth. One that changed me but I could never put into words that would capture the breathtaking awe of the place or the metamorphosis I undertook while there.

He writes, and when I have nothing left to say—or no ability to speak more—he sets down the document, now covered in his chicken scratches. No one will be able to read his transcription, but it motivated me to stay here, in this room, for a few hours more.

Lafayette-Robert shakes his head. I don't know if he's impressed, disgusted, or just in disbelief. Perhaps he doesn't know what to make of me, because all he says is, "'The Truth'. That's your title."

"Comme tous les rêveurs, je me suis trompé désenchantement de la vérité."

"I don't..." He is saying something but I can barely hear his words now. He is but a blur. I try to focus on the vibrations coming from his mouth, seeing the waves as they approach my ears. Peripheral vision hears, "I think you're speaking French. I don't know any language but English."

I sigh. The pain is worse. He relights my joint for me. A couple tokes later I manage, "The only truth I have is the truth that is eating me from inside out. My illness is the truth. The truth has consumed me."

My guardian angel holds my hand in consolation. "Honey, the truth is what consumes us all. And then it sets us free." I'm not sure if he's making fun of me, but I am too numb to discern reality any longer.

"Will you sing to me?"

"As a matter of fact, I am a lovely chanteuse." He bats his eyelashes.

"Chanteuse, huh?" I manage a smile. "I thought you didn't speak French?"

"Chanteuse is French? Who knew?" he winks. Is he really here? Because I feel almost as though he's floating above me. His voice reverberates, "What do you want to hear?"

Before I can curb my insensitive sensibilities, I say, "Sing me a Negro spiritual."

Lafayette-Robert frowns. And then he lets out a solid baritone laugh that fills my chamber, my death chamber. I am not a racist. I just don't see the point of delicacy at this point. He parts his plump lips and inhales.

"She is coming... Get onboard," L-R puts the joint to my mouth and flicks the ash in a nearby saucer before bringing it back to me again. Another man presenting me his precious offering. "There's room for many more..."

My vision is bleary. But the pain isn't there. Or if it is there, then I have accepted its presence. The final submission, the submission for which I have been waiting my entire life.

My gaze drifts behind Lafayette-Robert... what was his real name? Jeffrey. His name is Jeffrey. I look beyond Jeffrey where a handful of hallucinatory holograms have hypostatized in a haze: Elise, whom I kissed when she needed it; Marilynn, who was too afraid to board the plane to JFK—or perhaps of the ensuing grief that would result from a trip east—to bid adieu in person; Richie, who loved me despite my implacable rejection; Ryan-Claude, who was never there for me despite how much I needed him; Hélène, who will mend her heartbreak with hatred for not knowing until it's too late; and Frank, who had moved to Sao Paolo a month before. They are the Greek chorus to my dénouement. I feel some drool come from my mouth; it slithers down my cheek and is troughed into the creases of my neck. I am embarrassed. *Don't look at me like this. If you don't know me by now, you will never...*

I turn my head to hide from them all, to die alone as these things are done... and *she* is there. As I flop like some quadriplegic attempting to regain movement—am I drowning? where is the air?—Hallee, the mother of the toe-headed boys, sits beside me. By the Grace of God, calm sweeps over me. She takes my hand, and I know then.

Everything turns out alright.

The End

Since leaving David Ormston-Meighton Architects Company, Incorporated, Hallee had sent out more than 90 resumes. She had managed to garner five interviews that went fairly well. Three of them netted a "We decided not to hire anyone right now, but we'll call you if we change our minds." She had maxed out all her credit cards, borrowed money from her mother, and had finally broken down and called Jeremy to ask him to send extra money so the boys had Christmas presents; to her ever-lasting shame, she lied and told her ex that she had been laid off. Nevertheless, he was quite decent on the phone, telling her that he had been a really awful husband and that he'd like to take the boys for a while, maybe next summer, if she were amenable. Time and distance had either mellowed him or softened her bitterness towards him. She hadn't forgotten the abuse, so she would have to consider long and hard whether or not she would let him see the kids. However, it was nice to talk to him "as an adult," and Hallee knew the boys could only benefit from the two of them having reasonable civility towards each other.

Regardless, Hallee still had the very real issue of needing to find employment. To make the days go by—and give herself something to do—she had been volunteering for a couple different non-profits. She had even applied for a retail job at the Godiva shop (at least there'd be chocolate samples). The manager had taken one look at her application and told her she was over qualified, but would she be interested in managing another store. She said if they still wanted someone after the holidays to let her know (she was afraid that "managing another store" meant working twelve-hour days, seven days per week through Christmas getting paid minimum wage only to be downsized after the holiday rush). She had broken down emotionally repeatedly, often in front of the boys. Surprisingly, Gavin had seemingly grown up overnight, helping out with the twins and trying to support his mom.

One night in early December, Hallee was feeling particularly low. She kept opening her cell phone to text Xavier and closing it over and over (they hadn't spoken since the phone call in October). Even if he didn't want to see her, he might be able to help her find a job. Or pay her rent. With that thought, Hallee was crying and feeling stupid for putting herself in this situation. It was Gavin who suggested they bundle up and head to Rockefeller Center to look at the Christmas tree. Although Hallee had no interest in going out, the twins were so excited by the prospect she agreed. There had been very little snowfall so far, but the lights in midtown were spectacular. There really was nothing quite like Manhattan at Christmas to put the seasonal spirit into even the most despondent person. Aside from the gargantuan tree above the ice skaters, there were huge dangling multi-colored ornaments from every lamppost, white and blue electric menorahs, and dancing snowflakes. Holiday music ("Carol of the Bells") played from a loud speaker somewhere in the distance. The crowds were thick, but everyone was in a festive mood. Hallee hadn't much money to spare, but she indulged in three hot chocolates from a street vendor to treat the boys and roasted chestnuts for herself. She had never actually tasted them before and admittedly didn't really like the mealy texture. However, the smoky flavor was just right on a night like this, so she ate the entire bag. They all sang Christmas carols on the subway on their way back to Brooklyn, and several of the riders joined in with them. Josh suggested he pass a hat because "mommy's out of work like those guys who always sing on the subway." At that point, Hallee just thought her youngest son both clever and funny, so she simply laughed at the idea instead of feeling humiliated for a change.

The next day Hallee was back at the volunteer job, handing everyone a copy of her resume, whether they worked there, volunteered alongside her, or were simply dropping by to get information about the organization. She would find something by Christmas. She had to, so long as it wasn't another personal assistant position. She had learned the hard way that she wasn't cut out for that line of work. If worse came to worst, she would pack the kids up at the mid-winter break in February and move in with her mother.

THE TRUTH

She hoped it would not come to that, but with the economy in tatters, many adult children were facing a similar fate.

The family's Christmas was modest, but Santa still managed to visit the Thompson household, much to the delight of her boys (Jeremy had come through with an extra $500, and the boys had a lot of new—okay, "gently used"—clothes and three new video games—one per boy—that would keep them occupied for hours). Only Gavin noticed that Santa had forgotten to bring Hallee a present. She suspected that Gavin knew more about Santa than he was letting on, because he volunteered not to open his video game so that "Santa could return it" and bring something to his mother instead. Hallee had sworn she wouldn't ruin Christmas by feeling sorry for herself; she was broke and lonely, but things were bound to get better. She told Gavin that Santa wanted him to have the gift, and if he wanted to, he could pray for his mom to get a present next year.

Even better than Christmas, for the boys, was the nearly two feet of snow that fell the day after Christmas. Fortunately, Hallee had been monitoring the weather, and with the ham and roast chicken (she didn't dare splurge on a duck and a turkey was too big for her and the boys) she had cooked for Christmas dinner—not to mention all the sides, a pie, ice cream and candy from the boys' stockings—there was enough food to last at least a week. Which was a good thing, because by early Monday morning, they were completely snowed in. The apartment had electricity, but stories abounded of elderly people trapped in their homes, unable to get out because of the deep and drifting snow. Apparently Brooklyn was not high on the "snow removal" list, because by noon there still were no signs of plows outside her window. Hallee looked at the whiteness of it all and recaptured some vague memory of her youth when a blizzard equated bliss.

There was a small platoon of variously sized and shaped snowmen lined up along the street, and some industrious child (adult?) had crafted a fort-slash-igloo structure. And, of course, there were the ubiquitous yellow blotches with paw prints leading toward and away. The thrill of the excess snow obviously had diminished, because no one was outside her window playing at the moment. It was nearing dinner time, and Hallee knew she should start reheating something before the boys were clamoring to eat. However, she wanted to watch the sun go down; its glassy reflection on what was left of unblemished snow was exquisite.

Her reverie was distracted by a figure in the distance. Hallee squinted to see how the person maneuvered so quickly through the snow. At last she realized he was utilizing snowshoes. *Who the hell has snowshoes in Brooklyn?* Hallee wondered. However, as the figure drew closer, Hallee felt her pulse quicken and her breath shallow. It was a man, for certain. He was carrying several canvas bags with what appeared to be wrapped gifts and food. He drew up under her window, and even if she could have ducked out of sight, she didn't really want to. He was using ski-type poles to trudge through the snow, which he now waved gently in her direction. He said something; from Hallee's perspective he was just mouthing words, but his breath was steamy. He motioned to the front of the building, as if asking to come in. Even if she didn't really want to let him in, she would have anyhow. He was trekking through Brooklyn in snowshoes, for fuck's sake.

Xavier kissed her lightly on the cheek when he entered the apartment. The boys were on him almost immediately. The snowshoes were a big hit, so he demonstrated how to put them on and let each boy have a turn. An even bigger hit were the three new Nintendo DS systems, along with three new games (or nine; Xavier had bought each boy his own, because he didn't want them to fight over them, "And you can play each other! The systems have Internet so you can battle your brothers!"). The part of Hallee that wanted to be angry at Xavier's presumption kept quiet; the boys would be enthralled for months to come at X's expense.

Hallee was unpacking the food from the canvas bags when he returned to the very small kitchen. "You know," Hallee laughed, "you really didn't have to bring food. We have tons of left-overs from Christmas. We weren't going to starve, even if they do take a week to plow the roads in Brooklyn."

"Well," he drawled and came closer to her, "it *will* be a week. And what's the point having the same thing night," he slipped his hand around her waist and turned her towards him, "after night," he kissed her gently, and whispered, "after night?" His tongue parted her lips and he kissed her deeply, pressing himself hard against her.

She pushed him back, but not harshly. She wanted him. Badly. She was so happy he was there she could hardly contain the emotion. He took up too much space in the small kitchen; she felt claustrophobic. She motioned for him to follow her to the boys' bedroom.

"Good idea," Xavier said after they entered the boys' room. He tried to pull her close, but Hallee backed away. "What? What is it?"

Hallee wasn't going to fight with him. She wasn't trying to irritate him. She simply wanted to know what he was doing there. "And don't tell me you were afraid we were stranded by the storm. You could have called."

Xavier just shook his head. "Do you want me to leave?"

"No!" Hallee shouted with a bit too much desperation in her voice. "I want you to stay." Xavier let out an exhale that was half way between a laugh and a grunt.

"I'm going back to Afghanistan," he said simply. "I need to follow up on some things for the documentary. It might turn into a second film."

"But it's so dangerous," Hallee had moved closer to him. This was the worst news ever. So, he wasn't even there to see her, just to bring her the bad news. "When do you leave?" She touched his cheek. He hadn't shaved in several days. She could barely see his blonde beard, but she could feel it. She wanted to feel its roughness on her skin. She felt weak and vulnerable all over again. Why did she have to be so affected by this man? By any man? Why couldn't she just stand and say, "No"?

"I leave in a week. I'll be back in April, maybe May," Xavier said. "When I made the decision to go, I had to see you. I had to tell you how sorry I was, about what happened between us."

"We just had a fight, that's all," Hallee said. "Do you want to sit?" He nodded and sat on Gavin's bed beside her. "Did you hear I quit the domicile?"

"Yeah. Arnie told me what happened," he said. "But you hated that job.

It's good you left."

"That's easy for you to say!" Hallee was not doing as well as she had hoped on her plan not to get into a fight with X. "You know he won that fucking Pritzker, right? The one I helped him get? The one that got me into trouble?"

"Hallee," Xavier had that condescending look yet again, "David won the prize. You did one hell of a presentation, but if he hadn't won this year, it would have been next. He's a great architect."

"Oh, my God!" Hallee took several short breaths. "Because of him, I've been unemployed for two months. I have kids, Xavier. Maybe you noticed!"

"Well, you weren't fired. You wanted to quit, right?" Xavier said, rather matter of factly. He seemed to dismiss her anger out of hand, as though her disapprobation of David reaching this achievement was simple jealousy or malice.

"I quit because of you," Hallee said, simply enough.

"What do you mean?" Xavier asked, a concerned look on his face.

Unable to look him in the eye, Hallee glanced downward to his chest. It was Xavier's best feature. Which wasn't saying much, as he really didn't have a bad feature. At least not physically.

"I have accepted that I need to be abused." There, she had said it.

Xavier shifted to catch Hallee's glance. He viewed her with curiosity. Hallee could tell that he wanted to understand her meaning, yet he felt uncomfortable by the implied notion that he was abusing her. Hallee took pity on him; she realized in this moment that she felt true love for him.

"You were right. You never hurt me intentionally," she admitted. "I now understand what you meant when you said I need to be abused. I have put myself in the role of victim, but I can do something about it. You taught me that if I am to be that victim, it should be for someone who will never, in fact, abuse me. If that makes any sense at all."

Xavier sighed with relief. "So, you want me back?"

Hallee shook her head. Men really didn't understand women.

"Okay, you don't," Xavier was backpedaling. "I was wrong. You were right. It was never about you." Xavier was wringing his hands, and for the first time Hallee realized that he had more to say to her than simply his plan to return to the war.

"Hallee, the truth is," he whistled when he exhaled. He took her hands and held them, as if he were going to propose... or break some more bad news to her. "The truth is I do need to control something. I have seen... seen so much..." His voice was cracking, and Hallee had to fight back tears of empathy. He let go with one of his hands and rubbed his cheek, resting a forefinger on his lip before continuing.

"Usually, when I see violence, Hallee, I can't do anything about it. I can't stop anyone's pain. I have no control." He paused again. Hallee considered interrupting but then thought better of it. "When I'm with you, when we have violent or painful or whatever kind of sex you want to label it, I am in control. I know I can make it stop. It makes me feel human again. I need it, Hallee."

Hallee held him close. She didn't know if the embrace was what he needed at the moment, but it was all she could offer while the boys were in the next room playing. Finally she looked him square in the eye. "Maybe we both need it, Xavier. Maybe I've been looking for this my whole life, a way to calm the chaos. You make me feel safe, because you are someone who will know when it's enough and make everything seem okay. Because I sure seem to be attracted to people who hurt me, and I don't want to do that anymore."

"Hallee, I want you to be that one thing in my life I have some control over," Xavier said. "Please. Please be mine. I'll do what I can to please you..."

Hallee cut him short. "But what if what pleases me, is pleasing you?"

"Then we please each other," Xavier said, and once again his mouth was upon hers. He tried to lean her back on Gavin's bed, but she stopped him.

"Later," she said. "After the boys are asleep." She started to leave the room, before turning back to ask, "You'll stay?"

"Until the snowplows come," he laughed.

They cooked dinner together in the small kitchen, using every opportunity to rub up against one another as they sliced vegetables and sprinkled cheese over a fresh pizza dough Xavier had managed to snag from a ravaged Trader Joe's. He charmed the boys even further by tossing the dough à la an Italian chef. Every time it frisbeed into the air, Hallee winced, sure it would end up on the floor and she'd be cleaning up the mess. However, he caught it each time without fail.

"More, more, Uncle X!" Drake had pleaded. Somehow or another they had decided that he was "uncle," which given that Hallee had no siblings probably made more sense to them than it did to her.

"No, Drake," X explained, never mistaking one twin for the other. "We're gonna cook and eat this pizza!"

Once they had finished dinner, X did the dishes—making the boys help—and then got them ready for bed, all of which was wonderful since Hallee wanted to take a bath and make herself more into a woman and less of a mom. It might have been a cliché, but she still didn't feel like she would ever get to "have it all," at least not in a synergistic fashion. She felt that she was making little compartments in her life for each of her needs. If that meant mother was separate from lover and co-worker was separate from friend, so be it. At least there was the hope that her life was starting to make sense at long last. Maybe Xavier wasn't the only one who needed to feel in control of something.

After the boys were put to bed and X was beside her, the sex was great, as always. Per his routine, afterwards X cracked the window and brought out his little pipe.

"How often do you get high?" Hallee asked, trying not to sound judgmental. She was learning to let go and accept what she couldn't change. Plus, she had to be honest that she had only cut back on her drinking the past few weeks because she hadn't had enough money to buy wine.

"Not as often as you think," X claimed. "In truth, I really like to get high after having sex. I feel great. This makes it exponential." He offered her a toke, but she declined.

THE TRUTH

"Do you remember when you asked me what rocks my world?"

"Yeah," he took another drag from the pipe before putting it away and sliding back beside her. "Of course I do. You had no answer."

Hallee wrestled for dominance, rolling X onto his back and pushing into his torso. Her soft flesh pressed against his muscular frame. He was stoned, and the romance of the moment was tempered by her subdued mood. She stared deeply into his gray eyes and whispered, "Ask me again."

Xavier viewed her with mock seriousness, he tossed her onto her back in one swift move. She laughed. "What rocks your world?" he asked, returning her stare. She blinked first. He kissed her cheek, then her neck, hopefully still listening while working his way down her body.

"Roasting a duck with acorn squash and chestnuts." Chestnuts were her new go-to ingredient in anything holiday related.

"Mmmm," he purred at her clavicle. "That's a good one. What else?"

"George Harrison's, *Something*."

"Two for two." Now he was at her breast.

"Your mouth." To that Xavier chuckled and captured a nipple between his teeth.

"And theater." That stopped Xavier cold. He leaned back and studied her face.

"Really?" he asked, as though waiting an explanation. Hallee felt what her mouth was saying was competing with how her body was responding for his attention.

"Yes, really," Hallee began, wondering if he would think her a complete fool after hearing more. "I don't mean Broadway, I mean theater. I actually wanted to be an actress when I was little."

"Don't all little girls?" Xavier replied.

"I guess," Hallee admitted. "But I did some community theater and I just loved how the sets went together and the lights made the mood and then all these people would file in and sit there in this artificial world. And for a couple hours, everyone shared that reality.

"Before meeting you," Hallee was near tears, "it was the only place I ever felt whole. I had forgotten. Almost as if I had repressed it."

"Then it's good you remembered after all this time." Xavier pushed himself even with her and kissed her deeply. "You know, there's a lot of theater in New York."

"Well..." she was making sure he was still paying attention through the fornication.

"Well?" he asked, moving back down her body again.

"I got a job with a theater?"

He had stopped short of her belly button and now was fully engaged by the conversation. "As an actress?" he asked with an air of disbelief.

"No, silly," she said, taking a swipe at him. X was too fast, catching her wrist and holding her arm back over her head. He then grabbed her other arm, binding her to her pillow. She squirmed with pleasure, but he wasn't giving in.

"Tell me," he commanded.

"Later," she said, trying to raise her groin off the bed. He trapped her lower body with his heavy leg.

"Tell me."

"It's managing an off-off Broadway place," she admitted at last. "I'll be wearing a lot of hats for not a lot of pay, but the best part is I'll qualify for benefits in 26 weeks."

"Six months?"

"Yes."

"That's not so bad," he agreed. "And maybe you'll actually *like* this job."

"I think I will," she admitted. "It's a lot of hands-on work and wasn't easy to get..."

"I can imagine," X sympathized. Perhaps the economy was partially to blame for him going abroad again.

"I must've given out 500 resumes," Hallee laughed. "I was literally forcing people to take them from me, like those guys who stand on the corner passing along flyers." Hallee had felt so desperate just a few days before, but the doom that had been closing in around her seemed muted now, even if it was still lurking, threateningly, like that tiger finally bound by a cage. Had she contained it? No one can predict the future; it's all just illusion.

"You know," Hallee said, "I'm not sorry about working for David." Xavier rolled his eyes. She struggled against him, but he still had her pinned to the bed, well, futon. Finally, a look of recognition in those grey eyes.

"Oh, you mean because of me," he smiled.

"Yes, I mean because of you." He released her hands, pulling her tightly to him, and cradled her until she no longer could feel him or anything else. The sleep of the dead.

Xavier was as good as his word. He didn't leave before the snowplows arrived. In fact, he didn't leave *after* the snowplows arrived. Hallee was starting her new job in the new year, so he invited himself to stay over until then. Hallee didn't protest and the boys enjoyed his company.

On December 31st, they watched the ball drop from Times Square. Xavier had access to one of the business suites overlooking the festivities, and Gavin managed to stay awake until midnight. X had arranged for a limo to drive them all back to Brooklyn where the streets were now mostly clear of snow.

They both helped put the boys to bed, each of them carrying a twin with Gavin more or less sleep walking between them. From the fridge Hallee grabbed a cheap bottle of Prosecco she had bought earlier in the day, and set it on the side table next to her bed. She offered Xavier one of the two glasses (Hallee didn't own flutes, so they were regular wine glasses), hoping he would join her.

"You once told me you'd share Champagne on New Year's," she coaxed.

"I did now, didn't I?" He popped the cork, pouring the effervescent wine first into her glass and then into his own.

Before he had the chance to propose a toast, Hallee stopped him. He put the glasses back on the table and waited for her.

"Xavier," she spoke slowly. "Don't go back."

He looked at her with brows furrowed.

"I do not want you to go back to Afghanistan," she said. "Please stay here with me."

Hallee knew what he would say before he said it. Yet some small niggling voice in the back of her head made her think Xavier might say something unpredictable.

"Hallee," Xavier explained, "I thought you understood who I am, *what* I am. I haven't changed. I'm not going to settle down and be your boys' dad."

Hallee was struck breathless. She had finally relinquished the Prince Charming fantasy, and she had landed on her own feet, finding another job without exploiting Xavier's connections. Her boys were doing pretty well in New York City. She was okay. She honestly didn't need Xavier anymore.

"Well, then," she said, "I guess we've loved well enough."

"Don't do that..."

"Do what?" she snapped

"Turn us into some literary contrivance."

Hallee was crying. On New Year's. Talk about a bad start to a new decade. "I'm scared you won't come back to me," she whispered through tears.

Xavier smiled. "Why wouldn't I come back to you?"

"It's Afghanistan!" Hallee was trying to keep the emotion at bay because she feared she was bordering on hysteria.

"Oh, that," Xavier nodded. "You could get hit by a bus tomorrow. New York is not exactly known for being the safest place to be in the world."

"It's not the same," Hallee replied.

"No, it's not," Xavier said. "But if I can come back, I will. And I will want to be with you when I do, and I will be here for your sons, too, if that's what they need. I get it; you're a package deal. But please don't ask me for more than I am willing to give."

The man before her wasn't trying to save her or change her or do anything other than accept her for who she was. He was only asking the same in return.

"I asked you to move in with me, Hallee. I may have done it clumsily, but when you said no, I should have respected your choice. I do respect that choice. It just took me awhile to come around. I'm here now, and I hold you in respect. Truly."

For some reason, Hallee flashbacked to being on her knees in front of David's apartment door, Janine having just christened the entryway with chutney. Why hadn't Hallee run away, cut her losses then and there? Why did she allow herself to be denigrated and just stay put for as long as she had?

Hallee was on the verge of epiphany. She realized she hadn't stayed with David Ormston-Meighton Architects Company, Incorporated, (*How may I direct your call?*) because she had been afraid of being without work. In truth, even now she still wasn't 100-percent confident that leaving Jeremy had been the correct course of action. Had she weathered his abuse, her boys would still have a dad. But would they still have a mom? It was a valid question. She had endured abuse for so long that standing up for herself, whether in her personal life or her professional, simply felt wrong. Morally and colossally wrong. *I need to be abused*, still echoed in her mind.

Now lying beside her was a man who didn't feel wrong. Nothing about him felt wrong. He was no closer to—or further from—perfect than she. The "rightness" of the situation had been there for all the months the two of them had been together, and Hallee had felt that something was wrong only when they were apart. When she had tried to please him, he had been pleased. When he tried to please her, she had felt guilty or in denial. How fucking ridiculous she had been these many months not enjoying the delight he presented in her life? Now, hoping there would still be a chance to appreciate all he had to give to her, she vowed to let go the only part of her past that had remained: That "need" to be abused. Xavier only wanted to love her. Could she actually allow herself to be loved? She looked at him with hope.

"I deserve the best," she said, not entirely sure she yet believed it.

"You do, so keep saying it," he said, now kissing her face gently. "All I can promise is that if I'm alive in May, I'll be right back here. With you. If you still want me." She laughed at the thought she wouldn't want him back. But even she wasn't going to predict where the future would lead.

X had swung the sexual pendulum in the exact opposite direction towards tenderness and treated her body with the lightest of touch. He would never be boring in bed: a man who could be both nasty and nice to her. He kissed the nape of her neck, her décolletage, her breasts, her belly, working his way lower and lower. She was on her back now, melting into the lumpy futon. He stopped and gazed up from her pubis.

Hallee was grateful that what could possibly turn out to be the last time she had sex with Xavier was so tender. She would never forget this night. How could she? It was New Year's Eve 2011. The boys were sound asleep. The week had been among the best of her life. The future would unfold as it always did—unpredictably. Tomorrow Xavier would pack up and go back to his brownstone. In a few days he would be on his way to the Middle East. And Hallee would resolve to be happy for a change.

Xavier remembered the lingering champagne. He passed along a glass to Hallee, who sipped more from the thirst of the moment than in celebration. The brut was dry and crisp, and its taste belied the cheap price. They drank. They kissed. He clinked his glass into hers.

"Happy New Year, Hallee."

21979802R00136

Printed in Great Britain
by Amazon